# GETTING MAMA OUT OF HELL

# OTHER FIVE STAR TITLES BY LAURIE MOORE:

*Deb on Air—Live at Five* (2013)
*Wanted Deb or Alive* (2011)
*Couple Gunned Down—News at Ten* (2011)
*Deb on Arrival—Live at Five* (2010)
*Woman Strangled—News at Ten* (2009)
*Jury Rigged* (2008)
*Constable's Wedding* (2005)
*The Wild Orchid Society* (2004)
*Constable's Apprehension* (2003)
*The Lady Godiva Murder* (2002)
*Constable's Run* (2002)

# GETTING MAMA OUT OF HELL

## LAURIE MOORE

**FIVE STAR**
*A part of Gale, Cengage Learning*

GALE
CENGAGE Learning·

Farmington Hills, Mich • San Francisco • New York • Waterville, Maine
Meriden, Conn • Mason, Ohio • Chicago

# GALE
## CENGAGE Learning®

Five Star™ Publishing, a part of Gale, Cengage Learning.

Printed in the United States of America
1 2 3 4 5 6 7 18 17 16 15 14

# GETTING MAMA OUT OF HELL

# CHAPTER ONE

Blaring police radios roused me into consciousness. My first thought was a primitive one—unbearable pain.

*Where am I?*

*What happened?*

*And this pain in my side—excruciating. Can't remember ever hurting this much.*

*Lying flat on this hard surface makes it hard to breathe.*

Sounds of panic filled the night.

I cracked open my eyes and viewed the unfolding calamity in increments. Beacons of red, white and blue, strobing from emergency vehicles, bounced off the darkness. The odor of petrol fumes carried on the breeze. Bystanders gawked behind crime scene tape.

I blinked a few times, and a looming silhouette came into focus. A policeman.

He kneeled and leaned in close to my face. "I warned you, Sylvester, if you continued these crime sprees, you'd either end up in prison or dead." He gave the thumbs-down gesture. "You're on the highway to Hell," he said through the raspy chuckle of a heavy smoker. "You'll end up spending eternity playing basketball in a gymnasium of embers, surrounded by a moat of molten lava."

*This man is an American, but he makes no sense.*

A flash of memory helped me get my bearings.

*I'm on holiday with Elizabeth, my only child. In Texas.*

*Where's my daughter? Is she injured, too?*

Above me, a black velvet sky sparkled with a million mirrors, reflecting the desires of dreamers.

*Is this a bad dream?*

"Stay with me, Sly." The cop gave me a reassuring pat on the head.

*Who's Sly?*

*My name is Eloise Winthrop.*

*Elle for short.*

*He obviously didn't check my passport. My handbag must be missing. Is that what happened? I'm a mugging victim?*

I sharpened my gaze, then winced at the knifing pain in my side. Lightheaded, I tested the severity of my injury with a gentle touch. Dizziness washed over me, along with a blinding sting that electrified my body; my fingertips came away sticky.

*Was I stabbed?*

"Don't move. Not that I'd mind if you bled to death. Last thing we need is another peewee gangsta ripening on the vine." The cop gave my shoulder an avuncular squeeze, revealing a thread of kindness within the bluster. "Stay with me, Sly."

*Who's Sly, and why does he keep calling me that?*

*Anyone seeing me at close range wouldn't mistake me for a man even if I do wear my blonde hair a bit on the shorter side—well, shoulder-length anyway.*

*These curves, alone, should've been a dead giveaway.*

Reflexively, I lifted a hand to my breasts.

*Gone.*

Hand to head, I sucked in a sharp intake of air.

*I'm absolutely gobsmacked—I've been maimed.*

*How could this happen?*

*What else is different?*

I swallowed hard. Something's gone terribly wrong.

*I'm the grown-up version of Goldilocks.*

*Only now my silky tresses have the texture and feel of newly sheared lamb's wool.*

*Where's Elizabeth?*

*Can this man help find my daughter?*

As I cleared my voice to speak, a commotion broke out near the curb. Uniformed police officers struggled to restrain a hysterical black woman.

"Sly, Sly," she screamed into the night. "Is my baby dead?"

"See what I mean?" The big lawman braced his meaty hands against the asphalt for a quick lean-in. The sharp smell of onions on his breath couldn't mask the odor of a decaying tooth. The stench hit me like a punch in the face. "Your mama loves you— Lord knows why. If you make it, this'd be the time to turn your life around."

It dawned on me this Sylvester fellow must've been close by. Although I couldn't see him, the burly officer was clearly speaking to him, not to me.

Snippets of memory fell into place.

My twenty-five-year-old daughter and I were driving from Fort Worth to the DFW airport. Rain had made the roads slick. The truck in front of us veered hard right. I swerved to miss a van stopped dead in the road. Then everything moved in slow motion. Our car smashed through the guardrail. Smears of blue and green passed before my eyes. I remembered the sickening sensation of tumbling.

*I accept that we've been involved in a terrible crash.*

*It hurts to breathe. Probably broke my ribs hitting the steering wheel.*

Reflexively, I moved my hand to my buttery soft leather skirt to ensure that it hadn't ridden up around my hips. Instead, I touched denim.

*I've never worn denim in my life.*

"Mum? Mummy?"

9

My daughter's distress cry filled the air. She had to be nearby. Why couldn't I see her?

"Elizabeth?" The voice that moved past my throat seemed to belong to somebody else.

"Mummy, where are you?"

"Over here, lovie." I raised my hand enough for her to vector my location. Instantly I recoiled. Stabbing pain prevented me from hoisting myself up to take in our surroundings, but I saw enough to concern me.

Huge high-top tennis shoes pointed skyward where exquisite leather Ferragamos should've been. My eyes traveled up my legs, past cargo pants riding below my hips, to—

*Blimey—plaid boxer shorts? Since when did men's trolleys and undercrackers become fashionable for women to wear?*

*I'm gobsmacked.*

My heart thudded.

*This is a very bad dream.*

*I need to wake up and end it.*

*Perhaps I can incorporate good things into this nightmare, such as . . . I'm Elle Winthrop and I'm receiving the Nobel Peace Prize for my humanitarian work in Texas ghettos. There, that's the stuff.*

*Now give me my trophy.*

The stocky cop pushed down my outstretched hand, urging me to remain still.

The annoying flash of a camera went off near my head. When I craned my neck to see, a plain-clothes detective pointed a video camera at me. I lifted my hand to shield my eyes against the glare of the light and—

*Flaming Nora!*

I flinched as the black fist stopped short of my face.

The hand was attached to my arm—also black.

*Did my car catch fire?*

*Is this soot turning my skin black?*

*Have I been charred beyond recognition?*

I didn't feel burned. I pinched the other arm with my black hand. The skin was soft and smooth and it hurt when I twisted it.

The most dreadful thought occurred to me. That I'd turned into a black lad.

*No. Simply not possible. Bad dream. Wake up.*

"Mummy, where are you?"

My daughter's panic skewered my thoughts. When I inclined my head to hear better, the only female near enough for me to see—besides this kid Sly's panic-stricken mother—was an old white lady. She clung to her handbag, a lovely Italian number made of alligator hide . . . like the one I used to have that I donated to charity for a silent auction.

The old lady sported a black eye the shade and circumference of my fist.

"Mummy," cried the elderly woman. A couple of uniformed officers attempted to calm her. The old bird put up quite a struggle as they urged her to sit in the front compartment of a patrol car. "Mummy, where are you?"

*That isn't my daughter.*

*But that's Elizabeth's voice. I know my own child's voice.*

*Is that wrinkled woman a ventriloquist? I don't understand.*

"Right here, darling," I lifted my hand so Elizabeth could find me.

"What kind of crap are you pulling, Sly?" The broad-shouldered cop towering over me glowered. "And what's with the British accent?"

*Of course I have a British accent—I'm British.*

Before I could speak, he accused me of impersonating people.

The whoop of an ambulance rent the air.

The policeman rose and turned his back to me. "Over here."

"Mummy, where are you? I can't see you," Elizabeth called

11

out, frantic. "I can't see you."

"Here, Lillibet." Big hand wave. Then realization dawned.

*My side doesn't hurt.*

*I can breathe without pain.*

The old woman peered past me, eyes darting about like pinballs. Her mouth was a red gash against her puffy face. The alligator handbag hung by one strap. Someone must've slugged her quite soundly. I forced myself up on one elbow. No wonder I smelled fumes. I'd been lying near a string of petrol pumps. Neon beer signs glowed through the windows of a nearby building.

*This is a convenience store.*

I could see the old lady quite clearly now. Her pale blue dress shimmered beneath the glow of the fluorescent lighting from the canopy overhanging us.

I took a visual inventory of myself.

*Where did this disgusting T-shirt come from?*

*The shock value alone probably violates American hate laws.*

*No wonder the policeman's annoyed.*

*And these baggy blue jeans sliding past my hips?*

*What is this—"in your face" crime fashion?*

*It's like I'm in a parallel universe.*

I sincerely hoped the blood on these clothes belonged to someone else and not me. I examined myself more closely.

*My blood.*

I averted my eyes to keep from fainting.

*Blood and gore makes my stomach queasy.*

*It's the main reason I didn't go to medical school.*

The back-up whistle on the ambulance chirped. Its rear doors moved in closer.

"Lie down, Sly," said the cop. "Try not to move. They're taking you to Our Lady of Mercy. Don't worry, you'll be fine."

"I'm fine now. I want to go home." I rested on both elbows,

and took in my surroundings in a glance. This sudden absence of pain could be a symptom of shock . . . or impending death.

"You're not going anywhere but the hospital," the brawny officer said.

On the curb, the screaming black woman yelled, "Don'tchoo die, Sly. Don'tchoo dare deprive me of killing you myself."

"Who's the shrieking harpy?" I asked. But what I really wanted to know was the reason she was shaking her fist at me.

The cop waved a beefy hand in front of my face. "Don't you even recognize your mama, boy?" He touched my forehead. "Just as I thought—you're faking it."

I closed my eyes in exasperation.

*I'm a middle-aged white woman with a traffic-stopping body and this fellow keeps calling me "boy."*

*Men in the UK actually use the words "drop dead gorgeous" to describe me. American men say I'm "hot." Or they remark that Elizabeth and I look like sisters and mistake us for being in the fashion industry.*

*My features are on the delicate side.*

*I wear mascara to make my lashes stand out and my blue eyes appear larger.*

*My legs are toned and shapely.*

*So how can this husky oaf mistake me for a boy?*

*And why does he keep saying "sly"—that loudmouthed woman, too? Is this supposed to be a name or an accusation? They don't even know me. How dare they malign my character?*

"Where's my daughter?" I demanded, chilled by the notion that Elizabeth might be injured—or dying.

"Are you kidding?" The big cop wore the dumbstruck look of a man who'd left Las Vegas with a fanny pack full of cash and a hooker, and awakened in a seedy motel with a half-consumed drink and his pants crumpled around his ankles.

Ambulance attendants rushed to my side carrying medic kits

the size of fishing tackle boxes.

Before I could shoo them off, they opened their cases. Out came the rescue gear. One tried to lift my shirt, but I slapped his hand away.

*I'm a woman of dignity.*

*How dare that man tug at my clothes?*

*Especially with the burly law officer leering over me.*

*I'm proud of my breasts but not enough to show them off to anybody who wants a peek; besides, people are milling about.*

Then I remembered.

*I'm flatter than a crepe.*

A tiny cry rose up from my throat.

"Settle down, pardner. We need to take a look at that bullet wound," said one of the paramedics.

*Bullet wound?*

*I've been shot?*

My only discomfort came from the stiffness of being proned out on cold asphalt. I looked at my wrist to check the hour on my Piaget timepiece and found a cheap plastic imitation of a scuba watch in its place.

*Someone stole my birthday gift.*

*Lifted it right off my wrist.*

*Probably a sponger taking advantage of my bad situation.*

*I should file a complaint.*

The paramedic who hiked up my shirt shined a light over my blood-crusted ribcage while his assistant unscrewed a bottle cap and saturated a gauze pack. Antiseptic chilled my skin. The pungent solution felt so cold to the touch that for a moment it seared with a fiery sensation. After a few swipes against my wound, he discarded the bloody cloth.

Shrewd eyes narrowed into slits. He directed his attention to the policeman. "I thought you said he'd been shot."

"That's right. Either that, or somebody stabbed him." Then

the officer did a double take. The skin beneath my shirt—*the shirt with a bullet hole in it*—was undamaged.

"Can I go home now?" I asked, no longer sure anymore where home was.

"After we book you into juvie for attempted murder," said the cop.

He grabbed my arm and hoisted me to my feet. I glanced around. The old woman sat in the front seat of the police cruiser, but the door remained ajar, and her feet stayed firmly planted against the pavement. She appeared dazed and confused. A uniformed policeman who'd been interviewing people at the scene stepped away from the crowd, and handed her something that appeared to be the size of a driver's license. She stared at it with cold scrutiny, and her mouth went slack. Then she placed the item in her purse, and her gaze shifted to me. She quickly clutched her broken handbag to her bosom, and gave me a pointed look.

"Mummy?"

"Lillibet?"

The big bruiser, who'd been patting my head and calling me Sly, spun me around and ratcheted on the handcuffs. Then he marched me over to his squad car.

Squealing tires alerted me to danger. A metallic-blue Jaguar bounced into the car park with such a vengeance that I glanced back over my shoulder. It screeched to a stop a few meters from the police car containing the old lady. A tuxedoed man who appeared to be in his forties bailed out of the driver's side at the same time his passenger, a bejeweled female wearing a formal gown, wrangled out of the passenger seat with her processed blonde hair upswept in a chignon. The man took long strides, heading directly for the aging lady, with the glamorous woman in tow. I noticed a wedding ring on his finger, and assumed the regal woman gliding past in a fragrant cloud, with queenly posture, must be his wife.

"What the hell are you doing, Adelaide?" he challenged. "You're not even supposed to be up this time of night. How in the devil did you get out here?"

"Who are you?" asked the elderly woman, whom I now assumed to be Adelaide.

My breath caught in my throat. Adelaide spoke in a cultured British accent. The couple from the Jaguar did not.

*Elizabeth.*

The stylish fashionista wearing the elegant ball gown said, "Mother, I demand to know what happened. Get out of that car this instant." She did a quick eye scan of the area, as if searching for something or someone. "And Richard's right—how'd you get here? Did you take my car?"

Adelaide said, "And, who might you be?"

Then the man I assumed to be Richard spoke in a harsh, no-nonsense tone. "What the hell are you doing out here, Adelaide? If you wrecked Priscilla's car, you're not getting out of the house for a month, do you hear me?"

Adelaide clung tighter to her purse. She sat, gobsmacked—unable, or unwilling, to budge. Then Richard grabbed her arm as the policeman looked on, and angrily pulled her to her feet. In the violent momentum, she steadied herself against the door frame. When he hauled her up on tiptoes, she winced painfully.

"He shouldn't be touching her that way," I told the big cop, but he hauled me up on tiptoes, too, and steered me past the unfolding domestic drama. To Richard, I yelled, "Oi, mate—stop manhandling her this instant." That's when the policeman soundly shoved me against the boot of his patrol car.

Richard shot me a lethal glare. Then he returned his attention to Priscilla. "That's it, I'm done. Your mother's senile. First she talks in a British accent. What's next—a nod to Italy? Then she acts like she doesn't recognize us. Who knows what else she's done? You should go over her checkbook. I caught her watching that televangelist on TV the other day. She's probably sending him thousands of dollars. We're putting her under a guardianship before she spends all of your inheritance."

They pulled Adelaide toward the Jaguar as if they hadn't even noticed the purple mouse plumping beneath one eye, and I found it appalling that neither bothered to ask how badly she'd been hurt. Nor inquire as to who did this to her.

An unexpected voice caught me off guard. The silky baritone belonged to my fiancé, Allen.

As Richard opened the back passenger door of the Jaguar, the old lady gave me a quizzical stare. A flicker of recognition passed between me and her, and then to Allen, before it settled, once again, on me.

"Mummy?" she mouthed without sound. But she pointed a finger directly at me. Then she mouthed, "Allen," and shifted her finger to the police detective sauntering into the chaos.

*This is odd.*

*Why would Allen be out here on Airport Freeway when police headquarters are in downtown Fort Worth?*

*Did someone call him?*

"Allen, save me," I cried.

Instead of coming to my rescue, he stared right through me.

*Why isn't he helping me? He's supposed to love me.*

*The old lady senses this, too. Look at the worry knitting her brow.*

"Allen—please. There's been a terrible misunderstanding."

He looked at me slitty-eyed, as if we were complete strangers.

"Allen—it's me—Elle."

Instead of scooping me up in those big, strong arms, he showed me his fist. I blinked back tears.

*I don't understand. A few days ago Allen professed his undying love for me, and proposed marriage.*

*I said yes.*

17

After Officer Toughguy completed a brisk pat down on me, he motioned me toward the caged compartment of his patrol car. I glimpsed my reflection in the glass and reflexively jumped aside. Instead of a white woman with a palomino mane pulled back in a ponytail, a black lad in gangsta garb stared back at me.

I tilted my head to the right and saw movement reflected in the glass. I straightened my head and tilted it to the left. The image in the window did the same. I looked away quickly, then back again. The image shifted in sync with each turn of my body.

My stomach roiled.

The previous week, I'd watched an *I Love Lucy* rerun with Lucille Ball and Harpo Marx where they reenacted the famous mirror scene from the Marx Brothers film *Duck Soup*. At the time, I howled. Had a rollicking good time, in fact.

*Now, it's not such a riot.*

*It's as if I'm starring in my own sitcom, only this isn't funny.*

*Because instead of Harpo, there's a spooky-looking black lad copying my motions.*

*Who is this boy?*

I blinked in disbelief but he held me captive with his unnerving stare.

Like jerky frames from an old reel of film projected onto a blank screen, snippets of a near-death experience flashed in my memory. I studied the burly cop's face with cold scrutiny. Recognition kicked in.

*He's the same policeman who investigated the accident scene when our rental car plunged over the guardrail.*

Goosebumps popped up on my arms.

*He was there when the ambulance arrived.*

Little hairs on my arms stuck straight up.

*This is the same policeman who said, "Too late. They're both gone."*

*I think I'm going to be sick.*

# CHAPTER TWO

"Name and address?"

I guess I took too long to answer because the lady at juvenile hall, wearing the Tarrant County sheriff's deputy patch emblazoned on her black shirt, looked up from the booking form. The brass name tag pinned slightly above her shirt pocket read: Hanson; so, I assumed I'd be doing business with Deputy Hanson.

"Well?" she demanded.

I saw no way out of this sterile, one-story building, and cleared my throat. "I'm Eloise Winthrop, of the Clive Winthrops—Elle for short."

Her face went from boredom to disgust, as if the rice cake she'd been snacking on had just turned into fried crickets.

"Very funny. Mister comedian. What's your real name?"

"Elle Winthrop. From the UK."

The big cop piped up. "Always a smart ass." To the deputy, he said, "This little imposter is actually Sylvester Gooch. He's got a long rap sheet." He traced a finger up his arm to indicate the length of the criminal history printout. "Feel free to look it up on the computer because you won't get the truth out of him."

I hated having my character maligned—I'm not a liar—but I was more disturbed by the name he saddled me with.

"Gooch?" I said with a face scrunch.

"Rhymes with pooch. Which is what you screwed when you

20

tried to mug that old lady."

He frisked me, running his hands over my pockets, which he then emptied out. A handful of coins rolled across the counter. "Any machine guns, bazookas, machetes . . . ?"

He thought this was a riot, and apparently so did the lady booking me in, because he clearly earned entertainment points at my expense.

Computer keys clacked at her touch. "Age?"

"Forty-five." My voice vibrated as meaty hands finished the pat down.

"He's around twelve," said the big cop.

Her fingertips flew over the keyboard. She leaned in close with her face bathed in the glow of the computer screen. "Here we go." She shook her head, *Tsk, tsk,* and spun the screen my way. "You've been a busy little booger. Bicycle theft, motorcycle theft, auto theft, theft of service . . ." Her eyes slid upward from the monitor. "Is your mother coming to get you?"

"My mother's dead."

Her gaze flickered to the cop. He shook his head.

She returned her attention to the monitor. "Says here she lives on Avenue J. If she's not here to see the judge by docket call, which is at nine in the morning, you'll be held over."

Realization dawned. "Oh, you mean Mrs. Gooch." I said this on a whoosh of air.

"Knock off the British accent, Sly. Nobody's buying it." The policeman unhooked the handcuffs and pointed to a holding area, poking me in the back to spur me on. I took a seat on a cold metal bench, and massaged the numbness out of my wrists.

*I'm starring in my own nightmare.*

*Unless I've gone crackers. Which would be worse.*

I pinched my arm to wake up.

*Yikes. Hurts.*

*So . . . nightmare, it is. Should've known it wasn't mental problems. I would've at least given myself a more cultured identity if I'd been delusional, right? Like royalty. Then, again, I'm having a conversation with myself inside my head, aren't I? So, we can't exactly rule crazy out.*

The booking officer shifted her gaze in my direction. "What's your mother's occupation?"

"Before she died? My parents owned a farm in England. Now it's mine. We raise Belted Galloways."

"Got it. No job." Without taking her eyes off me, Deputy Hanson put a pen to her mouth and began chewing the tip. I'd temporarily lost her.

"A Belted Galloway is a hardy and distinctive breed of Scottish cattle with a band of pure white fur evenly distributed around the middle of an otherwise totally black animal."

Now they both gave me salamander blinks.

"Fanciers of the breed refer to the 'Belties' as Oreo-cookie cows. You know, chocolate on the ends, white in the center?" No, they didn't get it. Carry on, I told myself. "At the invitation of the Southwestern Cattle Raisers Association, we shipped two calves from our farm over for inspection. If our Belties passed muster, a few wealthy members of the association wanted to order matched sets of breeding age for their children to raise and show at the Fort Worth Stock Show and Rodeo. But I digress. My mother left us for the bright lights of Hollywood."

She huffed out her disgust, and I instantly realized she wanted to know what *Mrs. Gooch* did for a living. "I have no idea."

"Knock off the accent, Sly," snarled the big cop. "You're not fooling anybody."

I almost shot back that he was the one with the accent, but I restrained myself. "Look, if you'd be so kind as to call Detective Allen Carswell and ask him to come here, I'm sure this can all be sorted out."

"How do you know Carswell?" asked the booking officer with

mild interest.

"He's my fiancé." Shoulders erect, and with the pulse thudding in my throat, I waited with every muscle in my body tensing to see if they'd honor the phone call request. The lady deputy's expression hardened.

The big cop narrowed his eyes. "If you were a man, I'd knock the crap out of you."

"Allen can clear this up if you'll just get him over here."

But their heads shook in unison, as if they were puppets connected by an invisible string.

"I ain't callin' him," said the blustery lawman in a down-home bluesy baritone.

"Jolly good. If you'll give me back one of those quarters and show me to a phone, I'll call him myself."

"He's been through enough."

My mouth opened to protest, but he cut me off with a glare. "Allen's no queer and you're not his fiancée. And I don't know how you know Elle Winthrop—probably stole something from her—but if you so much as mention her name around him, I'll personally knock your block off."

"You don't have to get huffy. Besides, this is between me and Allen."

"And why's that?" he challenged.

"Like I said, I'm his fiancée."

"Shut the hell up, you lowlife. His fiancée's dead."

And that's where jailers found me—collapsed in a sniveling heap, on a disgustingly dirty bench in juvenile hall—when the events of my death came roaring back to me.

By the way, I'm being charged with injury to the elderly—a felony. I'm told that's an easier charge for prosecutors to make than aggravated robbery or attempted murder; and the penalty is just as stiff.

# CHAPTER THREE

After a jailer escorted me to my cell, I thought long and hard about the bizarre events that landed me in this horrible dungeon.

All right, in fairness, it's not a dungeon. From my place at the double-paned window with wire mesh sandwiched in between, I can see a car park—what Americans call a parking lot—which happens to be empty at the moment, and in the distance beyond, an industrial area. The window is about the size of a breadbox, making it impossible to climb through even if I had a blunt object to break it out—which I don't. Jailers took the trainers off my feet—a policy to prevent hangings by tying the shoelaces together—and exchanged them for rubbery slides. After accepting that I'm here until the judge arrives, I tried to process this sudden memory overload in increments.

At first, events from my life bombarded me like a frantic, ethereal round of channel surfing. Images materialized, then vanished, only to be replaced by others that flashed in and out, and back and forth, with no semblance of rhyme or reason. Recollections flickered like nonsense lightning . . . shifting from past to present to future and back again.

My twenty-five-year-old daughter, Elizabeth, and I had return tickets to London, and we'd set out for DFW Airport to catch our flight home. Sadly, my family's business venture with the Southwestern Cattle Raisers Association turned out to be a disaster because the locals placed fewer orders than we'd expected. The personal part of the trip, however, was a rousing success, making the return home bittersweet. I'd met a Fort Worth policeman named Allen Carswell, and Allen asked me to marry him. Elizabeth and I planned to return to the states once I had a chance to sit down with my father, and interview a foreman to run the farm in my absence.

If only I'd remembered to rewind my eighteen carat Piaget, then we wouldn't have been running late. And I wouldn't have been speeding in a blinding rainstorm. And when the truck in front of me slammed on the brakes and swerved hard right, I would've had more reaction time to move into the other lane. I wouldn't have overcorrected. And we wouldn't have plunged over the guardrail.

I shuddered at the memory.

Reliving each detail wilted my spirit: groping for Lillibet's hand; the noise—so much noise; so many sirens; raindrops pelting my face . . . and Allen.

Someone called for Allen—and there he was—rain soaked and cradling my head. Telling me not to leave. To come back to him.

Dear Lord, please let this be a delusion from the onset of schizophrenia.

Jolted back into the present by the clang of a slamming cell door at the other end of the corridor, I reviewed my predicament. A tear rolled down my cheek and splattered onto the khaki jumpsuit I'd been forced to wear while in detention.

I just now placed the hulking lawman. He's the one who pulled Allen to his feet and ushered him away while paramedics tried to revive me.

I remembered his voice as clearly as I heard it that fateful night. I watched him as I lingered above the wreckage of my rental car. For a moment, it seemed like Elizabeth had a fighting chance to live out her life, and to become the amazing person she was meant to be.

Then the big cop came over and gave Allen the bad news. He said, "They're both gone."

Now I know where I am, and why I'm here.

I died and went to Heaven that night. Following an unpleasant conversation with St. Peter, my daughter and I have returned to this mortal coil for thirty days.

My mother's in Hell. A Get Out of Hell Free card will save her from eternal damnation, but only if we successfully complete our task. And, while I'm not suggesting we've been set up to fail, apparently God has a sense of humor. Either this is God's little jest, or there's a shortage of suitable forms for us to occupy while we're here. Otherwise, why else would our souls have been placed into the bodies of an elderly white lady and an adolescent black lad?

# CHAPTER FOUR

I don't like to dwell on things I can't change, but I really must sort this out in my head.

The night of the car crash, a blinding light enveloped Elizabeth and me, propelling us deeper into its brilliance. We had no fear. I only glanced back once, but when I saw Allen weeping in the brawny arms of the big cop, I knew I had to return long enough to say good-bye.

I urged my daughter to wait, but as soon as I turned, Elizabeth ascended farther into the light with an ethereal smile riding on her face. As she faded from my vision, Allen's silhouette grew larger and more pronounced. I looked toward Elizabeth, then glanced back at Allen, and knew what I had to do. I caught up to my daughter and we ascended into Heaven.

Well, not exactly Heaven. It's more like a way station.

But there were mansions everywhere, and Elizabeth and I were led to ours by a guide—an odd little fellow named Thomas—who was small in stature and might've been a dwarf. I didn't notice any wings but they could've been concealed beneath his tunic.

At the way station, the skies were azure blue and the grass, emerald green. Thomas showed us to our house—a grand Tudor like the one back on our farm. Belties grazed in the garden.

Thomas said, "I trust the accommodations are to your liking, Madame, Miss. Let's have a look, shall we?"

As he opened the door and stepped aside to let us pass, I

walked inside and took stock of the interior.

The foyer had exquisite marble floors laid out like a chessboard in black and white tiles. A marble-topped Italian console with gilded carved wood and a rococo mirror lay to my left. The chandelier had to be Baccarat. Rainbow colors cast by the crystals played on the trompe l'oeil wallpaper—a Zuber mural painted with centuries-old wood blocks that formed a Venetian scene with statues of Greek gods and goddesses and pillars like the Parthenon.

The formal living room had several settees upholstered in silk damask with down-filled cushions and fauteuil chairs like the ones I grew up with. A stunning porcelain Capodimonte chandelier with sixteen branches decorated with hundreds of applied rosettes in various pastel shades hung from the ceiling, illuminating the room's eighteenth-century canvases.

The lounge had the comforting feel of a country club inglenook, with overstuffed leather club chairs and plenty of rich mahogany furnishings. I particularly fancied the eighteenth-century drop-front English secretary, but the fabulous Boulle period pieces with their tortoiseshell and brass inlays were as stunning as any museum-quality pieces I'd ever seen.

I could live here forever.

"This is our home?"

Thomas nodded.

I took a closer look. The interior seemed much smaller than it appeared from the outside. I gave him a strained smile. "It's a wee bit small for two people, don't you think?"

"Miss Elizabeth's accommodations are downstairs. Yours are upstairs, Madame."

I left our guide at the front door, and walked through the house to familiarize myself with the layout. When I'd finished nosing around, I returned to the living area.

"There's no kitchen. Where are we supposed to eat?"

Thomas gestured to his right. I hadn't noticed the massive dining table with a lavish display of my favorite foods.

"Brilliant," I squealed. "Chocolate truffles. And coconut shrimp. Beef bourguignonne. Green beans and new potatoes." Steam rose from the food as if it had just been prepared. "But where am I supposed to cook? How do I purchase groceries? How far are we from the market? Are these éclairs? May I have one?"

Thomas smiled. He spoke in a clear British tongue. "Madame, you do not need to go anywhere for food. Simply decide what you want, think about it, and it will appear to your liking."

"How much is this going to set me back? And what are we supposed to use for money?"

"It's free."

Elizabeth screamed from a different part of the house. Not the bloody-murder kind of scream, but the joyous, happily-ever-after kind.

She bounded in with excitement. "Mummy—I have a cinema. And video games. And the beach comes up to my patio."

I stared at Thomas.

"Shall we see if the rest of the house is to your liking?" Thomas said, and whisked his hand through the air with a flourish. A flight of stairs I hadn't noticed before appeared out of nowhere; together, Thomas and I ascended the steps.

My bedroom looked exactly like the one I grew up in. But I'm an adult now and the room seemed smaller than I remembered. Still, I didn't want to complain. A look of apprehension had settled on Thomas's face; it occurred to me that he might be held accountable to his superior if I didn't like it here. And I did love my room. The happiest times of my life were spent there, exploring other cultures through books.

"It's a wee bit small." I winced, not wanting to sound ungrateful. "Where's the wardrobe? Do I have clothes? How do I get things I need, like makeup and lipstick—I need mascara or people won't be able to see that I have eyelashes. There are other people up here, aren't there? Do I get to meet them?"

"In due time." Thomas stared at the door behind me.

"I once had this amazing turquoise silk dress," I reminisced. "And shoes to match. Got my picture in the society page wearing that gown, that I did." As I flung open the wardrobe, the rest of my sentence caught in my throat. I let out the same blood-clotting scream that I'd heard Elizabeth deliver only moments ago, as I stared into a room that appeared larger than the entire house. It must've been as long as three rugby fields.

Thomas grinned. "Welcome to the Imelda Marcos suite."

I'd moved into the wardrobe without being aware that I'd done so, surrounded by hundreds of thousands of beautiful shoes—all in my size.

I squealed, "I'm in Heaven."

According to Thomas, the way it works is different for everyone. For Elizabeth, who loves the beach and can recite movie lines, it's the ocean, a cinema and a stable of horses out back for long rides through the countryside. For me, it's shoes, fine food, and books. And the Belties. And my childhood home. And my friends.

But when I wished for Allen, he didn't appear. The dawning realization made me ask, "Are Elizabeth and I by ourselves?"

Thomas laughed. "Of course not. There's a banquet in your honor later this evening. I'll be back to escort you and your daughter. Tonight, you'll be reunited with your relatives and friends who've gone before you."

I spent the rest of the afternoon taking inventory of book titles in my personal library and trying on shoes. Most of the shoes and matching handbags were Italian. But I found a collection of Judith Leiber bags, too.

When I called down for Elizabeth to join me, she claimed she was swimming with dolphins and promised to come up later.

I didn't want Thomas to leave but he had others waiting to be escorted to their respective homes.

"If you want anything, just concentrate," he called over his gnomish shoulder. Then, he quietly evaporated.

In the quiet of my lounge—my informal living room—I munched on a burrito and other Tex-Mex cuisine similar to the food I was introduced to during my stay in Texas. As I reflected on my life, I realized that I'd forgotten to ask Thomas about pets.

I missed my beloved Pembroke Welsh corgi, Cassie, whose untimely death resulted from tainted chow from those bloody Chinese dog food–poisoning cases.

Unexpectedly, the skittering of claws sounded against the hardwood floors, followed by a luxurious blur of red and white fur.

My dog Cassie.

*My dog Cassie!*

I welcomed her with open arms. She bathed my face in the comforting smell of doggie breath. We lay on the down-filled cushions of a chaise lounge getting reacquainted. After what seemed like the passing of mere seconds, I gradually became aware of our guide standing beside me.

Thomas had arrived.

Elizabeth stood next to him, dressed in a beautiful cashmere tea-length dress in a gorgeous shade of camel. Her white-blonde hair glistened in the light like a halo. Sapphire-blue eyes sparkled brighter than the necklace and earrings that dangled near her face. My daughter looked as radiant as I'd ever seen her.

"I'm not ready," I said, but when I looked down at the slacks I'd been wearing, they'd been replaced by my favorite green silk dress. And matching Italian handbag. And matching shoes that felt so buttery soft against my feet that it hardly seemed as if I wore shoes at all.

"Where are we going?" I asked. "Is it close by?"

Instead of answering, Thomas drew his hand through the air and we were miraculously transported to—my breath caught—a place that resembled our country club.

An orchestra played soothing background music. People I'd never seen, dressed in period clothing, mingled all about.

"You didn't say it was a costume party." I cupped a hand to my mouth and did a quick lean-in. "I think we're in the wrong place, Thomas. I don't know anyone here."

"They're your ancestors, Madame."

Elizabeth whispered, "Cool."

"I'm related to John Adams?" A short portly gentleman with white hair bunched in a twist, with a pink English face and stocking-covered calves spoke to a young diminutive woman in medieval clothing. "Is that . . . ?"

Thomas confirmed my thought. "Joan D'Arc? Why yes. She's a pleasant young lady. Make sure you spend time with her."

Uncertainty set in. "But she's French. Does she speak English? Because I don't speak French."

"Speak from the heart. You'll understand each other."

Elizabeth, who'd disappeared without my knowing, reappeared breathless with excitement. "Mummy, Buddy Holly's here. He says he's supposed to play for you."

Sure enough, when I turned, Buddy Holly was talking to George Harrison and John Lennon. I inclined my head in their direction, and their words resonated as clearly as if I'd been standing next to them.

Buddy said, "I'm the headliner."

John challenged him. "She fancies us more," he said, thumbing at himself before turning his thumb on George.

"I'm her favorite singer. If you don't believe me, ask her."

Buddy removed his thick black eyeglasses, fogged the lenses with his breath and wiped them clean with the corner of his jacket before reseating them onto the pink indentations on the bridge of his nose.

"Maybe we will."

Buddy gave them a dismissive wave and tuned a guitar string. "You fellows wouldn't even have gotten as far as you did if it hadn't been for me."

Then Elvis swaggered in and all hell broke loose.

A winged referee swooped down, separated them and yelled, "Best you be thinking about where you'll be seated in eternity— smoking, or nonsmoking?" Jolted by the thought, they slunk off stage, not to be seen again for the rest of the night.

Except for Buddy.

"Do you think he'll play "Rave On"—because I love that song," Elizabeth said. Abruptly, she clutched her throat. "Mummy, look," she cried, "it's Teddy."

Teddy McLain had been Elizabeth's boyfriend back home. He died of a brain tumor a year before we left for the United States. That accounted for the main reason I insisted Elizabeth accompany me. The tumor, which was inoperable by the time doctors discovered it, had distorted the dear lad's face. But tonight, as Teddy played back-up guitar for Buddy Holly, his face was perfect, and the blond hair that had been ravaged by chemo had grown back.

Elizabeth headed for the stage.

A wave of sadness washed over me. Everyone at my reunion was dead.

Including Elizabeth and me.

# CHAPTER FIVE

I spent the rest of the evening getting to know distant relatives and ancestors, and visiting with my contemporaries.

I met Abigail, in her floor-length wool dress and white bonnet tied securely under her chin, who perished in the witch trials of Salem Village in 1692. Her crime? Contracting smallpox, and passing it along to the rest of her family. They died; she didn't. Which led the town to respond as if she'd deliberately started an epidemic. Which she hadn't. As a matter of fact, the colony folk were terribly sorry after tying her to a pole and submerging her underwater until such time as she admitted to being a witch. If she drowned, *Oh well, guess she wasn't a witch after all.* If she survived, she'd be burned at the stake or hung. Although the townsfolk expressed sadness and guilt for their mistake, fat lot of good that did, according to Abigail.

I met a Trappist monk in a long brown tunic cinched at the waist with a hemp rope, carrying a bottle of ale. As I listened in on the conversation he was having with a bass guitarist from the band, I overheard the musician say, "Sects, sects, sects—is that all you monks ever think about?"

I'd been told my family was related to Winston Churchill. Sure enough, I recognized his blustery presence at my reunion. In a conversation with John Adams, he said, "I am ready to meet my maker. Whether or not my maker is prepared for the great ordeal of meeting me is another matter."

A man I believed to be Albert Einstein stood in the corner,

talking to a geeky-looking young man with clear skin and a bad haircut. I eavesdropped on their conversation.

"Photons have mass? I didn't even know they were Catholic."

I turned away and came face-to-face with my nose. It was sitting on the face of a woman about my own age, who'd dressed in jodhpurs, a competition jacket, helmet and boots. She identified herself as my great-aunt Bettina. I searched my mind for a distant memory. My father's aunt Bettina had been fatally injured in a riding accident when I was small.

I met a minuteman, a Confederate soldier who carried the flag at the Battle of Shiloh and a Scotsman dressed in the kilt of the MacDonald clan. The clansman joined the monk, trying to talk him out of the bottle of ale.

"When I died, I wanted to be cremated and my ashes scattered over Kelly's pub. That way, I'd be sure my brothers would stop in to see me every night." He fist-chucked the monk's arm, then doubled over with laughter.

What an interesting lot. Can't pick your relatives, I thought.

Of course I got to see my contemporaries—cousins, aunts, uncles, both sets of grandparents and their parents and grandparents. I even met a young lady who looked a lot like Elizabeth.

And then the most amazing thing happened.

My father walked in.

I did a double take, grabbed Thomas, who'd migrated over to the impressive buffet for the lobster, and pulled him aside.

"What's my father doing here?"

Thomas beckoned me nearer, until I practically bent over at the waist to hear what he had to say. Staring serenely into my eyes, he spoke in a voice that was undertaker-soft. "The news of your passing was just too much for the old gent."

Then Thomas vaporized, leaving me alone to sort out my thoughts.

In a way, this reunion became cathartic. I never imagined what it would be like to have all of my family gathered together in the same room. I wanted to get to know most of them better. Some—like the drunken clansman—not so much.

By now, Elizabeth had turned into a social butterfly, making the rounds and greeting our friends and family members. Before I could run to my father, she appeared at my side dragging Teddy McLain by the hand.

"Mum, did you see Grandpapa? He's not sick anymore. His heart's fine. He wants to know where the golf course is."

I shook my head in wonder. Before my eyes, his clothing changed from the suit I assumed he'd been buried in, to bright plaid slacks, and a jaunty little hat. He grabbed my great-uncle Nigel and they headed for the door, dragging their golf clubs behind them like tails.

Then the obvious hit me. I hadn't seen my mother anywhere in this crowd.

"Have you seen Grandmummy, Lillibet?"

My daughter shook her head.

"Try to find her for me, will you?" The words had no sooner left my mouth than she took Teddy's hand, and off they went in a new direction.

Thomas reappeared. I knew he'd been at the buffet because of the powdered sugar stuck to his lips.

"Wedding cookies," he said, "I love them."

"I didn't see any wedding cookies."

"Do you love them?"

"They're not exactly my favorites."

"That's why you didn't see them. You have your favorites; I have mine."

I must've made a ghastly face because Thomas's smile dried up.

"What is it, Madame? Isn't everything to your liking?"

36

"It's . . . I . . . my mother."

Thomas's eyes thinned into a shrewdness I hadn't noticed before. "What about her?"

"She's not here."

He shifted his gaze to the dessert table.

"Thomas?" I couldn't tell if he'd spied a treat, or if he craftily refused to make eye contact. I pinched the sleeve of his tunic and gave it a spirited tug. "Thomas, why isn't my mother here?"

"It's really not my place to say, Madame."

But this was Heaven. Or something close to it. I was supposed to be *happy*. But how could I be happy with my mother missing from the festivities?

"I *demand* that you tell me where my mum is."

Thomas sucked air. He pursed his lips and made a whistling sound. His eyes darted around the room like pinballs.

"I want Mama," I said with the petulance of a five-year-old.

He coupled a sad headshake with a one-shoulder shrug. "Yes . . . and people in Hell want ice water."

# CHAPTER SIX

When I arrived home, I found Elizabeth and Teddy sitting out on the patio swing, catching up.

"Hello." I announced my presence. "Elizabeth, I need to speak with you."

"But, Mum, Teddy and I—"

"It's important." When I looked back where Teddy had been standing, he was gone.

"You can't just go around doing that, Mummy . . . making my friends disappear."

"We have an appointment with St. Peter. It's about Grand-mummy."

"What about her?"

"She's missing."

"Perhaps she didn't feel well."

"People in Heaven don't get sick. You saw your grand-father—no more heart problems."

She took this under advisement. "Do you think something bad happened to her?"

"Why, yes." Edginess brought out the sarcasm in me. "And we're going to find out what that is."

I took Elizabeth by the hand. In seconds, we were standing inside the lobby of—where else?—the country club.

A female guide, dressed in a tunic similar to the one Thomas wore, floated over to assist us. She directed us to a waiting room.

Fearing the worst for my mother, I asked, "Do you know what Hell is like?"

She answered in the drawl of a Southerner. "Wouldn't want to be there, that's for sure. I'm pretty sure Hell's a place where the motorists are French, the policemen are German and the cooks are English." Then she glanced down at her clipboard and her eyes drifted over the page. "It says here that you came to us from Texas, during summertime."

"That's correct."

"Well then, I reckon you already know what Hell's like, don't you?" she said with put-on sweetness.

She motioned us into overstuffed chairs. As we sank into fluffy cushions, Elizabeth reached for the coming issue of *Celebutantes and Stars* magazine.

She said, "Cool. Turns out Angelina prefers women. Who would've thought?" Leafing through the pages, she paused. "I knew that marriage would never last." Her eyes drifted to a fashion article. "I knew my knotted-scarf idea would catch on."

The door cracked open and a sliver of silvery light poured out.

"Mrs. Eloise Winthrop and Miss Elizabeth Winthrop may come in now."

Lillibet and I exchanged awkward glances.

We entered an area with fog so thick that it obscured our surroundings. The heavy scent of incense hung in the air.

I sniffed. "Does that smell like pot to you?"

Elizabeth took a deep breath. "It smells like lilies."

And it did.

Until I decided I liked the scent of freshly squeezed citrus better.

Now that I had a better understanding of how things worked around here, I knew that an individual could control his or her own Heaven. Elizabeth smelled lilies; I smelled the zest of Meyer lemons.

Without warning, the fog dissipated and one of the handsomest men I'd ever seen came into view. Actually, this imposing presence didn't *come* into view so much as the vapors disappeared to reveal him. He stood tall, decked out in a bright green polo shirt, khaki slacks and freshly shined loafers with argyle socks.

He shifted a golf ball from his right palm to his left, and then extended his hand for me to shake.

"I'm Peter."

"Peter . . . ?" I waited for him to furnish a surname. When he didn't, I said, "I have an appointment to see St. Peter."

"Guilty as charged."

He flashed the brightest smile, like actors in dental commercials on the telly. Which reminded me, how come I don't have a television?

"It's in the entertainment center," Peter said.

"Beg your pardon?"

"The TV."

"You know what I'm thinking?"

"Of course."

"Then why am I here?"

"You asked Thomas for the meeting."

"Yes. Right." I hope he didn't read my thoughts when I eyed him up. My reference point for good-looking men includes, well, you know—the good stuff. "I'm Elle Winthrop and this is my daughter, Elizabeth Winthrop."

After we made each other's acquaintance, he motioned us into chairs that I hadn't previously noticed. In fact, I'm certain they weren't there when we entered the room. We sank into cushions as squishy and comfy as the ones in the foyer.

"I have a tee time, so let's make this quick. You're here

because . . . ?" His voice trailed, and I knew he knew what I knew he knew.

Just trying to diagram the sentence in my head made me dizzy.

"I went to my family reunion and my mother was missing. Is she sick?"

"Not that I'm aware of," he said, seemingly unconcerned.

"On holiday?"

"I rather doubt it." Accompanied by the universal palms-up-shoulder-shrug move.

"Then why didn't she come to my party?"

The room's interior dissolved before my eyes, replaced by a golf course. Now, the three of us were sitting in a golf cart, speeding toward the first hole.

"My game's about to start," he offered apologetically.

"My mum's missing and you want to tee off? Well, I'm a wee bit teed off myself, if I do say so. What sort of place is this?"

Elizabeth put her hand on my knee to calm me. Or warn me.

"I want my mother."

There's a stubborn streak that runs in my family. My voice contained a harsh sort of edginess that I hardly recognized, and didn't much care for, and wouldn't have put up with in someone else if they'd directed it at me. As a newcomer, I wondered if such petulance would jeopardize my standing.

"She's not here."

I attempted to jog his memory. "I don't understand. She died before we did. She should've already been here. Do you often lose track of people?"

Peter shook his head, emphatic. "Sorry. Not here."

"Isn't there someplace you can check? Don't you keep a log-book?"

Elizabeth's fingernails dug into my knee.

"Not necessary." Peter slowed the cart. I grabbed his sleeve and hung on. He cast his eyes downward and the fabric came away in my hand. When I looked back, his sleeve hung as perfectly as before I had manhandled him.

"Then there's been a mistake."

"No mistake." He alighted from the cart and lifted out his clubs.

"Don't you have a caddy?"

"Certainly. It's Thomas. But he's afraid to come here until *we* finish talking business."

"I want my mother."

"She's not here."

"Like I said, there's been a mistake," I insisted.

"We don't make mistakes."

Elizabeth and I exchanged ghastly looks.

My voice trembled with the effort of speech. "Please. Check again."

"Your mother's not here. Silence. I'm about to tee off."

"I'm already teed off." My chin quivered. "Where is she? Where's Mama?"

But I knew. I didn't *want* to know—but I knew.

Then Peter said, "Come back in an hour," and got into his stance, and proceeded to swing.

# CHAPTER SEVEN

How long is an hour? I wouldn't know. Cosmic time isn't the same as what I'm used to. For one thing, there aren't any clocks where I am—and why is that? Don't these people keep track of time? It seemed like the passage of mere seconds before Thomas arrived at our Tudor and ferried us away in a golf cart. In the blink of an eye, we arrived at the T-box at the seventeenth fairway as Peter teed off with a *thwack*.

Had he really played sixteen holes of golf since we'd left?

He shielded his eyes, tracking the ball as it sailed through the air. When we were transported to the green, the ball teetered at the lip of the cup. Peter tipped it in.

"I can't seem to get any distance on my drive," he said.

"I thought this was Heaven." For no good reason, I glanced down at my hands and thought how nice it would be to have a manicure and pedicure.

"What can I say? I'm new to the game."

"How do you resist the urge to—you know—" I did a little finger wiggle to symbolize nudging the ball into the hole— "cheat?"

"Heavenly golf is no different from Earthly golf. You play against the course. Cheaters can't fool themselves."

"One more coat," I said to the nail tech as she wiped the excess polish against the stem of the bottle.

Peter frowned.

"Oi, you have your version of Heaven; I have mine." The nail

43

tech adjusted foam separators between my toes and gave the bottle of polish a good shake.

"Touché."

The nail tech evaporated. I wiggled my fingers, admiring her good work. "So what about Mama?"

"What about her?"

"Look—Thomas promised our stay here would be perfect." Frustration set in. "If Mama's not here, then it's not perfect."

"She didn't make the cut."

"I get that." My sarcasm brimmed. "So what do we need to do to get her here?"

Elizabeth whimpered. "We're not going to be happy if my grandmum isn't here."

"Make do," said Peter.

Hand to mouth, I sucked air. "Your answer to our happiness is *'Make do'*? What kind of place are you running here?"

Peter did the palms up, shoulder shrug. "What would you have me do?"

"Let Mama in." Hand on hip.

"Can't."

"Why not?"

"She doesn't deserve to be here." Exactly what I'd been afraid he'd say.

"But I've done lots of great things in my life. I gave money to build a wing at the children's hospital. My family built new restrooms in the children's annex at the church where my parents married. I'm talking hands-on labor. I did relief work in Africa during a plague, without any thought to my own personal safety."

"But those were *your* accomplishments," he challenged, "not Mama's."

Elizabeth bottom lip quivered. "I won't be happy . . ."

My chin corrugated. My bottom lip quivered. "Nor will I . . ."

I don't know how long I spent trying to convince Peter to help us get my mother up here; I only know that the longer it took to convince him to reunite me with my mum, the more I seemed to be losing ground.

Peter gave us the visual once-over. "Are you a betting woman?"

My eyebrow arched. Curiosity made me want to know more.

He took out a thin gold box from his trouser pocket and pulled out a card.

"Here's how it's going to work." He laid out the details. His conditions got spookier with each delivery. "You must be very careful with this. If you lose, there are dire consequences."

He handed over the card. Dread washed over me. If we failed the challenge, would Elizabeth and I be forced to give up our positions here?

"Be absolutely certain this is what you want. There are things that cannot be undone." When he finished, I accepted his challenge.

In the time it took to blink, he vaporized, and Elizabeth and I were back "home" in our wonderful Tudor.

# Chapter Eight

Dressed in powder-blue silk pajamas, Elizabeth sat cross-legged on our living room floor. Her seal point Siamese cat from childhood had shown up unexpectedly, and she stroked Jasmine's beautiful coat while my dog, Cassie, slept on the chaise lounge at my feet. Cassie was experiencing her own doggie heaven through thin snores and leg jerks, which only added to the suspicion that she was chasing rabbits through a meadow.

I turned over the card that Peter had given me. On some level, I expected the printing on it to disappear like invisible ink from a practical joke. But when I flipped it over to perform a closer inspection, it looked exactly the same as when he'd given it to me.

The card was about the size of a standard business card, with the look and texture of a Monopoly "Chance" pass—like the one from the board game that read: GET OUT OF JAIL FREE. Only instead of orange, the card was white. And instead of a message written in black unraised ink, one appeared in a jagged font that looked like flickering flames—a hologram of sorts—colored in iridescent shades of red and orange. It had a mesmerizing effect on me.

The longer I studied it, the more it pulsed and licked like flames from an actual blaze.

The longer I held it, the hotter it felt to the touch.

I could almost hear it crackle.

This was no ordinary card.

In letters formed by fire, it read: GET OUT OF HELL FREE.

And it bore a clause: *This card may be kept until needed or sold.*

Elizabeth cuddled the cat. The animal responded with a loud, steady purr.

I thought of the consequences of the arrangement I'd made with Peter. Naturally, Elizabeth didn't have the same vested interest as me when it came to getting my mother out of Hell. Elizabeth didn't *know* Mama, not like I did. She'd only been around Mama a handful of times, mostly during brief trips to the states. I also understood why she went along with this caper. My daughter wanted me to be happy.

I didn't abandon Elizabeth the way my mother abandoned me in search of a movie career; even at the tender age of eight, I couldn't fault Mama for the magnetic pull of Hollywood. When that didn't work out, she moved to New York City. Then, like a social butterfly, she flitted off to Dallas. The last place she lived was Fort Worth. I grew up believing she'd carved a niche for herself as a wealthy socialite. And by then I *did* fault her. Hugely.

"Lillibet—"

She looked up expectantly.

"—I think we should have a plan."

Big eyebrow arch. She's thinking *Worrywart.*

"Seriously," I said, "because we don't know when we'll go back. And if we get separated, we need to be able to find each other."

"He said we'd leave in an hour."

"You forget we're on cosmic time. How long is a cosmic hour? There aren't even any clocks here."

"I get it," she said with a nod. "Like the song."

"What song?"

"You know the song." She made a flip-flopping hand gesture in an attempt to jog my memory. "It's the one where the man asks God, how long a million years is in Heaven. And God tells him, 'It's about a minute.' And then the man wants to know how much a million dollars is in Heaven. And God tells him, 'It's a penny.' So the man asks God if he can have a penny, and God says, 'In a minute.' "

She grinned big.

Caught up in the moment, she launched into another theory. "Perhaps where we are, time is calculated in dog years—you know, one equals seven. So an hour would be . . ." She ciphered in her head.

I closed my eyes, not wanting to follow this train of thought. Math makes me dizzy.

"Or maybe it's like when you dream."

I blinked, unable to follow this new logic.

"You know," she waved her hand in a shooing motion, "like when you dream, it seems like the dream lasts all night. But really it only takes a few seconds—a couple of minutes at most."

I swear my daughter's more beautiful than I've ever seen her.

"The backup plan," I prompted, steering the conversation back on track. "We need to discuss it. Get our ducks in a row."

I was open to suggestions, but I had no idea what memories we'd carry back with us. What if we got separated and it took a month to find each other? We only had thirty days to accomplish this feat, this extraordinary task set upon us by an even more extraordinary St. Peter. Hard enough just to do what *he* had insisted upon—conceivably, we could spend the entire time searching for each other.

A horrible notion occurred to me.

Before I could speak, my daughter echoed my thoughts. "What if we don't look like ourselves? How will we know each other?"

"We should have a code word."

"What's our word?"

"I don't know. But we should think of one."

As she sat, free-associating, with Jasmine climbing her shoulder, a look of panic crossed her face. "Mummy, what if we don't speak the same language? How will we communicate?"

I tried to hide my chagrin. "We'll find a translator."

Elizabeth's eyes watered. They sparkled so shockingly blue they were luminous.

Now I'm worried. I knew this task wouldn't be easy, and I expected a few handicaps, but this venture could end up being a catastrophe. Not to mention we'd been warned of perilous consequences if unsuccessful. I shuddered, then reached down to pluck a bonbon from a box of chocolates that hadn't been there a moment ago and popped one into my mouth—and now I'm plagued with thoughts of failure.

"Will they give us money? Because if they don't, how can we hire a translator?"

My daughter was right. I hadn't thought this through. The only thing I was clear on was the object of our mission: If we wanted to bring my mother here with the rest of the family, we had to find five people to complete an extraordinarily good deed in Mama's name without disclosing the reason for the good deed.

*Good deeds? In Mama's name? Heaven help us.*

Peter and I had sealed the deal with a handshake before all the particulars had been ironed out. I knew, with certainty now, that I'd made a huge mistake. My mind cast back to our last conversation.

*"How will we know if we're on the right track—if the good deed counts?"*

*"It'll rain. Not just any rain. It'll be what Texans call a gully washer."*

*"Will we get our old bodies back?"*

*"You know better than that. But I'll find suitable vessels for you to occupy."*

Looking back, I remembered the way he chuckled without humor when I tried to find out how we'd look upon our return. A disconcerting feeling washed over me. I had a duty to Elizabeth for dragging her into this pact, so I'd pressed for more details.

*"You're not going to make it difficult, are you? Like giving me the body of a ninety-year-old quadriplegic in a coma?"*

*"You don't get to choose. You take what's available. Let me know when you're ready."*

And on that scary note, Elizabeth and I exchanged glances and said in unison, *"We're ready now."*

That's when he gave us an hour to get ourselves in order.

At best guess, it feels like only a couple of minutes have elapsed. But like I said before, we're on cosmic time.

"Think." My voice went strident. Only now did I realize what a very bad idea this had been. "Bounce ideas off me, Lillibet. Come up with a code word. Let's figure this out while there's still time. For all we know, we could be sitting here talking and—*poof!* Off we go to some third-world country without even the slightest warn—"

# CHAPTER NINE

Let's just say I'm not fond of this American jail and leave it at that. I wouldn't have liked it any better sitting here as Eloise, and as Sylvester Gooch . . . well . . . enough said.

But what I liked even less than imprisonment was the body cavity search they put me through before issuing me hideous coveralls and nasty-looking vomit-colored rubber slides that aren't even new. Ironically, beige makes me look dead.

Nine o'clock rolled around and a Tarrant County sheriff's deputy appeared at my cell.

In a voice that sounded both melodic and taunting, he ordered me to my feet. The bars clanged open and he led me to a holdover tank with other lads. They tried to make conversation, but I couldn't follow their gangsta talk and hand signals, and I figured my accent would only jeopardize my safety. I pretended to be deaf, and faked my own little version of sign language to show them I meant business. If you lock a monkey in a room with a typewriter, eventually he'll bang out a novel. I figured sign language works like that. At least I have a passing familiarity with the universal gesture for *Bugger off,* and in a place like this, finding ways to keep bigger lads at bay could come in quite handy.

It didn't occur to me to use the loo before I left my cell. Now I have to drop my underpants in front of this hulking band of cutthroats, and use the toilet in the holdover. I've never even seen my new bollocks and willie, much less handled them. What if I couldn't hit the toilet?

"I need the loo," I said to the deputy.

"Best I can do is let you talk to the senior officer."

I realized my mistake. "Not your lieutenant. The toilet."

"Can's over there." He pointed to an aluminum commode.

I shook my head. "Bashful bladder."

"Get un-bashful. Look, son, you're at the Crossbar Motel. If you want hotel treatment, go stay at the Four Seasons."

I decided to wait.

My huge clown feet were freezing. The thermostat must've been set on glacier mode, and they issued me these cheap flip-flops without socks.

Deputies led us to the courtroom. Bailiffs called our names, and we filed in one at a time.

When they brought me in and stood me before an empty podium, I sneaked a peek into the gallery. The shrieking black woman from the previous night sat in the front row with her graying hair strained back from her face in a bun. She'd dressed in brown polyester knit that fit like a tube—a big misshapen tube—and that reminded me of a National Geographic documentary I once saw where a reticulated python swallowed an entire gazelle carcass. Fury blazed in her eyes as she tried to incinerate me with a look. I swallowed hard. When a woman like Mrs. Gooch flares her nostrils so wide you can park a couple of Citroëns in them, well, you know she thought I'd taken a piss on her.

I felt an unexpected swirl of air. My attention shifted to the big wooden doors sucking open at the back of the courtroom.

The brawny cop from the crime scene entered, and checked in with the bailiff. At the same time, a woman strutted in from a side door, pulling a dolly behind her like a tail. I took in her presence in stages: the severe blue suit with a pinpoint oxford shirt; a mother-of-pearl cameo pinned at the collar; the way she exuded confidence as she extracted a stack of cases from the cardboard box she'd toted in.

This was the barrister—the state's attorney.

*I'm screwed.*

She called out, "Detective Stone, could I see you for a moment?"

With a knifelike look meant to cut me dead, he ambled over to the desk.

*That's Detective Stone? I know him.*

Correction. Know *of* him.

Stone is Allen's best friend. Some fellows introduce their fiancées to their parents, but Allen's parents are dead. So the most important person in his life, besides his son, was Chip Stone. He'd wanted me to meet Chip, but I never got the chance. Each time Allen set up a meeting, Chip got called out on an investigation.

Detective Stone—I still think of him as Chip because of the big build-up Allen gave him—pulled up a chair at the barrister's table and they had a little chat. As the state's attorney glanced over my file, Stone studied me through eyes with cold depths.

Then it got worse.

The last person I expected to enter that courtroom that morning was Allen Carswell.

The sight of him whipped my breath away. Hand to mouth, I stood dumbstruck and lovesick. I clutched at my throat, unable to help myself. Tears welled as I cried out, "Allen, darling," and tried to wave, but with my hands secured to a clattering belly chain, they only flapped uselessly at my waist.

Instead of sharing my delight, Allen scowled. Church-like pews comprised the seating in the gallery, and he slid into one of the rows, sat near the aisle, and focused his electric gaze on me.

"No, don't do that—don't be angry, darling, it's me—Elle.

Don't you know me?"

Detective Stone nearly upended his chair. Beet-faced, he stalked over, grabbed me hard by the scruff of the neck and jerked me to my tiptoes. The rest of my outburst slid back down my throat. He pulled me centimeters from his shopworn face and spoke in the low, throaty rasp of a heavy smoker. "Quit fucking with him or I'm gonna knock your block off."

"But he's my . . ."

*He's my what?*

*I keep forgetting I'm in the body of a twelve-year-old black lad.*

*But if I could only talk to him, I'd convince him I am who I say I am because I know things only Allen and I know. Intimate details. And yet . . . how could I do it?*

The prosecutor shot Chip a look of disapproval. He unhanded my clothes and backed away, still looking as if he'd enjoy the opportunity to thrash me.

Then a lady judge wearing a flowing black robe swooped in through a side door. The bailiff hopped to his feet and announced, "All rise," and four spectators leapt from their seats as she climbed a couple of steps and took her place behind a large wooden podium. The elevated platform, which had been finished in a lovely fruitwood stain, allowed her to preside over the courtroom with ease, while the other lads and I stared up at her.

*Black really isn't her color. It makes her look dead. Someone should tell her.*

"I say . . . that's lovely fabric. Is it silk?"

Her eyes thinned into slits. "Mr. Gooch, flattery will get you nowhere. I'm immune to it," she said, clipping her words.

*Well—I never.*

*Most ladies would consider it a kindness—like when you tell someone they have breakfast mortared between their teeth. I suppose she wouldn't appreciate hearing how my hairdresser could fix that bad cut, either. Makes those birdlike features seem practically sinister.*

She slid a pair of half glasses onto the bridge of her nose, and opened a thick file.

*My file.*

Her face visibly changed. "I remember you." Her voice developed an edge. "You were ten the first time we met. It was after Christmas and you stole a bike. Remember that?"

I shook my head. I had no memories of crimes Sylvester Gooch committed because I'm not him.

"I asked you what your mother thought about what you did, and you said she was a religious woman who dragged you to church all the time. Then I said you must've missed the lesson on 'Thou Shalt Not Steal'. Remember what you told me?"

I shook my head.

The judge burst into derisive laughter. Then she tightened her jaw and tapped a fingernail against the report. "I actually wrote this down because I couldn't believe my ears." She drew her finger across the paper as she read the documentation. "You said, 'When I was six I asked God for a bike for Christmas. I didn't get it. My mama said God doesn't work like that—you can't just ask for something and expect to get it. Then I realized He didn't work that way so I stole a bike and asked for forgiveness.' "

I barked out a little laugh. I couldn't help it. What a cheeky monkey, this Sylvester Gooch.

The judge sobered me with a scowl.

*I'm screwed.*

Her gaze drifted over the pages. "It says here you tried to mug an elderly woman—a Mrs. Hollingsworth . . ."

The door to the courtroom swung open; she stopped reading and glanced up.

I turned to look.

*Adelaide.*

The old lady from last night walked in, dazed and bruised, with a phalanx of wrinkles fishnetting her face beneath the harsh glow of the fluorescent lights. I realized she must have been at the police station all night, giving a statement against me, because she still had on the same pale blue dress with a rip at the waist and dirt on one side and carried her alligator handbag by its broken strap. The single black eye I remembered had doubled. She surveyed the courtroom through raccoon eyes that had turned a violent shade of indigo. After several seconds, she moved near the wooden pew where my fiancé sat. He gradually became aware of her eyeing him up and scooted in farther toward the center of the courtroom to allow her enough space to sit.

Her presence sent a chill through my heart.

*She's here to testify against Sly.*

*Against me.*

"And this must be Mrs. Hollingsworth," the judge announced to the room at large. She gave the old woman a curt nod, but I doubt if Mrs. Hollingsworth noticed. She was too busy fawning over my beautiful Allen.

"Your Honor, may I approach the bench?" The state's attorney, looking annoyed and rubbed raw from the yoke of public service, strolled up beside me.

I whiffed her perfume, an extraordinary scent that I just had to learn the name of before they hauled me off to do serious time. "I say . . . your fragrance . . . is it specially blended?"

"What?" She stared as if she'd misheard.

"Your scent." I sniffed her. "Is it custom blended?"

She shot me a look of utter disgust. "Judge, this little miscreant, Sylvester Gooch, is charged with attempted robbery. We may even bump it up to attempted murder. Detective Stone made the arrest, and Detective Carswell was present at the crime scene, and both are here to testify, if necessary."

The judge acknowledged each officer with a curt nod. "And the mother's present, as well?"

The black woman stood. She held up a hand. "I'm Myrna Gooch, Judge. Sly's mother."

"Please approach the bench, Mrs. Gooch." The judge wiggled her fingers. *Come hither.*

With Mrs. Gooch standing in front of the podium and the judge peering down over her glasses, the conversation moved with the speed of a tennis volley. I barely followed the gist of it. My beloved Allen, who was ripping out my heart by pretending not to know me, distracted me.

Snippets of "Got no money to pay for lawyers," and "Got two other kids to feed," floated to my ears.

This normally would've tugged at my heartstrings. But thoughts of kissing Allen overwhelmed me. I remembered his touch. And the way he used to . . .

Mrs. Gooch burst into tears, shearing my reverie.

With her emotions flaring, she flung out an arm and pointed to me. "I try so hard to make Sly behave, but he don't stop his evil ways. This the most selfish boy ever—" she wagged her finger "—and me, all the time, having to work so hard, Judge . . ." She raised three fingers. "I got three jobs, Judge, on account of Sly's father, he in the pen. He don't help on account of he's a no-account. And this boy, he gonna turn out just like him if he don't change his sorry ways."

After listening in stricken silence to this woman run me down throughout her crying jag, I could only stare in disbelief. Next she'd be wanting a firing squad.

A voice I didn't recognize came from behind and to the right—a British voice. Perhaps they'd called in the British Embassy. The old bird from the night before stood with her hand raised as if she'd been called to take an oath—or to ask the teacher's permission to visit the loo.

Which reminded me . . . I pressed my knees together and did a little jig in place.

Then a head popped up behind her and to the left, and I sucked air. "Thomas. Is that you, Thomas? Oh thank heavens you've come. Get me out of here."

The little man was small in stature, but I saw, too late, that he definitely wasn't Thomas.

The judge barked at me to be quiet. "Good morning, Mr. Kaufman, I didn't realize you were here. Why don't you stick around if you want to be appointed to this case?" She dismissed him with a pointed look.

"Your Honor, may I have a chance to speak?"

It was the elderly lady again, boring a hole through me like I was a sheep-killing dog.

The judge scanned the paperwork. "Adelaide Hollingsworth? You may approach the bench, Mrs. Hollingsworth."

It took a few seconds for the old woman to step past the single swinging saloon door and hobble to the podium. She had a spry gait for a woman her age. Still, I had the feeling she wanted the judge to put me away for life.

"I don't want to bring charges." Then she looked me dead in the eye.

*Do what?*

I almost blacked out from the shock.

*Did she say what I think she said?*

My jaw went slack. My mind raced ahead.

*If they let me go, maybe I can catch Allen before he leaves. I have to talk to him, I just have to.*

"I don't understand, Mrs. Hollingsworth. Are you saying this young man didn't assault you? Didn't try to snatch your purse? Try to rob you?"

"Well, you see, Judge, I think maybe what he needs is to speak to me in private so we can get this all sorted out before things get too out of hand."

"Mrs. Hollingsworth, things have already gotten out of hand. You have two black eyes."

"And I'm not real keen on that, but if you'd give me a moment to speak with the lad—"

"This is highly irregular."

"Please indulge me. I'm only asking for a smidgen of time. Five minutes. Can't we take a break?"

The judge looked at Mrs. Gooch. "You're the mother, what do you think? Would you have a problem with the victim in this case speaking with your son?"

Mrs. Gooch's eyes turned shrewd. "She ain't gonna hit him, is she? Don't nobody hit my boy but me."

"She isn't going to lay a hand on him." To Mrs. Hollingsworth, the judge said, "You realize I can't leave you alone with him, right? I'll allow Detective Stone to sit in while you talk to Mr. Gooch."

But the old lady said, "If it's all the same to you, Judge, I don't have a problem with Detective Stone, but I'd much rather have Detective Carswell sit in."

The judge shifted her gaze to Allen. "Would that be all right with you?"

Allen gave a derisive grunt. He wore a stunned facial expression—the kind routinely seen on police reality television shows, when a thug has fifty thousand volts of electricity surging through his extremities from Taser wires sticking out of his torso—only without the seizures.

Reluctantly, he agreed.

"Very well." She raised the gavel and hammered it down on a little wooden block. "We'll take a five-minute recess."

# Chapter Ten

The bailiff ushered us into an anteroom no bigger than the cell I'd spent the night in. The old lady and I sat opposite from each other in molded plastic chairs with a round government-issue bistro table between us. We eyed each other up, making quiet assessments, as Allen closed the door and propped himself jauntily against the frame.

This Mrs. Hollingsworth was going to send me to the electric chair. Or the gas chamber. Whatever they had in Texas. Lethal injection—that's it. The needle.

She did a quick lean-in. "Is it you?"

"Beg your pardon?"

"Is it you?" She looked at me, then cut her eyes to Allen before shifting them back to me. In a strange ventriloquism that proved difficult to locate its source, she recited the opening line to a child's rhyme:

"Trot a horse, trot a horse . . ."

I stared, dumbfounded, as she started the rhyme over, this time incorporating a series of complicated hand movements by patting her knees and clapping her hands together.

"Trot a horse, trot a horse, on a shell road." She carefully modulated her tone to conceal the words, as if she'd invented the secret Masonic handshake, and had to perform it in the presence of an outsider. Hand claps and knee pats increased in speed. "Baby . . ."

She paused, staring a hole through me with eyes so shockingly blue that they cut into my soul like lasers.

"Baby . . ." she prompted me.

My heart fluttered. I knew this rhyme by heart. The hand gestures, too. I knew it because I'm the one who taught Elizabeth when she was a wee tyke.

*This is code!*

All choked up, I joined in. "Baby Lillibet's going to town."

She smiled. Worry lines in her face went slack. Tension drained from her shoulders as if she were a blow-up doll with its plug pulled. For several seconds I didn't realize I'd been holding my breath.

Then we chorused, "Watch out, baby Lillibet, horsy may fall down."

We both came up out of our chairs like a couple of jack-in-the-boxes. Disguised as an old woman, my daughter embraced me from across the table.

"So it *is* you?" my Lillibet said expectantly.

"It's me." I held out my hands as far as they would go with the belly chain still in place, to show I wanted to hug her, too.

Allen stared, unable or unwilling to move. His face contorted into a grimace as if he'd been presented with a plate of something vile, and had to eat it.

We turned to Allen.

"It's us," I said, "Elle and Elizabeth."

"And the blue fish swims upstream . . ." He moved in slow motion, the way one does when talking to a crazy person. Put his hand on the doorknob and reared his head back.

"Don't you see," I said excitedly, "I'm Elle. And this is Elizabeth. We came back. They let us come back."

He answered in halting speech. "Who let you come back?"

"Peter. *Saint* Peter. He gave us a Get Out of Hell Free card— not for us—for Mama. And we have thirty days to find five people to do extraordinarily good deeds in Mama's name and then we can redeem the card and Mama gets to join us. In Heaven."

His upper lip curled into a sneer. One eyebrow fishhooked. "Uh-huh. I see. Well, good luck with that." He tapped a finger against the crystal on his watch. "Time to go."

"Don't leave." Taking little geisha steps, I came from behind the table, wanting to hug him. I didn't expect a hand block to the chest to hold me at bay. "I want to talk to you before you go."

"Right," he said, but his expression said *Absolutely not.*

When he opened the door to let us out, I spotted a loo directly across the hall and announced the need to visit it.

But when I tried to enter, Allen grabbed the belly chain and yanked me back. "Hey wise guy—down the hall. That's the ladies room, you little pervert."

*Well I knew that.*

I expected him to wait at the door, not to follow me in. But in he came and there I was about to burst, and trying not to explode. "Could I have a bit of privacy?"

"This is as private as it gets, buddy. And what's with the accent? Stone says you're a kid from Stop Six, not Trafalgar Square."

"I'm from Shropshire." I gave him an aristocratic sniff.

Allen set his jaw. He gave me the most evil glare, walked over to the toilet and unzipped his trousers. I knew I shouldn't look but my eyes strayed of their own volition.

He caught me staring. "Knock it off, you little homo."

"I'm not a . . . that."

I don't even want to go into what happened after that. Let's just say I wee'd on myself and Bob's your uncle. That's like Americans saying it's just that simple.

Back in the courtroom, I was feeling brilliant about my chances of leaving. Lillibet put her excellent oratory skills to work, and the judge seemed to be swayed by her persuasive speech.

We were home free.

It didn't occur to me that things could actually get worse.

But then I hadn't counted on Mrs. Hollingsworth's daughter, Priscilla, flinging herself through the courtroom doors, shoehorned into a pair of Jimmy Choos, wearing silk Capri pants, a gossamer blouse opened over a tank, and dripping in jewelry. For a few seconds, activity faltered as everyone took in her presence. No one said anything, but everyone watched her carefully, especially the windblown, straw-like hair that could've used a strip of crime scene tape around it.

Then the door opened a second time, and the insufferable Richard strutted in wearing a dark blue suit with a red tie. He took a seat in one of the pews, but Priscilla stood behind the bar, directly behind the prosecutor.

The judge said, "Who are these people?" She gave Adelaide a pointed stare. "Is this your family?"

Elizabeth answered with conviction. "I have no idea who these people are."

At the back of the gallery, Richard said, "That rips it. We're putting your mother in a home."

Priscilla, who'd hand-patted the wildness out of her hair, now looked like a runway model. But she acted like an anorexic, untranquilized badger.

In *voce fuerzo*, Priscilla announced in the drippiest Southern accent I believe I've ever heard, "Don't listen to a thing my mother says—she has dementia and Alzheimer's—and we're in the process of having her committed."

Before anyone had time to absorb this new disruption, the bailiff angled over and slipped the judge a note.

With a curt, "We'll be in recess while I return this call," the judge turned her attention to Priscilla and Richard. "Have a seat in the courtroom. Do not talk to any of these witnesses while I'm gone." She stepped down from the podium, shot me a wicked glare, and glided to her chambers like a graceful little bat. When she returned a short time later, she addressed me in a peevish tone. "So you're quite the basketball star."

A laugh bubbled up before I could squelch it.

"No need for modesty," she announced, clearly irritated, "I just spoke with your coach." She shifted her attention to the state's attorney. "I'm afraid without Mrs. Hollingsworth's testimony, the best the state's attorney has is a CHINS offense." I must've looked puzzled because she said, "Child in Need of Supervision. CHINS."

The prosecutor stared, slack-jawed.

The judge's gaze cut back to me. "You're very lucky, Mr. Gooch. I hope you realize that." Then she smacked the gavel and announced to the room at large, "We're adjourned."

I'm not sure what made the judge hold off on charging me with attempted robbery. Perhaps she'd seen enough drama for one morning. Maybe dealing with Sly had exhausted her. Then again, it might have to do with that cryptic phone call from the coach. Whatever the reason, I'm relieved I don't have to spend the next thirty days in kiddy jail.

# CHAPTER ELEVEN

I don't know why the judge didn't lock me up and swallow the key to my jail cell, but it's probably due, in part, to Lillibet's brilliant oratory skills. To be clear, the judge didn't outright release me; I have to see a probation officer first. Mrs. Gooch went on her way, though, and that's a blessing. Allen left, too, and it hurt my heart that he wouldn't even bother to stick around after I asked nicely.

Euphoria ended at eleven o'clock that morning.

While sitting at the barrister's table with thoughts of freedom vibrating off the top of my head, a tall, skinny fellow with thinning brown hair arranged in a comb-over swaggered into the room. Looking anxious and vaguely resentful, he pushed his wire-rim eyeglasses up the bridge of his nose and strolled my way carrying a fat brown folder tucked under one arm, and a cup of coffee in his free hand.

I gave him a bland smile.

"Well, well, well . . . if it isn't the poster boy for the failure of the criminal justice system. All right, Sylvester, let's get down to business." He dropped the accordion file onto the tabletop, pulled up a chair, and seated himself across from me.

"And you are . . . ?" I waited for him to introduce himself.

"Knock it off. You know perfectly well who I am. And cut the crap with the British accent. It sounds affected." He opened my file.

"When can I leave?"

He snorted in disgust. "You're not going anywhere."

"But the judge said I wouldn't be charged—"

His voice overrode mine. "With attempted robbery." He reached for his Blackberry, all brisk and efficient, and ran through a checklist of my recent crimes. "But this is a CHINS offense—Child in Need of Supervision—so you'll be fitted with an electronic monitor around your ankle, and you'll have to attend school every day." His face creased into a broad smile.

*Ankle monitor?*

*School?*

I felt a chunk of ice where my heart should've been. I knew enough about those contraptions from hearing Allen talk about them. The probation office would install a machine about the size of a DVD player in the home, and if you walked beyond range, it would send an alarm to a central monitoring system, and the law would come looking for you with the vengeance of Nazis.

"I can't wear an ankle monitor," I shrieked.

The concept was as uninviting as a pudding cup made with mouthwash.

He slurped his coffee, paying no attention to my objections. "Frankly, I'd hoped you'd do time for this latest offense. Then you wouldn't have to worry about anything but stamps, envelopes and commissary." Between sips, his face cracked into a thin grin. "By the way, just so you know, if you keep up with that accent you're going to get the crap beat out of you—or worse. Don't say I didn't warn you."

Jail had immunized me to indignity with the body cavity search. I could hardly fathom the possibility of anything worse. Then he wiggled his eyebrows and made a fist, which he forced into the circle he'd formed with the thumb and forefinger of his other hand to indicate a violent and extremely personal assault.

Realization dawned.

I placed my head in my palms, massaging my headache, unsure of how well I could imitate a Texas accent. Then it came back to me, the things the bigger boys said in the holdover cell, and I decided to try them out.

"Yo. 'Sup? How's it hangin' dog?"

I could tell he wanted to punch me out. Wanted to slap me so hard I'd end up across the pond, to Ireland, perhaps, picking out togs to replace the coveralls he knocked off me.

"I guarantee—" he paused to consider his empty cup "—if that old lady had wanted a piece of your hide . . . if you weren't the star of your basketball team, and there wasn't an All-City tournament riding on your ability to play in tonight's game, you'd be rotting back there in a cell." He made an over-the-shoulder thumb gesture at the door behind him. "But apparently your coach called and made a big stink, so here we are."

I barked out a laugh, and a leggy brunette who'd darted in to pick up a stray file twisted around to see if I'd gone off my trolley. Then I cackled so hard my face hurt.

The probation officer must be confused.

I've never played basketball in my life. Wouldn't know the first thing about it.

"Bottom line, you're getting fitted with an ankle bracelet," he explained in a loud, slow voice as if we'd never met before, and he thought I had a low IQ.

Then he opened the accordion file and pulled out a gadget no bigger than a pager. "This is an active-monitoring, three-ounce tamperproof ankle bracelet." He dangled it in front of me by one strap. "It's a portable tracking device lashed to the ankle and tracked by a global positioning satellite. The information's submitted every few minutes by cell phone to a tracking center, and has the ability to track the movements of a little recidivist such as yourself in real time.

"You can shower in it, do just about anything you want in it.

What you can't do is cut it off. Your mother already left. She had to let the technician into your house to set up the monitor, so I'll run you over to your school."

Talk about feeling sick.

"What grade am I in?"

"Very funny. You're never going to make it to the eighth grade if you keep this shit up. You'll either end up dead or doing time in the Texas Youth Commission."

I knew about the Texas Youth Commission from Allen. It's prison for bad kids.

My probation officer had me sign several documents; apparently, I have to check in with him on a regular basis. Then he gave me his business card with the time of my next appointment penned on the back. That's when I learned his name.

*Barney Geeslin.*

Mr. Geeslin found a big T-shirt and pair of blue jeans from the donation pile for me to change into since my blood-soaked clothes had been confiscated as evidence. Before he took me to school, he fitted me with the ankle monitor, and stood guard over me beneath the portico outside while he enjoyed a cigarette.

I drifted in and out of the conversation, alternately comparing Geeslin's comb-over to the "curlies" caught in the shower trap of a dingy motel, and fretting over the prospect of attending an American junior high school. This new body I've inhabited puzzles me. I can't think of anything worse than showering in a locker room after physical education class with a bunch of lads whose sole purpose is to contribute to the greenhouse effect by trying to outdo each other emitting bodily gasses.

I dropped onto the top step, miserable, while Mr. Geeslin blew smoke rings out of his mouth and talked basketball.

According to him, I'm a forward on one of the All-City basketball teams, whatever that means. When I didn't show up for school this morning, the headmaster notified the truant officer. Mr. Geeslin said the officer tracked me here after a series of phone calls—the first to my mother, the second to the homicide unit, and the third to juvenile hall.

Also, according to Mr. Geeslin, I'm what's known as a badass. A badass on the highway to Hell. But even worse, a badass whose only socially redeeming quality is that I'm the star player for my team, with an important basketball match on the line tonight at my school. Apparently the Highlanders are one match away from the regional championship, whatever that is, and the only reason I'm getting out of the can at all is because Coach Dodson convinced the judge that they needed me to win.

The irony was hardly lost on me. Unless you count riding on the back of a horse with your eyes squeezed shut, death grip on the reins, and screaming bloody murder an athletic activity, I've never played sports in my life.

Besides, if I attend school, when will my daughter and I have time to find five people willing to do an extraordinarily good deed in Mama's name? We've already wasted over twelve hours.

What I really wanted to do was to find a pair of scissors to cut this awful thing off my leg.

On our way out to the car park, we ran into Detective Stone. After a brief exchange, Mr. Geeslin asked if Detective Stone minded running me over to school. Apparently, Stone would rather eat glass.

I visualized my probation officer having a nervous breakdown. Instead, he pulled Detective Stone aside and growled something unintelligible under his breath.

Stone reluctantly gave in. He led me to the patrol car, and seated me in the caged area, slamming the door with an authoritative clunk. With him behind the wheel and me slumped downward against the seat with my head propped against the window and my nose fogging the glass, I watched the scenery roll by and plotted my escape. Neither of us spoke above the police radio squawk until I got a brain wave to ask about Allen.

That set him off.

"What are you bringing up Carswell for?"

I shrugged. "I'm worried about him."

"Yeah, well you don't need to be picking at sores now that they've finally started to scab over." Seeing my confusion, he said, "His old lady died in a car wreck. It almost killed him getting the news. We practically had to shoot him with rhino darts just to get him under control. So don't go fucking with his personal life, because I'd hate to have to beat you senseless."

I closed my eyes, lulled by the drone of Chip Stone's voice as he accelerated through the amber lights, belittling and trying to threaten me into good behavior.

We approached a red light, and I discreetly tried to open the door.

*Locked.*

*Donkey.*

*What shall I do if we wreck and the car catches fire?*

We made eye contact through the rearview mirror. He flashed a brittle grin from a mouth that seemed feral; in an instant, I understood how the three-man trapeze troupe, the Antares, felt when Gilles Gommeton plunged to his death during an aerial performance without a safety net at Paris's famous Cirque d'Hiver.

The traffic signal changed. The driver of the car behind leaned on the horn. Stone's window hummed down, and I looked away as he stuck out his hand. Then his radio crackled to life. He grabbed the microphone and spoke in police code.

When he finished, he said, "So your old man's in prison? You trying to end up just like him?"

Suppressing a loud intake of air, I entertained cruel fantasies that grew more pronounced the longer he railed against so-called bad acts committed by yours truly. After he finished running me down, I kept my vision mostly cast to the floor, no longer willing to look him directly in the eye.

Evidently silence frustrated the man, because he resorted to benign conversation in an attempt to draw me out. "So what do you like to watch on TV, kid?"

I started to tell him I'd happily stare at the electronic snow of a dead channel, listening to its hiss and crackle, if it'd get me out of this car. But the mere act of studying his tightly clamped jaw covered by skin the texture of old alligator luggage warned of a dark and volatile danger lurking underneath. No good could come from a chat with Stone. The detective possessed the kind of mind that can bend spoons, and extract false confessions.

I closed my eyes, and an image of Allen appeared behind my eyelids. I thought of our last intimate moments together, lying between passion-rumpled sheets, and could almost feel the caress of his hand on my breasts, hot breath against my ear and the tickle of cool air from the ceiling vents drying our sweat-covered bodies.

Then I fretted. How would I find Lillibet again?

Lulled by the drone of tires on the asphalt, I dozed.

# Chapter Twelve

A half hour later, Chip Stone turned me over to the truant officer, a jolly sort who joked as he escorted me to the classroom, and stood guard over me at the door as we politely waited for the teacher to acknowledge us. A dark-haired woman who didn't look much older than Elizabeth wrote on the dry-erase board with a colored marker. She gave us a sideways glance and nodded acknowledgment. As I entered the classroom, I heard the lock snap shut as the truant officer closed the door behind me.

One of the students called the teacher "Mrs. Lang," and I assumed she taught history, judging by the information she'd scrawled across the board.

Activity faltered when I came even with her desk. Everyone gave blank stares.

"Nice of you to join us, Sly," Mrs. Lang deadpanned.

A wave of giggles rolled through the room.

"Why, thank you," I said, "thank you so much. Lovely day, isn't it?"

She stared through narrowed eyes.

I stared back—such a lovely scarf. Wonder where she bought it? It's silk, with a white background and red, green, blue and yellow geometric splashes of color that set off her stunning green eyes and rosy cheeks.

*I simply must have one.*

She barked out my name. During my descent into scarf-rapture, she'd said something and I missed it.

Now, she had my complete attention. "What's with the accent, Sly?"

"What accent?"

Raucous laughter filled the air.

She pelted me with rapid-fire questions. "What? Is this your theme for the day? You're being British? Take your seat. And where's your history book? No-no—let me guess—" her voice oozed sarcasm "—you can't get your locker open, because you forgot the combination, right? And judging by your empty hands, I bet you don't have your homework, either, do you?"

"I don't know."

"You don't know? How do you *not* know?"

Peals of laughter filled the room.

I came up with the best explanation I could on short notice. "If I find it, I'll turn it in."

She huffed out an exasperated sigh. "You know, Sly, I'm sick of you never coming to class on time, never having your homework and never paying attention. But I'm not going to *harass* you, as you're so quick to accuse me of doing. Did you ever stop to wonder why teachers don't bother to discipline the problem students anymore?"

I shook my head, and ventured a guess. "They're lazy?"

"Because they've come up with a more ingenious way to get even with slackers like you. As long as your antics don't disturb the future doctors and lawyers and financiers of the world, we'll let you do what you want. And do you know why? Because when you reach my age and you've shortchanged your education, see how you like digging ditches in hundred-degree weather; or wasting away in an un-air-conditioned prison; or dying at the hand of a crack head in the back alley of some Godforsaken neighborhood where everyone's on meth . . ."

She ran out of steam.

Tears jeweled her eyes.

Clearly, my reputation had preceded me.

For a second, I thought she might fall into a crying jag. She'd worked herself up until her cheeks glowed neon pink, and turned blotchy.

"I'm sincerely sorry for the interruption," I said, my voice cracking.

She shot me a galactic glare that should've disintegrated me from its force field alone.

I did the only thing I could. Took the empty chair closest to the back of the room, as far away from Mrs. Lang's wrath as I could get.

"That's not your seat." She eyed me with contempt.

I got up and moved to another row.

"That's not yours, either."

This raised pointing and laughing to a feverish pitch.

By process of elimination, my desk turned out to be in the front row, right under her falcon-eyed stare. Over gales of laughter, I slid into my chair.

Mrs. Lang took command of her classroom again. "All right, for the rest of you who are actually excited about the role you'll play in changing the world, let's pick up where we left off." She glanced around. "Who can tell me about America's governing bodies?"

A precocious classmate raised her hand and spoke.

For the next minute or so, I was in and out of the conversation, trying to figure out if Mrs. Lang stored scissors in her desk, when she asked a question that perked me up. "And how does that compare with British Parliament?"

I sat erect and raised my hand.

Mrs. Lang laughed without mirth. "Sly." My name rolled off her tongue like undigestible food. "You want to field this question?" She barked out the cackle of a madwoman. "Right. Of course you do."

I took a deep breath.

We locked gazes.

Distress puckered her lips. She leaned against the chalkboard, weary with resignation, holding a colored marker like a pocketknife. "Knock yourself out."

I took the marker and drew a diagram on the board.

Once I finished, I spoke. "The parliament of the United Kingdom and Northern Ireland is the supreme legislative body of the UK and the British territories located overseas. It has parliamentary sovereignty, conferring ultimate power over the UK and the rest of the territories. And Queen Elizabeth—I love that name—Elizabeth. Elizabeth Regina of the House of Windsor, or Elizabeth Mountbatten-Windsor, since she married Philip Mountbatten of Greece, is the head. Parliament is a bicameral operation—that means it has two parts—with an upper house known as the House of Lords and a lower house, the House of Commons. Much like America has a President, a House of Representatives and a Senate, yes?"

Mrs. Lang's jaw dropped. She gave me a dedicated eye blink.

I glanced around and noticed everyone staring at me. You could've heard a strand of hair crash to the floor. "Shall I go on?"

In a voice less contemptuous, she said, "Please do."

"There are two types of members in the House of Lords— the Lords Spiritual, which includes the senior bishops of the Church of England—and the Lords Temporal, which includes members of the Peerage. Those members aren't elected by the general population but are appointed by past and current governments. The House of Commons is a democratically elected chamber with elections every five years." Then I made the comparison between Parliament and Congress. I paused for breath. "Shall I continue?"

Mrs. Lang wore the dumbfounded expression of an animal

trying to figure out why it had a tranquilizer dart sticking out of its shoulder.

"No, that's fine." She swallowed. "Very nice, Sly. See me after class, would you?"

I spent the next forty minutes calculating how much time it would take to unlock one of the windows, and estimating how far the drop to the ground would be in the event I made it past the sill.

Then the bell rang. Everyone made a mad grab for their books, ricocheting off each other while trying to leave. A busty blonde girl wearing a tight sweater with the name *Stella* emblazoned on an oval patch walked up and touched my shoulder. The knitted fabric accentuated her voluptuous breasts and she wore a short enough skirt to keep the waxer in business.

"Hi, Sly." She flashed a coy smile. "Ready for the big game tonight?"

I blinked. Something terrible was happening—it felt like I had a snake coiling in my crotch.

She leaned in close, grazing a breast against my shoulder. In a husky voice, she whispered, "If you cinch the All-City Playoffs for us, I'll wait for you behind the bleachers."

She nonchalantly hooked a thumb into the waistband of her skirt and pulled it away from her belly enough to flash her piercing, siphoning off the rest of the oxygen from my lungs. After shifting a precautionary glance at the teacher, she mouthed, "I'm all yours," and lewdly flicked her tongue at me.

My eyes widened at the silver bolt piercing her tongue.

A light-headed rush filled my head. I squeezed my eyes tight. I thought I might be turning into a lesbian until I accepted the fact that I'm a twelve-year-old boy with testosterone raging through my system.

When my eyes popped open, Stella was gone, and Mrs. Lang

was closing the door behind the last student. She crossed the room and perched on her desk in front of me.

Her expression turned cagey. "What's the deal?"

"Beg your pardon?"

"You studied."

I gave her a little shoulder shrug. I grew up watching the BBC. Some of it stuck. What can I say?

"Why don't you try this hard all of the time?"

Another shoulder shrug.

"You could turn out to be a contributing member of society if you'd put forth a little effort."

"Yes, Mrs. Lang."

"So why don't you?"

Shoulder shrug.

"I'm giving you an 'A' today for class participation. If you do this every day, it should bring your average up enough to get you a passing grade."

I nodded. "Do you by chance have a pair of scissors I could borrow?"

There must've been something scary about the thought of us in the same room with the door locked, with me holding scissors, and her probably wishing she had a whip and a chair, because she denied having any.

I decided to do damage control for Sylvester Gooch. "Mrs. Lang, I think you're a good teacher."

Her eyes misted. "That's nice of you to say, but the kindest thing you can do for me is to pay attention, complete your assignments and show me respect."

"You're right. I'll work on that."

She braced her arms across her chest. "I meant what I said about ending up in prison."

"Yes, Mrs. Lang. I intend to do better." And then, "By the way, where'd you get that scarf?"

"It was a gift from my husband." I nodded, and her eyes narrowed into slits, "Do you really like it? Or are you just saying that to suck up to me?"

"I was thinking maybe I'd try to get one for my mama. She works three jobs," I parroted what I'd heard in court that morning, "and my daddy's in prison on account of he's a no-account. And my mama thinks I'm pretty sorry, too. It'd be nice to get her a scarf like that to apologize for the wrong I've done. I guess a scarf like that would cost a lot of money, though . . ."

Which reminded me, I have no money. Not even enough coins to drop down the chute of the pay phone to call my probation officer and ask for the address of the old lady I'm supposed to have mugged. Not that he'd give out that information to a thug, but I'd already invented my cover story. I decided to tell him I was writing a letter of apology, and needed to know where to send it.

Lost in thought, I didn't realize Mrs. Lang had unknotted the scarf until she handed it to me.

"Oh no." Wide-eyed, I waved my hands. "I didn't mean you should give it to me. And your husband . . . I couldn't."

"If it'll make things better at home so you can study more, it'll be worth it."

My eyes misted. It felt like a golf ball had lodged in my throat.

"Why, Sly—are you crying?"

I wiped my eyes with the back of my hand. "Allergies." I rose and headed for the door. With a backward glance, I said, "Mrs. Lang, you're my favorite teacher."

She dismissed me with a wave, like shooing away a bothersome pet. I planned to leave but had no idea which direction to head off to. Not that it really mattered—my feet wanted to move like they were on fire. If I could just get off the school grounds, I could snip this monitor off my ankle.

A truant officer standing outside the door wrecked my plans.

I tried to put him at ease. "I can get to my next class, but thanks for caring."

"Let's just go." Said nastily.

This went on the rest of the afternoon until physical education class rolled around.

Now I think I might die.

I'm supposed to go into a locker room and change into gym clothes? The thought of having to shower with thirty naked boys made my head spin like an afternoon on the circus tilt-a-whirl.

Since I walked into gym class tardy and with an escort, I managed to dress in relative privacy. It took several attempts to find the right locker but I located the basketball uniform for Sylvester Gooch, and a set of freshly laundered gym clothes.

After tucking away Mrs. Lang's silk scarf with my street clothes, I dressed quickly in a pair of shorts and wore the T-shirt that Mr. Geeslin gave me. While everyone else gathered around the instructor, I had to run laps for being late.

I hate running. I suppose it's better than, say, being mauled by a tiger or having gang members chase you—or being subjected to a body cavity search like what happened to me at juvenile hall—but that's about it.

Sly, however, quite enjoyed it.

I'd completed my fifth lap around the gym when I heard my name called out. It came from behind and to the right. When I looked back, a huge black man wearing Kelly-green sweats motioned me over.

"You ready for tonight's game?" Light bounced off his shaved head, giving it the sheen of a scoop of dark chocolate ice cream.

Which reminds me.

I can't remember the last time I ate, and I'm starving. For some reason, I crave a double-meat, double-cheese burger with potato fries and a shake. The thought jolted me. I rarely eat that stuff. It's toxic. I prefer salads, or fish and chips, and the occasional glass of wine for my light meal.

"Gooch, what the fuck's wrong with you?" Black eyes burned a hole through me. The man spoke fast and chopped his words. He reminded me of those drill sergeants you see on the telly in old war movies.

Inspiration struck. "I don't feel good. I think I got a bad case of flu."

"Come down with it tomorrow. Tonight, your ass is mine."

"I don't think I can play."

"Listen up, Gooch, you've got no choice. Without you, we're in the shitter. I've waited my whole career to have a team with a chance to make the state playoffs. I'm counting on you. Do not let me down, Gooch."

This must be Coach Dodson. He had the brawn to snap my neck like a toothpick.

The bell rang, effectively putting an end to my misery. But instead of letting me go, the black chap in the green sweats made it clear I'm eating dinner in his office "so you don't boogie"—whatever that means. I wasn't much for chatting so I asked Coach Dodson if I could nap on his sofa. I've suddenly become very tired, and a nap will lend credibility to my story that I'm sick.

# CHAPTER THIRTEEN

"I don't understand you, Mother. You could've been killed," said Priscilla Hollingsworth to Addie as they left juvenile hall. "And then you go and tell the judge that you don't want to press charges against that little monster? What's wrong with you? Never mind—don't bother to answer." Her hectoring voice disintegrated into mutterings.

Elizabeth Winthrop knew better than to get into a protracted discussion with the haughty socialite, after all, Priscilla had launched a plot to put her mother under a guardianship. Or have her committed to an asylum. Or force her into a nursing home. And Elizabeth didn't want to make things worse for the old girl.

Under the circumstances, Elizabeth thought it best to keep her answers as short and innocuous as possible. What she really needed was peace and quiet, and possibly a telephone. She needed to hunt for Sylvester Gooch.

"Don't ignore me, Mother. This is *not* going away."

"You shouldn't worry, dear. I wasn't killed," Elizabeth said, posing as Addie with put-on sweetness.

Priscilla, still in a filthy mood from court, looked down her nose. "I'm taking your car keys away. This isn't an easy decision, but you simply cannot be trusted. Richard says—"

"Richard?"

"You don't remember Richard? Is this going to be one of those days?" Fueled by exasperation, Priscilla peppered her

conversation with expletives. "I don't understand this Alzheimer's business. We live in the same house. You see him
everyday. How can you not know who Richard is? It's like you
have Swiss cheese for brains."

*Uh-oh. Bad mistake.*

"I know who Richard is," Elizabeth snapped back. "What I
want to know is what he has to do with these decisions."

"He's my husband. He gets a say-so in this."

"I don't know why. He's not even family."

"Did you just hear me say Richard's my husband?"

"I heard you. But Richard's not blood kin. He's replaceable.
Your mother is not."

"I won't let you shame me." Priscilla pressed the remote and
the door locks popped open. When Elizabeth attempted to open
the front passenger door, Adelaide's daughter became even
more snappish. "I'm sitting up here. I always sit next to Richard. Or did you forget?"

Elizabeth studied the skirt of her dress. Expensive fabric, but
ruined. Much like these wretched people who called themselves
Priscilla and Richard.

She said, "Where are we going?"

"Home."

With her body aching, and her joints creaking, Elizabeth
wrangled her way into the back seat. She'd already assumed her
role as Adelaide Hollingsworth; now, she embraced it. As soon
as she yanked the door closed, the driver's side opened up, and
Richard slid in behind the wheel. They locked eyes in the
rearview mirror.

"What are your plans for the rest of the day?" Priscilla stared
straight ahead, as if she didn't really care.

Elizabeth and Richard gave simultaneous answers: "I might
ring up a few of my friends."; "Golf."

Priscilla said, "I was talking to Richard."

"I'm going to the country club," he said.

"That's your answer to everything."

"I need to relax. This whole business with your mother is putting a lot of stress on me."

"What about work?"

"Forget work. As for you," he said, as he slid Priscilla a sidelong glance, "you'd better be spending the morning making phone calls."

Elizabeth didn't need to ask. Poor Addie. What had she done that was so bad that these people wanted to get rid of her?

Tires droned along the roadway, lulling her into a hypnotic trance. She settled back into the seat and closed her eyes. Maybe if she feigned sleep, Priscilla wouldn't pry, asking questions that she couldn't supply answers for. Elizabeth certainly knew better than to ask her own questions. To do so would only mean digging a deeper hole. Better to just listen. Get a feel for things before deciding on a course of action. No need to do anything that would leave the real Adelaide Hollingsworth in a worse position once the thirty days were up.

Then, she dozed.

Priscilla's voice jarred her awake. "We're home."

Elizabeth's lids popped open. They'd parked in front of a beautiful two-story, French style house that clearly had architectural and historical significance. Red bricks, appointed with contrasting wrought-iron details in a lovely shade of dove gray, turned what might have been an ordinary mansion into the jewel of the avenue. Hundred-year-old pecan trees shaded the sprawling-but-beautifully-landscaped gardens, while box-woods and seasonal flowers in festive shades of periwinkle blue and red bloomed in the beds.

She alighted from the metallic-blue Jaguar.

A lawn jockey painted in the style of Black Americana welcomed them onto the porch with an outstretched arm that dangled a lantern.

A question rolled off Elizabeth's tongue. "Do we like black people?"

Priscilla, looking quite efficient, stood tall and erect. "If we didn't, we wouldn't have Jessie, now, would we?"

"Who's Jessie?"

"The cook."

"Of course." Elizabeth cupped a hand to her ear. "Because I thought you said Tessie and I don't believe I know anyone named Tessie."

Priscilla did a heavy eye roll. "You deal with her," she told Richard, and walked on ahead of them.

Elizabeth studied Adelaide's daughter from arm's length. She took in the woman in stages: pretty, fortyish, with pale, flawless skin and classic features; but reed thin to the point that the starving-orphan look gave her hollowed cheeks a certain severity. Her unpleasant disposition only added to the bitter image.

Anger pinched the corners of Priscilla's mouth. She unlocked the front bolt with her key, shouldering the massive wooden door to dislodge it. Accompanied by a prolonged squeak, the door gave way with an inward swing.

"Damned that lazy Perry anyway." Priscilla inspected the frame. "I told him to oil these hinges. It's a wonder I didn't dislocate my shoulder. You should fire him, Richard. Jessie, too. They're old and they're slow. See?" She traced a finger over the hardware. "Nothing. Not even a hint of lubricant. Let me tell you, Mother, I've found a wetback named Pedro who will keep up with the yard for half the cost; and his wife, Maria, can clean house. They work for cheap, you know, since they're—*not from here.*"

Elizabeth let the silence speak for her. She trailed Priscilla inside, and gasped as she glanced around in awe.

They stood in a marble-tiled entry with a mural-covered wall that had been covered in hand-blocked Zuber wallpaper and friezes. She recognized the maker immediately. Her decorating class had toured the Zuber factory in France, where even the building had been considered a historical monument. Original woodblocks from the seventeenth and eighteenth centuries were still currently used but at a cost that proved prohibitive for most individuals. She'd seen Zuber in the White House, though, and at the home of a filthy rich oilman in Argentina.

And now at Hollingsworth Manor?

She estimated the value to be around fifty thousand pounds, roughly a hundred thousand US dollars.

"These walls are lovely. Just absolutely fabulous," she said through a reverent breath.

"Yes, well, you'd better like it since you're the one who picked it out," Priscilla said grudgingly. "Daddy didn't want it. I'm surprised you talked him into it. It's one of the few times you went against him, and I'm sure that contributed to his stress." She held out her hand, palm up, in demand. When Elizabeth didn't respond, Priscilla prompted her. "Your car keys."

Elizabeth bosomed her broken handbag.

"If you don't give me the keys, I'll have Broderick take the car to the dealership, and get the ignition switched out."

*Broderick? Their son? Or maybe* my *son?*

*Who'd name their kid Broderick?*

*A psycho, that's who.*

Well, that wouldn't do, now would it? Because it'd be far easier to relocate the keys than it'd be to figure out how to hot-wire a car.

Sylvester Gooch, on the other hand, probably knew how to boost a car. But since that wasn't Sylvester Gooch inside his body, Elle Winthrop certainly wouldn't know.

With a pout of defensiveness, Elizabeth opened the bag, fished out a key fob and handed it over. Priscilla took the entire ring and deposited it into a porcelain bowl with applied cherubs and roses—probably Meissen—that had been centered on a marble-topped Italian console. Elizabeth peeked inside. The keys lay atop a smattering of business cards in various shades and fonts—similar to the one St. Peter had given them.

The Get Out of Hell Free card.

She remembered why she'd come back, and set her mind on reuniting with Sylvester Gooch.

"Don't even think about getting those keys back."

"But what about my house keys? What if I want to take a stroll and need to get back inside?"

Priscilla screwed up her face. "Take a stroll? You don't take walks. You don't even go outside without a hat. Which reminds me, where's your hat?"

Elizabeth gave her a one-shoulder shrug. "I'd like a plate of food and a spot of tea, if you don't mind?"

"A spot of tea? What's this British crap? You've been talking like a Cockney ever since we rescued you from that awful crime scene."

*Cockney? Of all the lowbred things to say.*

Elizabeth ground her molars. Members of the Clive Winthrop family were not working-class East End Londoners. Neither were they born within earshot of the Bow Bells, the bells of St. Mary-le-Bow church.

"That's probably what it is," Priscilla said to Richard. "That punch in the face probably caused it." She sighed. "Well, no matter. We won't have to put up with it much longer."

"Perhaps I enjoy talking this way," Elizabeth said, feeling suddenly colder. "Is it hurting you?"

"It's weird, Mother. You've been doing lots of weird things this past year."

"Such as?" Elizabeth challenged her.

"Forgetting who we are, for one thing. Losing things. Forgetting the date, the time and the place. The freaking President of the United States."

"I'm under stress."

Priscilla barked out a laugh. "Stress? You want stress? I'll give you stress—" A round black woman waddled in, and Priscilla's unpleasant shrill came to a screeching halt. "What is it, Jessie?"

The cook ignored Priscilla. " 'Morning, Miz Addie. I heard you say you was wantin' a bite to eat."

"Yes, please."

"I made you a plate. So if you wants to follow me into the kitchen, I'll show you what we got." Jessie turned to leave, and Elizabeth trailed her.

With a dismissive glance, Priscilla nabbed Richard's arm and strutted off down the corridor. When Elizabeth was certain Priscilla had headed off into another part of the house, she excused herself long enough to pluck the key fob from the bowl and pocket the keys.

## Chapter Fourteen

When Elizabeth caught up with Jessie, the spread being prepared on a wooden worktable looked disgusting.

"Is that porridge?" Elizabeth asked. "I despise porridge."

"It's your oatmeal. And you love it."

Elizabeth shook her head. "Ummm—Jessie? I'm sorry you went to all this trouble but what I want is a big, juicy burger with potato fries. And—may I have a look?" Without permission, she angled over to the refrigerator and opened the door.

"I reckon it's yo' house, Miz Addie," said Jessie, "but Miss Priscilla's gonna be mighty mad. Miss Priscilla say the doctor say you have a cholesterol problem."

"Well maybe Miss Priss just needs to button it."

A smile cracked Jessie's stony face. "Now that's the Miz Addie I been knowing my whole life. Where you been, girl? Lettin' these spoiled children boss you around . . . umm, umm, umm." She shook her head. "You want a burger and fries?" She reached for a cast-iron skillet from the pot rack overhanging a butcher block island in the middle of the kitchen.

Elizabeth took a seat at the breakfast table.

"Oh, no, Miz Addie." Jessie set the skillet on the countertop and pulled Elizabeth to her feet. "Better not let Miss Priscilla see you in here hob-knobbin' with the help. You take yo' place at the dining table. I'll wait on you."

She pointed to a swinging door. Elizabeth reluctantly passed through it.

According to the antique grandfather clock, fifteen minutes passed before Jessie sashayed in with a cheeseburger and fries.

"Thank you, Jessie." She took a huge bite, savoring the mouthful as she chewed.

"Whatchoo want to drink?"

"What do we have?"

"The usual. Bottled water, liquor, wine, lemonade, milk for your osteoporosis on account of the doctor say you got brittle bones."

"I'd like a milkshake. Chocolate."

"Got no chocolate. But we got vanilla on account of I keep my own private stash, and I don't mind sharin'. It's so nize to see you eatin' again, Miz Addie. Been a long time since I watched you wolf down yo' food like a field hand. Umm, umm, umm."

She waddled back into the kitchen. Elizabeth heard the refrigerator open and close, followed by the whir of a blender. Jessie returned with a milkshake she'd poured into a large Baccarat water glass.

"Better not let Miss Priscilla catch you eatin' that." Jessie's gaze stopped on the last remnants of burger. "Lordy mercy, Miz Addie, you done finished?"

Elizabeth's eyes fell to half-mast—now *this* was Heaven. Jessie stood guard while she popped fries into her mouth.

Elizabeth patted the table. "Sit."

"Oh, no, Miz Addie. We don't sit at the dining table with the family. Me and Perry, we eats in the kitchen."

"Who's Perry? And who's Broderick?"

A sad look settled onto the cook's face. "Miz Addie . . . Perry—he work in the yard. He the gard'ner. Broderick's yo' driver."

"I have a driver?"

Jessie nodded. "For three months now."

Jessie had a melodic way of speaking, dropping consonants off the end of her words, and often in the middle, as well.

"Do I like them?"

"Oh, yessum. You love Perry. He been workin' here five years more than me."

"How long have you been here?"

"Nigh on thirty years. You and Mr. Buzz, you got us when we was young."

"Mr. Buzz?"

"Yo' husband. Don'tchoo 'member?"

Elizabeth feigned surprise. "Of course I remember." She did a conspiratorial lean-in and touched Jessie's hand. Perspiration dotted her dark skin; plump hands shimmered with grease. "Sometimes I play dumb."

But Jessie shook her head. "Miz Addie, if you know what's goin' on 'round here, you should say so. Miss Priscilla and Mr. Richard, they just lookin' for a reason to get you outta this house."

Elizabeth ventured forth a thought. "But the house is mine." There. She'd made a bold statement and sat back to see how it'd go over with the help.

"The house is yours, but Miss Priscilla and Mr. Richard got a life estate in it. Means they get to stay here unless they stop payin' the taxes on it, or abandon it."

"A big house like this must take a lot of money to run."

"You know that's right." Jessie punctuated her statement with a curt nod. "But if you get married again within five years of Mr. Buzz dyin', or move out any time before five years is up, Miss Priscilla and Mr. Richard get the house all to themselves—no limitations." Jessie sat back and folded her arms across her ample breasts. "Says so in the will."

"Why would he do that? Mr. Buzz, I mean."

"Mr. Buzz—he a jealous man. Didn't wantchoo triflin' with

none of his rich friends."

Elizabeth checked her wrinkled hands. The gnarled fingers. She pinched a piece of parchment skin and lifted it. Instead of snapping back when she released it, it oozed back into place like melted wax.

"Do you remember the day my husband died?"

Jessie gave a resigned sigh. "Like it was yesterday." Her attention strayed to the ceiling. Without prompting, she recited the date.

Only three and a half weeks away from reaching the restriction her dead husband had saddled her with. If Jessie was correct, then the house would be hers outright. No wonder Addie's daughter and son-in-law were trying to exercise control over her. Priscilla and Richard planned to stick her in a nursing home. Or the nuthouse.

"Jessie, do you know where my checkbook is?"

Big headshake. "Miss Priscilla took it away 'bout three months ago. You get a 'lowance."

Smart, the two of them keeping the old lady dependent on them for money, feeding her crappy food, and watching like a hawk so she couldn't get wriggle out from under their collective thumbs.

"Jessie, where's my bank?"

"Up at the end of the street. Turn right and go a block. Bank's on the left."

Elizabeth wrapped her hand around the cook's wrist and tightened her grip. "You won't tell anyone about our conversation, will you?"

"No, ma'am. I ain't sayin' nothin' 'bout nothin'."

"Jessie, why do you think I put up with Priscilla?"

"I reckon it's 'cause you feel a sense of obligation. Much like you do with me and Perry now that we're old and slow."

"Are you and Perry married?"

Jessie hooted. "Miz Addie, you be knowin' this better'n anybody. Wasn't for you, Perry woulda never *got* married. You the one made him axe me."

To hear Jessie tell it, she and Perry once lived in the Hollingsworth house.

"Not anymore. Not for six months now. Not since you started forgettin' stuff and Miss Priscilla and Mr. Richard made us move out on account of they said we got enough money from workin' here and didn't need room and board."

"Where do you live?"

"Stop Six. On account of we couldn't find anything cheap enough on this side of town. So now we get up two hours early so we can get dressed and catch the bus. And we get home an hour later."

"How'd you like to move back in?"

"Miss Priscilla, she say she gonna get rid of us when you go to the nursing home, on account of we don't move so fast, and they need people who can get twice as much done in half as much time. She already interviewed a couple of illegal aliens to take our places 'cause she say they more affordable."

Elizabeth nodded. "We'll just see about that. Now don't you fret. Show me to my room, and find me a phone book. I have calls to make. And Jessie—" she locked the cook in her gaze "—don't you worry. You and Perry aren't going anywhere as long as I'm alive. And for dinner tonight, I want fried chicken and mash. With real gravy."

"Miz Addie? How long you gonna be British?"

Elizabeth grinned. "For a while. It suits me, don't you think?"

"Sho' nuff do."

# CHAPTER FIFTEEN

Around seven o'clock that evening, distant vocal rumblings awakened me from my nap. The door to Coach Dodson's office banged open, and the coach angled in and tossed a team uniform to me.

"Up and at 'em, Gooch. Let's go out and kick some ass."

I didn't ask where he got the uniform, just shucked down to my knickers and hopped on one foot as I tried to stuff a toe into the bright green shorts. With an overhead gyration, I slipped into the green and gold tank with my name emblazoned across the back. Made me want to throw up. A series of disgusting things popped into mind in this feeble attempt to finagle my way out of the match.

Then a couple of teammates I recognized from physical education class trotted up and cuffed me on the arm before I could run away.

"Where you been, dog?"

This fellow had red hair, pasty skin, and a freckled face, but he talked as if he'd been raised in the ghetto. Music leaked out of the ear buds to his CD player.

"Been chalking your pool cue?"

*Chalking my pool cue?*

I frowned.

His mate, a black lad, said, "LaVon, he been lookin' everywhere for you. Say he gonna kill you if you talk to Stella again."

I tried my best to mask my British accent and decided I'd be able to pull off this masquerade a whole lot better if I kept my answers to a minimum.

I remembered the way the lads in jail spoke and tried to imitate them. "Yo, home boy. Stella-Who?"

They bent over with knee-slapping guffaws.

"Dog, she yo' woman."

The freckled one said, "Nah, she not yo' woman—she yo' booty call."

I shook my head and copied their speech. "She not my booty call. She nothin' to me."

"Yeah, well, she somethin' to LaVon 'cause he say he gonna kick yo' ass."

I looked on, speechless, as they high-fived each other.

It took a couple of beats before my memory jogged. Stella was the blonde from history class, the one who offered to meet me behind the bleachers. To listen to my home boys tell it—I'm catching onto this slang—LaVon and Stella go steady. Well, they didn't exactly use that term. They called it hooking up.

A rumble from the stands filtered through the locker room. I have no idea what this sport's about, but now I know why I'm on the team. It's my height. The tallest teammate is six inches shorter than me. I was looking around for a place to hang myself when Coach Dodson came up.

"Feelin' better, Gooch?"

"No. I'm really, really sick." I grabbed my abdomen and pulled a face.

"Bull . . . loney," he snarled, cleaning up his insult for the news reporter who'd entered the locker room to cover the game. "The only way you're not playing is blood or death. Your blood. Your death. And believe me, Gooch, I can make that happen." He balled up a fist and shook it. Neck veins plumped like garden hoses. "Now you dudes quit chalking your pool cues and get ready to play ball."

Spare me the indignity of retelling what happened after that, other than to admit we were down by ten points at the end of the first half. By the end of the third quarter, the Pumas had a twenty-point lead over the Highlanders. Apparently if you bump one of the lads, it's a foul and they get a free throw. So that makes me responsible for the Pumas getting four free throws, which they call 'sinking the ball' if it passes through the hoop.

Coach Dodson looks like he wants to murder me in front of all these witnesses. This whole thing's making me so upset I'm delusional. I actually visualized a coil of steam rising from the top of his head.

Good news though—the match is almost over.

"Gooch." Coach Dodson screamed my name and thumbed at the court. I pointed to myself to make sure he actually wanted me, and not the invisible lad sitting next to me. "Don't make me come over there."

I have no idea what I'm doing so I keep running with the ball—this is called dribbling—and it's a penalty if you run with the ball and don't bounce it—that's called traveling. So far, the ball has turned over four times because I did that—traveled with the ball.

I ran down the gymnasium with my teammates close by, so sweaty that I could feel my uniform top tacking itself to my back. I turned in time to see the ball, airborne, coming my way. I don't even know which hoop I'm standing under, theirs or ours, so I threw it back to the player I got it from. He looked at me like I'd lost my mind. Turns out I was standing right under our hoop. The ball circled the rim and dropped through the net.

The crowd cheered.

The ball was in play again. I followed my team down to the other end of the court, lingering enough to make it less attractive for my teammates to throw me the ball. A tall white boy from the Pumas turned, and I saw the name CARSWELL stitched onto the back of his uniform.

Chills swarmed my body. Allen had a son in junior high. Cody Carswell.

I looked around the stands, hoping to catch sight of Allen in his purple cap. But how would I find him in a sea of purple?

"Outta the way, nigger." The Carswell boy slammed me hard. A whistle shrilled, and the referee trotted over.

Now I knew how it felt to be called a derogatory name. "I'll bet your father, the policeman, would be so proud of your name-calling, you big bully."

*How humiliating. I know he didn't learn to talk that way from Allen. Allen's a gentleman.*

I wanted to protest that I didn't do anything. That it was him—Carswell.

But the ref tossed me the ball without me having to tattle. The gym fell deathly quiet. Blood thundered between my ears.

A girl cried, "Sink it," and when I looked over at the cheerleaders, there was Stella, sticking her chest out and mouthing something nasty. My groin didn't even stir, now that I knew about the thrashing LaVon wanted to give me.

With my hair damp, and sweat trickling down my ribs, I bounced the ball as others had done. Then I flung it at the basket. It bounced off the rim, and the room resounded with the collective gasps of Highlander fans. Cheers erupted from Puma fans. The referee bounced the ball back to me.

Apparently I get a do-over. Lucky me. Talk about prolonging the agony . . .

I bounced the ball a couple of times and inwardly gave myself a pep talk.

*I can do this.*

*It shouldn't be this hard.*

*Besides, the score's tied. If I miss, the clock will run out, and Bob's your uncle.*

The noise in the stands died down to a hush. The only movement I could hear at that moment was the sound of the ball smacking the floor in cadence with the rhythm of my bouncing heartbeat. A drop of sweat rolled off my forehead and into my eye. As I rubbed away the burn, a high-pitched screech came from the bleachers.

"Mummy."

Lillibet's cry reached my ears.

Someone shouted, "Shut up and sit down—you're blocking my view."

My attention flickered to the stands. An old woman with a face that needed ironing flailed her arms at me. Addie Hollingsworth, dressed in a riot of color flashier than the organ grinder's monkey, shouted my name and pointed toward the illuminated exit sign.

As if by telepathy, we shared a mutual understanding—*run.*

The clock had ticked down the last five seconds. I turned to sprint off the court and realized I still had the ball. I did what anybody in my situation would've done—treated it like a hot horseshoe and got rid of it. Made a backward throw and broke into a dead run. The crowd screamed my name as I fled toward the exit. My daughter fought her way through the crowd behind me.

And just as I made it to the big metal doors, I glimpsed Allen consoling the boy who'd called me a bad name.

# CHAPTER SIXTEEN

*"Gooch, Gooch, Gooch."*

The name roared through the gymnasium and reverberated off the walls as I crashed against the safety bar and fled through the exit. With cheers rumbling in my head and the sweet taste of freedom on my lips, double doors opened like a huge, cavernous mouth. Outside in the car park, blood-clotting rock music pulsated from jumbo speakers of a gangster-mobile.

Home free.

"Yo. 'Sup?"

I turned at the sound of a velvet voice. Two black lads popped out from behind a pillar. The bigger one put his shoulder into me, knocking me to the ground.

I tasted the pavement. Shock paralyzed me. My heart mimicked the sound of hooves on a dirt racetrack.

*This must be LaVon.*

He delivered a menacing accusation. "Heard you's meetin' Stella behind the bleachers."

The snick of a switchblade echoed in my ears.

Cold pinpricks started at the nape of my neck. With an anger so strong it whipped my breath away, he grabbed my throat, digging in his fingers enough to make me hunch involuntarily.

I shrieked, "Run, Lillibet," and hoisted myself to my knees. But instead of charging off like a horse out of a paddock, an ominous hiss erupted from Addie's hand.

LaVon grabbed his face and recoiled. His mate backed away

in response to LaVon's girlish screams.

I jumped to my feet and grabbed Addie by the wrist. We took off like a couple of gazelles—more like one gazelle and a lame springbok—angling toward the car park with no particular direction in mind.

"This way." Addie pulled me past a metal fence. We zigzagged through several rows of cars before she abruptly stopped and flailed her arms. In the distance, headlights brightened.

A car slumped heavily toward us.

The champagne-colored Mercedes, a sleek, top of the line sedan with dark tinted windows stopped directly in our path.

Whatever Lillibet sprayed on our tormentors wore off. They stormed the car park like marauding Vandals.

"Get in," she said. We both ran around the luxury car's bonnet to our respective sides: her, behind the driver and me, opposite.

When we jumped inside and slammed the doors, electric locks snapped shut.

"Floor it," Addie cried.

We accelerated out of the car park and roared off down the road.

I flopped back against the seat into buttery leather so soft it reminded me of a cloud. Just being in such an automobile made my heart race. I knew it cost around one hundred thousand pounds sterling—I doubled the amount and decided it would roughly cost around two hundred thousand American dollars. I'd wanted one ever since the new models came out, but couldn't afford it. Not that the Winthrops didn't have discretionary money to spend, but we've always been a bit on the frugal side, and as my father always said, if we gave generously to make others' lives better we'd reap our just rewards.

Giddy with excitement, my daughter introduced me to the driver. "This is Broderick."

I took note of him, estimating his weight to be about twelve and a half stones and his height at one hundred-seventy centimeters after deducting where the top of his chauffeur's cap rose above the headrest. I imagined a conversion chart and ciphered in my head to come up with one hundred seventy pounds and five feet seven inches.

She said, "Broderick's my chauffeur—for three months now," and swatted him, good-naturedly, on the shoulder.

Trying to fit the part, I said, "Yo. 'Sup?" But to Lillibet, I said, "Bloody hell, where'd he come from?"

She giggled in a melodic, old lady chuckle that sounded like plucked violin strings tuned too tight. "Turns out I'm rich."

"Broderick, this is . . . what shall we call you, Mummy?"

Broderick's jaw flinched. I heaved a resigned breath. Lillibet and I were having the same problem assuming our new roles.

"Sylvester. Sly for short."

The chauffeur studied us in the rearview mirror. "Where to, Madame?"

Elizabeth turned to me. "Where to, Mum—Sly?"

"Do we have any money?" I whispered under Broderick's intent regard.

Elizabeth pawed through her handbag, a lovely Italian number in a luscious shade of lime green, with a buttery leather flower slightly offset from the center. It matched her silk jacket exactly, and the leaves in her festive flower print skirt. It was exactly the kind of ensemble you'd expect a dowager to wear to an escape.

Elizabeth pulled out a book of cheques. *No, dummy,* checks. *This is America.*

"You have no idea what I've been through today. Priscilla, the daughter, is the most wretched cow. She doesn't trust me with money, keeps me poor, and she confiscated my car keys." She lifted her head, adding, "Isn't that right, Broderick?"

His eyes flickered to the rearview mirror, and back to the road. "Yes, Madame."

"Only I took them back before she could relieve me of them permanently." She cut her eyes to the driver. "Broderick won't tell, will you, Broderick?"

"No, Madame."

Elizabeth scowled, gripping my wrist and pulling me in close. "So, Broderick, why doesn't Priscilla trust me with money?"

Huge brown basset hound eyes made eye contact in the rearview mirror. "Because you give it away, Madame."

Elizabeth heaved herself against the seat back, slouching into the buttery leather. Before I could stop myself, the words in my head touched my tongue's hair trigger. "Don't slouch, Lil—Mrs. Hollingsworth. Addie."

She sat up straight. "What shall we do now?"

The ankle monitor had chafed my skin. I lifted my leg to show her. "I need a pair of scissors to cut this off."

Elizabeth eyed it with suspicion.

"It's an ankle monitor," I said. "Like a global positioning unit. The probation officer put it on to track me."

"I say, Broderick, might you have a pair of scissors on you?"

Wary eyes flickered to the mirror. "Sorry, Madame. No scissors."

Her face wilted.

"But will a pocket knife do?"

"Brilliant." Elizabeth perked up. "Let's have a look."

He dug into his pocket and pulled out a Swiss Army knife with everything one needed to survive. I opened it to reveal a sharp blade and proceeded to saw away at the strap on my leg. It came off with ease. I dangled it in front of us like a dead rat.

"See here, Broderick," I said through a sigh of resignation. They'd be looking all over for me now that I was on a steep trajectory to kiddie prison. "Can you find us a skip?"

"Skip, sir?"

I snapped my finger. "What you Americans call a dumpster."

With a head bob of acknowledgment, he took the next exit, wheeled into a car park and drove around to the back of a restaurant. I jumped out long enough to toss the monitor into the trash bin and dust off my hands for a job well done.

When I returned to the back seat and closed myself in, I caught the tail end of the conversation between Addie and the chauffeur.

"How will you ever explain having a, *ahem,* black boy with you, Madame?"

"I shouldn't have to explain. We'll just sneak him into the house and they'll be none the wiser."

"But Madame, Miss Priscilla and Mr. Richard will be waiting up for you."

Neither of us said anything. I realized we had a problem but we also had plenty of time on the drive to come up with a solution.

My daughter seemed to be enjoying the ride, like when we first toured the area with our guide from the Southwestern Cattle Raisers Association. We didn't have to lift a finger to get to the tourist attractions, or decide where to eat. They took care of everything.

She said, "Tell me something, Broderick, why do you wear that silly cap, and that stuffy uniform?"

Eyes to mirror. "Because you make me, Madame."

"Well take it off. It looks terrible."

"Thank you, Madame." He took off the hat and set it next to him on the seat.

"Broderick, I don't ever want to see you wearing that hat again, do you hear me?"

"Thank you, Madame." He hit the electric door button and the driver's window slid halfway down. He flung the chauffeur's cap out the window. It rolled across the road and disappeared into a ditch.

"Hey, don't mess with Texas, pardner," I said. My pride was about as convincing as my best ghetto accent.

With that, Addie gave him permission to wear whatever made him comfortable. Broderick suggested Hawaiian shirts and Safari shorts, and Addie pronounced the idea dandy.

"Home, Madame?"

"I'm not sure." She repeated the information she'd gotten from the cook earlier in the day. "Do you think we should seek refuge at Sylvester's house?"

I shuddered. "Not on your life. Did you see those lads back there? They probably know where I live."

I weighed our options. We had to stick together. White woman in a black neighborhood? Black lad in a white neighborhood? The latter might be the lesser of the evils.

Or a hotel.

I rejected that outright. If we went to a hotel, we'd end up with two sets of cops out looking for us. At least with Adelaide safely ensconced in her own home, the police would only be searching for me.

Elizabeth gripped the chauffeur's seat back, and hauled herself up close to his ear.

"What does my daughter do?"

He took a long, deep breath. "Well, Madame, to hear you tell it, she makes your life miserable."

"No, I mean what's her occupation?"

"Well, Madame, to hear you tell it, she's a selfish, gallivanting little slug who's been sucking off the commercial airline tit for years."

I barked out a laugh.

"I see. So why do I allow her to stay in my house?"

"Because according to the terms of Mr. Hollingsworth's Last

Will and Testament, Miss Priscilla has a life estate."

"Is there a way to get her out?"

"I sincerely wouldn't know, Madame. I would think you should speak to your attorney about such things. But I've overheard Miss Priscilla and Mr. Richard talking—quite by accident of course—"

"Of course. Do go on."

"And Mr. Richard said . . ." His jaw tightened. He drew in a deep breath as if to mentally brace himself before delivering this next part. "He said you'd gotten crazier than a rat in a drain pipe and he couldn't bear to be around you anymore. He said Miss Priscilla should get you to deed over the country house to them before you . . . before you . . ."

"I say, Broderick, do go on."

"Before you get so crazy the transfer of property could be attacked in court."

"But who'd want to attack it?"

"I believe Jessie and Perry would. They still care a great deal about you, Madame."

"How sweet." Addie settled back into her seat. "We have a country house?"

"You do, Madame."

"What does it look like? Besides being in the country."

"Oh, it's not in the country, Madame, it's just down the street. Mr. Richard just calls it that to be facetious."

"Mr. Richard likes to put on airs, doesn't he?" Addie said.

"That he does." Broderick's gaze flickered to the rearview mirror again, and he winked.

According to the chauffeur, the country house was about the same size as Hollingsworth Manor only it had declined over the years from being left vacant. Priscilla refused to live there once Walden "Buzz" Hollingsworth died. The house staff speculated it was because she thought she could squeeze Mrs. Hollingsworth out and take over the estate herself. Priscilla, as it turned out, was big into throwing parties on a grand scale, the kind the newspaper society section covered, where the only invited guests were the snootiest of snobs.

My daughter gave me a sideways glance, then refocused her attention on our driver.

"How much do I pay you, Broderick?"

Eyes to mirror. "Not nearly enough, Madame."

"Well, let's give you a raise, shall we?"

"That would be most appreciated, Madame."

"And just so we understand each other, Broderick, this is because you're my loyal employee. And loyalty means a lot to a Hollingsworth, doesn't it?"

"Indeed, Madame."

"How much of a raise shall I give you?"

His eyes flickered to the back seat. "Perhaps two thousand dollars a year would be in order?"

"Let's make it five thousand. And another five as a bonus."

Broderick's jaw gaped enough for us to see that he could use a bit of dental work.

I nudged my daughter. "Make it ten."

"Ten it is. A five thousand dollar raise and a ten thousand dollar bonus."

Broderick's eyes misted. "That's very generous of you, Madame, but are you certain?"

Addie nodded. She held up a finger to signal *Onward*.

"To the bank, first thing tomorrow, my good man."

For the next several minutes, we drove in silence as Addie contemplated our destination.

She opened her handbag and pulled out a checkbook, and opened the register. She revealed the amount in the balance column. "Do you believe this?"

I blinked. "I want new clothes. I can't wear this basketball uniform around. Might as well be a neon sign."

"Broderick," she said, "where shall we take Sly for new clothes?"

He glanced back expectantly. "One of the discount department stores would work."

I said, "Would you know if they carry Bally shoes?"

"Noooooooo," he said, drawing out the word. "I believe you'd have to go to Harkman Beemis for that . . . or as I like to think of it, Needless Markups."

"Splendid." Elizabeth clapped her hands in childlike glee. "We'll do that tomorrow, after breakfast, once we leave the bank. For now, the discount store will do."

Broderick took the next off ramp, and turned back toward the direction we'd just come from.

As the scenery flew by, Elizabeth continued to engage our driver in polite conversation. "So what do people call me?"

"Really, Madame, I don't mean to offend, but Miss Priscilla doesn't like it when the help gets into protracted conversations with the family."

We exchanged awkward glances.

"Well Miss Priss isn't here," she said. Our telepathically encrypted thoughts confirmed that we'd both seen him bite his lip to keep from smiling. "So what do they call me?"

"To your face, Madame?" He paused a few beats. "Your daughter calls you 'the old crone' behind your back. Your son-in-law calls you 'troublesome old bitch' and your friends call you Addie."

"And what do you call me?"

His eyes flickered to the mirror again. "I've been instructed to call you Madame, Madame."

"By whom?"

"By you, Madame."

My daughter reached over the seat and patted him on the

shoulder. "From now on, Broderick, you may call me Addie."

My daughter took my hand and dozed while I settled against the seat back, lulled by the swishing of highway traffic. I didn't dare sleep. I had no idea who these lunatics were, or whether our chauffeur would turn out to be friend or foe. Until we firmed up our plan, the last thing we needed was for Broderick to take us to the Hollingsworth house and notify Addie's shrew of a daughter that she'd taken in the black kid who robbed her the previous night.

I spied the store in the distance and relaxed a bit. Next thing I knew, my eyes succumbed to the hypnotic effect of the highway. I couldn't have been asleep more than a few minutes when Elizabeth's—Addie's voice—startled me awake. Broderick pulled off the freeway and the grand Mercedes slumped heavily into the car park. I needn't have worried that the people inside would eye me up for wearing a basketball uniform, since most of the customers had dressed like they came from another planet. Men wore women's clothes; women wore men's clothes. And a few were even missing clothes.

Within the hour, Broderick helped me pick out a new outfit, trainers, underpants, socks, pajamas and a Buddy Holly CD— enough to tide me over until we made a visit to Needless Markup's in the morning.

# CHAPTER SEVENTEEN

With Broderick's help, Addie familiarized me with the goings-on at the Hollingsworth household on the drive home.

According to the intelligence report provided by our driver, the main problem with spiriting me into the house once the family turned in for the night had to do with the security system. Part of Richard's habit included setting the alarm once the rest of the household retired to their respective rooms. Since Addie didn't know the code, they'd have to sneak me inside before the aggravating pair locked up the place.

"Or he could stay with me," Broderick suggested.

I gave a discreet headshake. This man was a virtual stranger. He might even be a child molester.

It turned out Addie's chauffeur lived in the carriage house at the rear of the property, in a rectangular one bedroom, one bathroom, lounge and kitchenette area that ran the length of the three-car garage below. And while he only had to be available from eight in the morning until five in the afternoon to squire Addie around town, Priscilla insisted he wear a pager for on-call periods and emergencies.

Panic must've settled onto my face because Addie said, "That won't be necessary. I'll figure out a way to get him inside without anyone noticing."

But I wasn't so certain. I had no knowledge of the layout of the place in the event we became separated before I received a guided tour. If Priscilla or her husband or anyone else, for that matter, caught sight of me, there were any number of violent endings I imagined for myself.

"Do they keep guns in the house?" I asked.

Addie glanced over expectantly. "Well, Broderick, do they?"

"I have no idea, Madame."

"Addie," she corrected him.

Addie looked me over with the shrewdness of a diamond appraiser. "Do we have a large box?"

"You want to put me into a box?" Just the thought of her guesstimating my size made me claw at my neck. I've always been a tad claustrophobic. No way would I climb, voluntarily, into a box.

"Keep your voice down," she said. She returned her attention to Broderick. "What time do these people go to sleep?"

"Sleep? I have no idea. But I know they retire to their respective rooms around ten o'clock because I see the lights come on in different parts of the house from the garage apartment." Anticipating my next question, Broderick checked his watch and said, "It's nine, Sylvester."

After circling the block several times, Broderick pulled into the back of the estate from a side street. He let the Mercedes idle while Addie and I got out of the car.

The night air had turned nippy. I briskly rubbed my arms to warm the goose bumps. With Broderick's help, we cooked up a plan.

We decided Broderick should go around the house to the front door with the bracelet Addie handed over to him. His job was to ring the doorbell and distract Richard and Priscilla by returning the jewelry Addie supposedly left in the car, while Addie sneaked me in through the back door.

Sounded good.

It was a stupid plan.

At the time, the idea seemed perfect, but it would've been

even more perfect if I'd been drinking heavily enough to slur my own name. This dangerous scheme made me so apprehensive that the nervous giggle I initially let out turned into a donkey bray of doubt. Nice to know that even with all the bad stuff going on I could still be convulsed with laughter. Addie looked at me with curiosity, probably wondering what part of the distraction I found most appalling. Then I started to get all fuzzy because I'd been warned not to overthink the plan, as if I should just smile mindlessly and nod in agreement to whatever these two plotted.

The problem stemmed from the notion of distracting Richard *and* Priscilla.

When Broderick appeared at the front door with the bracelet, Priscilla answered his knock. As Addie and I slipped in through the back door, a Rococo mirror of magnificent carvings, hanging on the dining room wall, reflected the shadowy movements of a man I took to be Richard. As he rose from the sofa, he picked up an empty dish and cut through the dining room on his way into the kitchen.

I started to bolt out the back door but Addie grabbed my arm and pulled me back. She opened the broom closet and shut me inside.

I watched Richard through the fretwork in the closet door. He was tall and husky with a voice to match, with dark hair silvering at the temples; and he appeared to be about my age—back when I used to be Elle Winthrop. When he flipped on the light switch, the sight of Addie startled him.

"What's going on?" he said dully.

"Nothing." The guilty look on Addie's face and the deranged glint in her eyes told a different story.

"You're not playing with matches again, are you?"

Big headshake. "I wanted a bite to eat. Ice cream. I'd like a dish of ice cream."

"You don't have ice cream."

Addie walked to the icebox. Richard followed.

She opened the freezer. "Imagine that." Triumphant, she removed a brick of ice cream and headed for the cupboard.

"That's mine, Addie." Richard spoke firmly as his empty bowl clattered into the sink.

"Surely you don't mind sharing."

"That's not the point. We all have our own treats. Ice cream is mine. Yours is . . . carrot sticks."

"Are you kidding me?" Defiantly, she pulled off the lid on a brand new carton and opened several drawers before locating the silverware. She selected a tablespoon, and had started to dip out a scoop, when Richard stepped up and seized her by the wrist. Addie winced.

Animal instinct washed over me with such visceral determination that it took all of my resolve not to bolt from my hiding place and choke him until his eyeballs popped out of his head like champagne corks.

He said, "That's enough."

Addie looked up expectantly. "Who do you think paid for this, Richard?"

His mouth rounded into an "O". She shook off his hand and dipped out a scoop.

Richard plucked the utensil from her hand and stuck it into his mouth.

My daughter narrowed her eyes. I wondered what she'd do. On the one hand, she needed to be Addie. On the other, I knew my daughter's love for ice cream would not be vanquished by this spoon-licking lout.

"Did you want me to put it back?" Addie said with mock innocence.

"Yes. That would be acceptable."

"I see." She picked up the lid as if she intended to replace it.

At the last second, she put the carton of ice cream to her face and swiped her tongue across the remaining Swiss Vanilla.

Richard sent the spoon clattering into the sink.

"You horrible old bitch. You ruined it."

"Want your ice cream back?"

"Not with your spit on it."

"Good. Then if you don't mind, I'd like to fix myself a bowl of ice cream and eat it by myself."

"Choke on it." He turned to leave.

A rumble of voices filtered in through another part of the house. I assumed this was Priscilla, getting the lowdown on the ice cream debacle. Their absence gave me time to come out of the closet, only to flee to a nearby area that turned out to be the laundry room. I found myself in a closet that housed the water heater, and wedged myself between the cylinder and the wall. Heat seared my back.

I heard a woman's voice in the kitchen.

"Mother, you're not supposed to be eating that."

"Let it go, Priscilla."

"The doctor said—"

"I'm old. What does it matter at this stage of the game?" Addie's frustration turned sarcastic. "I have an idea. Why don't you mind your own beeswax and get out of my hair?"

"What?" Priscilla's voice spiraled up in a shriek.

"You heard me. We've somehow managed to slip into an unpleasant role reversal in this household. You seem to be forgetting who's the mother, and who's the daughter."

My eyes bulged. I recall saying those same words to an angry teenage girl not ten years ago. I caught myself smiling. Made me proud to think she'd learned something useful from me.

A drawer slid open and the familiar clink of utensils rattled through the air. I suspected my daughter was eating directly from the carton.

My mouth watered. I could use a bite of ice cream.

"We have an appointment with the doctor in three days. I'm reporting this to him; believe me. He'll probably agree that you're a danger to yourself, and sign off on the papers."

Footfalls came toward me. My back felt like it was on fire. I needed to get out, fast.

Addie let out a shriek.

"What the hell?" said Priscilla.

The footfalls receded and I cracked open the door. From my place near the water heater, I saw Addie shoot me a look. I knew, on instinct, that she'd created an opportunity for me to change locations.

I crept around the corner, into the formal dining room, and kept moving. I knew I'd entered the formal parlor by the silk-covered sofa, and down-cushioned chaise lounge, not to mention marble-topped French commodes and chests with sterling silver pieces displayed on the tops. My eyes grew wide. Then my peripheral vision alerted me to movement. Richard walked past and I barely escaped being seen.

I tiptoed out of the parlor, into a den that had been decorated like a friendly corner pub, with leather-upholstered furniture, dark mahogany pieces, and Safari trophies mounted on the walls. Richard, with his slight build and affected mannerisms, didn't impress me as a big-game hunter. These springbok and gazelle heads, and the taxidermied grizzly bear that presided over the room from its place in the corner, were probably the works of Addie's husband.

Disoriented, I found myself in a hall and heard feet thundering against the hardwoods. I dashed through the first door to my right and realized that I'd entered a bedroom. As I groped around to get my bearings from the shaft of street light shining through a part in the curtain, a highly-lacquered dressing table felt cool against my fingertips. I contemplated darting back out again when the twist of a doorknob froze me. The closest place to hide was the loo. I shot through the entry as the bedroom door came open. Gingerly, I stepped into the bathtub and drew the curtain closed.

Footfalls followed me in. The light switch snicked on.

The lid to the toilet went up. The ominous ratcheting of a zipper sheared my attention, followed by a trickle and a groan. When Richard flushed, I thought I'd pass out.

Now *I* needed to use the loo.

The bedroom door opened again, and Priscilla flounced in.

"She's a fucking disaster," she announced to the room.

"Tell me about it."

"Dr. Bomar had better sign those papers, or we'll never get her out of this house. I actually think she's getting better. She was as lucid as I've ever seen her tonight." Her voice became soft, almost coquettish. "Richard, what are we going to do if the judge doesn't commit her?"

With a roguish inflection, he said, "I know what I'm going to do . . ." and I thought I'd choke on my own disgust. Bodies thudded against the mattress. Animal sounds erupted from the bed. The harder I tried to keep from imagining sex between Richard and Priscilla, the more it felt like a flock of sparrows just landed in my undercrackers. I finally did the only thing I could, given the circumstances—wee'd in the bathtub.

Then Priscilla said, "Turn out the light."

Richard got up from the bed and padded, stark bollocks naked, to the wall switch. The room went dark and the guttural sounds resumed.

What to do?

I stepped out of the bath.

If I opened the door, the light from the hall would sweep across the room. They'd see me and all hell would break loose.

Right then and there, I almost lapsed into a full-scale panic attack.

Then I caught myself.

Why worry? Richard would probably kill me in my tracks and mount my wooly head in the trophy room.

A slow vibration started in the direction of the bed, and I alerted. They'd resorted to the bob—battery operated boyfriend. It picked up speed, and then became conspicuously muffled as Priscilla simultaneously moaned.

I tried to block out the smutty banter, but Richard made it impossible. The more Priscilla responded, the filthier it got. I actually felt needles lancing my penis and realized I couldn't move if someone strapped a bridle on me and hitched me to a horse-walking machine.

# CHAPTER EIGHTEEN

After Richard left the bedroom to set the alarm, I tried to slip out of the room.

Priscilla dreamily called out.

"Come here." Her voice went suddenly demanding. I realized she'd mistaken me for Richard, and didn't like the turn this was taking. Still, I migrated over to the bed. She slipped a hand beneath my shorts. "Well, well, well, what have we here?"

I tried to mimic one of Richard's animal noises—the one that sounded like a rhino in heat. She shifted her face toward the edge of the bed. "Do you want me to—"

I made a noise that sounded like I'd swallowed my own tongue and moved away from the bed.

"Well don't say I didn't try," she announced haughtily. "I get credit for this, you know?"

A mewling kitten sound slipped out and I continued to skulk, in discomfort, toward the door. Instinct warned me to hurry. With the door ajar, I realized Priscilla had her face to the wall. I rushed out of their bedroom, and bounded farther down the hall. When I tried the next door, I found myself in a guest bathroom. Although I couldn't make out the conversation coming from Priscilla and Richard's bedroom, I gathered he'd made a run at her to continue the intimacy—and she wasn't having any of it.

I tried the last door, and for no good reason, the alarm went off. Quiet be damned, I launched myself into the room and found Addie sitting in front of a vanity, combing out her long hair with such vigor her upper arm jiggled.

"So, that went well, don't you think?" My daughter might conclude that I comically exaggerated the point about being smuggled into a house I viewed as a deathtrap, but deep down, we both knew.

She eyed me sternly and shook her sterling silver hairbrush at me. "Where have you been? You set off the motion detector."

"Don't start with me."

She jumped up from her tuffet and shooed me. "Quick—into the wardrobe."

I stood my ground. "I'm not going in another closet as long as I'm here."

"Then get into bed and pull the covers up over your head. I'll get in the wardrobe."

Self-sacrifice.

Footfalls thundered down the hall. I flung back the covers and dived under the plush comforter. Addie hit the light, and in seconds, the snick of the lock told me she'd made it to safety. The door cracked open, letting in an ever-widening sliver of light.

"Addie? You in here?" Richard.

I figured Addie and I would be discovered, and wished I'd grabbed one of the fireplace pokers before jumping into bed. Having nothing to bean him with, I did the next best thing—stirred beneath the coverlet.

"Did you set off the alarm?"

No response.

"Fricking alarm company," he muttered under his breath. The door closed, sealing me in a black abyss. I held my breath, waiting for more bad stuff to happen.

Neither Addie nor I moved for a good half hour. Somewhere between the time Richard left and Addie came out of the closet,

I fell asleep.

The nightlight switched on beside the bed.

For a few seconds, I forgot where I was. I blinked at the old lady in a pastel pink silk dressing gown standing beside the bed. Then Addie laughed at the expression on my face and I came fully awake. Everything came rushing back. Clearly, I found the entire evening disgusting, while my daughter thought it was horrifically awesome.

"I hope Peter's getting a big kick out of this," I groused, fisting my eyes from the glare of the bulb. Addie smiled a relaxed smile, the first I'd seen in almost twenty-four hours. "You're beautiful."

"Wonder when the last time the real Addie heard that?"

It didn't matter if my daughter was eight or eighty, she looked exceptionally lovely. Even with raccoon eyes. A pang of regret hit my heart that my Elizabeth would never know the joy of having children, or growing old.

After she drifted off to sleep, I switched on the nightlight and tiptoed to the door to make sure she'd locked it. On my way back to the bed, I felt the pull of the telephone.

*Don't do it,* warned the left side of my brain.

I took a closer step.

*Really, don't do it.*

I took another step.

*Nothing good can come of this.*

And then the right side of my brain weighed in.

It whispered, *But what if he listens this time?*

And that's all the persuasion it took to dial Allen's number.

# CHAPTER NINETEEN

Day two yawned with a butterscotch sunrise.

I slitted my eyes open as the first shafts of sunlight slanted through the split in the curtains, and officially woke up from the worst nightmare of my life. I dreamed my mother went straight to Hell, and Elizabeth and I had to save her. Oh, wait. That's for real. Addie was still sleeping so I tiptoed around my side of the bed and headed for the loo. I was sudsing in the shower when I heard my daughter say, "Well, I never. Doesn't a lady get any privacy in her own home?"

I grabbed the nearest towel and stepped out onto the bathmat. Now what?

Addie said in a loud voice, "I was merely letting the water run until it's hot enough. I want steam. It's good for the skin." And then, "You act like you pay the water bill." Followed by an embarrassed, "Well, jolly good then." And shortly thereafter, "It wouldn't do you any harm, Priscilla, to take better care of your skin."

The door opened, and Addie stepped in long enough to stick a hand past the curtain and shut off the tap. I stood perfectly still, chilled to the bone, with shower gel running the length of my body. Then she walked out, leaving me to drip-dry, shivering, like Bwana of the Jungle.

She fired her next canon salvo. "There . . . happy?"

Priscilla ignored her. "Did you make a phone call in the middle of the night?"

119

"No, why?" Addie appeared suitably surprised.

"Someone called here around two o'clock. It woke Richard up."

"Bummer," Addie said as I inwardly grimaced.

"Bummer? What are you—twelve? The caller insisted someone telephoned from this house."

Addie was quick on her feet. By the time she finished advancing her theory, she'd not only convinced Priscilla that she had nothing to do with the phone call, but also had her believing it was a slumber party prank.

Priscilla turned to leave. "Jessie sent me in to tell you your oatmeal is ready."

"That's another thing," Addie said. "I'm not having oatmeal."

"Of course you are. It's what you always have."

Addie huffed out her disgust. "Well today it comes to a screeching halt." Priscilla drew a bracing breath as Addie squared her shoulders. "You know how, in the old days, if you wound a watch too hard or too much you could break it? Yes? That can happen to people, too. Things are going to be different around here, Priscilla, and if you don't like it, you can move out and take that weasel with you." She pointed to the door. "Out of my room before I knock the living daylights out of you."

As soon as Priscilla left, I quickly rinsed the soap off, re-dressed in my Budget World clothes, and waited near the window to contemplate my next move. I'd already decided that a sudden dive out, headfirst, would only turn me into an eggplant and land me on a ventilator, not actually kill me, when the doorknob suddenly turned and Addie toed open the door.

"I can get it from here, Jessie," she said in a strained voice, and waltzed in carrying a tray with a silver lid on it, and highball glasses filled to the brim with a variety of juices. She back-kicked the door as I dashed through vapors of bacon and eggs, pancakes and grits to lock it behind her.

"Here, Mum. Brought you something."

I practically swooned. This was the first decent meal I'd eaten in a day.

"They treated me like a leper this morning. Gave me dirty looks and said there was no way I could eat a full breakfast and then order up a meal to go. I told them, 'Watch me.' " She unc-inched her dressing gown and headed for the loo. "I don't like Priscilla, but Richard's absolutely disgusting."

*Tell me about it.*

I gobbled every last bite of food, washing it down with orange juice, apple juice and a spot of hot tea with cream. When Addie came out after her shower wearing nothing but her old lady bloomers, I noticed the bruises.

"How'd you get those?"

She shrugged. "Don't know. Maybe from when Sylvester tried to filch my handbag."

Seemed plausible enough.

"Do you really think Sylvester did that? That he's a thug?"

She lifted one shoulder. "I don't know. The police say he did."

"They could be wrong. It could've been someone else. Sylvester just doesn't strike me as the kind of boy who'd harm an old lady."

"And you know this, how?"

"Because I'm living as him."

"No, Mummy, you're living as you, inside of him."

From my place on the bed, I glanced out the window in time to watch Broderick pulling the car around to the front of the house. Addie pawed through her wardrobe in search of something to wear. She selected a bright blue pantsuit with a blue and green silk scarf, and held her choices out for me to approve.

"Don't be jealous. We'll find you nice clothes."

"If I have to wear boy's clothes, I want Bally shoes."

"You could pick out some nice frocks, and we'll tell everyone you're into the 'tranny' scene." Addie winked to show she didn't mean it.

I threw my napkin at her.

We dressed quickly. Once she sneaked me out of the house—I went out the bedroom window this time—Broderick drove us to the bank.

Addie went in alone. When she returned, she had a big smile on her face and a boatload of cash in her handbag.

She gave Broderick the *Onward ho* sign and the car slumped heavily out of the car park. He made a right turn, and headed for the department store.

When we left Needless Markups, Addie nicknamed me Debtzilla. I was so thrilled with my clothes that it didn't even faze me. I had a dozen outfits, three complete suit sets, a super-comfortable pair of alligator Bally loafers, track shoes, house slippers and khakis. What a glorious experience to be shopping again for well-made garments, even if they were designed for a man.

But my favorite part of the morning had to be the trip to the mobile phone store. Addie bought wireless phones for us, and I was lucky enough to get my old mobile number reassigned to me, which made it easy for Addie to remember. On the other hand, we couldn't get Addie's old number back—they'd given it to someone else—but we got one with repeating sequences that made it user friendly.

Broderick dropped us off at the country club, a masterpiece of postmodern-style architecture featuring four vertical elements in the corners of the tower portion of the building. Our chauffeur pulled up under the portico, and several valets spilled out and opened our respective doors. While Broderick drove away with the intent to return in one hour, we entered the grand foyer with its marble floor tile, and came to stand in front of an impressive set of stairs that curled up to the second-floor ballroom. The scent of fresh-cut flowers hung in the air. Everywhere I looked there were vases of roses or gardenias and jasmine, even a centerpiece of magnolia blossoms and daylilies.

The rooms got their names from golfing terminology. We passed the Par, Birdie, Bogey, Double Eagle, the British Open, the Masters, the Sand Trap—an outdoor grill and snack bar— and briefly entered a tavern called the Nineteenth Hole. I smelled food, and the aroma gave me an appetite even though Addie had brought me a king's breakfast not four hours earlier. As we reached the main dining area, the Unplayable Lie, the club's director intercepted us a few feet from the entrance. He took one look at me and invited us to step into his office.

Unfortunately, our plan to eat soup and fork down bites of quiche tanked. The most unpleasant conversation followed.

It seemed the Unplayable Lie had run out of food—never mind that I saw tons of it spilling over the buffet table. Or that four ladies who arrived after us were seated promptly by the wait staff. Realization dawned—I'd been blackballed from entering the country club because Sly's black.

Addie gave me a hyphenated name and introduced me as Sylvester Parker-Wellington. For no good reason, she created the most fantastic pedigree for me where I'm an exchange student living on the Hollingsworth estate. When the manager's frown deepened, she told him I was a relative of Her Royal Highness the Duchess of Cornwall, Prince Charles's wife, Camilla.

Even that didn't serve as my entrée into high society.

In a state like Texas where oil is thicker than blood, I'd just discovered that I'd become something of an ethnic problem. The most unpleasant conversation followed. And while the

manager didn't say, outright, that Addie couldn't bring an ethni-
cally challenged lad into the club, let's just say he thought it
might alarm the other members.

I suppose in golfing terms, I've been DQ'd—disqualified.

As a consolation prize, however, he allowed Addie to give me
a quick tour of the facility.

I've been to a handful of American country clubs but none as
posh as the one Addie Hollingsworth belonged to. My daughter's
eagerness to scope out the place was positively brimming.

"May as well have a look around, yes?" whispered Addie.

I agreed.

While walking through the different rooms—even the tavern
and men's club—we passed a number of exquisite eighteenth-
century bureaus, secretaries, chinoiserie china cabinets and
butler's desks, all of English origin. And next to each piece, a
brass plaque like those that accompany Old Masters in
museums, read: "On loan. Property of Walden and Adelaide
Hollingsworth."

I dug an elbow into Addie's side. "Looks like we'll be eating
here after all."

"How do you figure that?"

"Darling, don't you see?" I touched her hair. "These people
may understand that Addie's been doing things that make it
seem like she's bonkers, but she's still holding all the cards."

She looked at me as if she'd taken a relaxing dip in the family
pool, only to find that the inflatable alligator seen floating
beneath the surface was actually real. "What do you mean?"

"What if . . . ?" I whispered the rest of my idea into her ear,
and off we went to see the manager.

# CHAPTER TWENTY

We spent the rest of the afternoon in the Kimbell Art Museum coffee shop, ringing up Mama's closest friends and inviting them to join us at the country club that evening for a special dinner given in memory of Fiona Slack-Applegate—my mother. Although none of the ladies knew Addie Hollingsworth personally, all seven agreed to attend.

Mama's friend Frances arrived first. Addie and I met her at the door of the Double Eagle, a sunny room with yellow walls and floor-to-ceiling windows. I actually liked this room best. It contained most of the chinoiserie pieces Addie had loaned to the club, and the black and gold furniture positioned against a backdrop of yellow gave the room an elegant, airy feel.

Frances introduced herself. We pretended to get acquainted even though we've known her for years. She still has the lingering accent of the Deep South on her tongue, despite the fact that she's lived in Fort Worth for two decades. Frances was the first person Mama wrote us about when she and Daddy divorced. Frances, a real estate magnate, helped her find a beautiful home.

Mama's other friends arrived soon after: Bitsy, Allyson, Thais, Emily, Dottie and Tosca. I made small talk with each of them before excusing myself to the loo.

On instinct, I entered the ladies' room.

As I realized my mistake, I lingered a few seconds admiring the down-filled chaise lounge and the beautiful peach-colored wallpaper against wainscoting of waist-high black marble. They even had posh disposable hand towels with the country club crest embossed along the bottom edge.

Then the door swung open, and I was forced to dart into one of the stalls. I pulled my trouser legs up around my knees but realized that anyone peeking under the door would see my alligator Ballys and argyle socks—not to mention hairy black shins—and realize that a man had entered. I slipped out of my shoes and pushed them to the back, then climbed upon the seat and perched there until the woman left.

My knees hurt, having been in such a crouch. I was about to step down when two of Mama's friends walked in. I recognized the voices as Bitsy's and Tosca's.

"A memorial for Fiona? Whoever in the world thought that up? Half the west side is dancing on her grave." Tosca.

"After she stole Sugie Rowenstein's husband—it's a wonder someone didn't hire a hit man, if you know what I mean." Bitsy.

"We still don't know that they didn't." Tosca whispered confidentially. "They never did find the body, you know. But really—I had no idea Fiona even knew Adelaide Hollingsworth, did you? Now there's a grand lady . . ."

Running water drowned out the rest of their conversation, but I did hear Tosca's parting shot as they went out the door.

"Let's just enjoy the free meal, tell them we'll do whatever they want us to do, and then don't."

Chills covered my arms. Fine hairs stuck up like needles.

Mama's friends almost seemed relieved that she'd passed on.

Yes, Mama was selfish, only thinking of herself when she left Daddy and me. But I understood because she was so beautiful. It would've been wrong not to try for a movie career, wouldn't it? Wee ones only hold you back, don't they? It wasn't as if she didn't love us.

True, Mama didn't have a lot of time for me. But she paid

for my visits to the states, and hired a nanny to shuttle me about so I'd see Disneyland, didn't she?

And yes, Mama may have given Elizabeth short shrift on the two or three visits to her home in Fort Worth. But she had a grand house to run, and not enough staff. And didn't she find neighborhood playmates so my daughter wouldn't be lonely, and didn't she pay their mothers to take the children to Six Flags?

I climbed down from my perch, dumbfounded, and stepped back into my shoes. Addie had bought me a Tag Heuer watch—something Sylvester could hock once he got his body back—and I checked the time. My daughter would be anxious to get on with this little soiree.

Then I reconsidered.

I pulled out my wireless phone and punched in Allen's number. I only wanted to listen to the message on his answerphone. Answering machine, rather. I really must pay more attention. I've almost lost all trace of Great Britain in my voice. No need to call unwanted attention to us. It only comes back when it's just Addie and me.

On the third ring, the machine came on.

Only it wasn't the machine. It was Allen.

I tried to hang up but couldn't bear to.

Neither did I wish to anger him.

I reclaimed my voice and spoke into the wireless. "Allen?"

"Yeah. Who's this?"

"Please don't hang up." I sensed him, bug-eyed, at the other end of the connection.

"Who is this?"

"I need to talk to you. But I'm afraid, you see, because I don't think you'll believe me."

"Believe what?"

"It's me, Allen. It's Elle. I called to say I love you and, darling, I've missed you so—Allen? Allen, I say, are you there?"

But I was listening, once again, to a dropped call.

Gathered inside the Double Eagle, we took our places around a large round table appointed with a buttercup-colored cloth, and napkins folded into swans; pale yellow Minton china, and heavy utensils with the country club crest hammered into the handles.

While others were being served their meals—filet mignon, blanched asparagus, garlic Yukon potatoes, and a choice of cakes and pastries from the dessert table, Addie did a quick lean-in.

"What's wrong?"

"Nothing." I did a little sniffle.

"I know you. Out with it."

I confessed that I'd phoned Allen.

Addie sucked air. "You're the one who made the call from the house. You have to stop doing that. He thinks you're a twelve-year old con artist."

"If he'd only listen . . ."

Tosca interrupted our private conversation. She asked how long we'd known Mama.

I said, "Over forty years," at the same time, Addie chimed, "Twenty-five years."

Seven confused ladies collectively blinked.

I wanted to thunk my head with a bread roll. "I meant Mrs. Hollingsworth knew Fiona over forty years."

Addie reached for her water glass and lifted it as if she'd made a toast. "Yes, and Sylvester's known Fiona for twelve years."

Frances screwed up her face and looked at me funny. "But you said twenty-five."

"Did I?" Addie said, "I must've been thinking of Sylvester's mother, my dear, dear friend, Lady Wellington-Parker."

"Parker-Wellington," I hissed.

"Oh yes, silly me. Lady Parker-Wellington. Eugenie Parker-Wellington."

Great. Another name to remember. I had to hand it to her, at least she was mostly sticking to names in the Royal Family.

I decided these were a wicked lot of old battleaxes when one of them suggested sharing amusing stories about Mama. By the time these torrid tales made their way around the table, I learned that Mama had not only stolen Sugie Rowenstein's husband, she'd also filched a beaded dress from Drea Hudson's wardrobe while house-sitting, pilfered a set of eighteenth-century candlesticks from a high-end antique dealer's home during a birthday party, shagged the woman's husband in a linen closet and tripped a blind woman to create a diversion while she snogged a couple of men at a Christmas party.

Only Fran had anything nice to say about Mama. "I once saw her give a stray dog a nice big hambone—"

*See? There,* I wanted to shout, *Mama may've had her problems but she wasn't evil.*

"—dunked in antifreeze."

Addie and I exchanged awkward looks. This had turned into a disaster.

Then Thais said, "Pardon me for asking, but weren't you married to Walden Hollingsworth?"

Addie mimed a smile. "Did you know Walden?"

"No," Thais hesitated, "but I read the newspapers."

Addie continued with her frozen smile as Drea elbowed Thais into silence.

"What she means," Frances said, "is that we're all a bit surprised that you, of all people, would do something nice for Fiona."

"I can answer that." I pushed back from the table and stood. Reached across my plate and picked up my water glass. Tapped the tines of my fork lightly on the edge until the snickering subsided. "I'm sure you're wondering why we invited you here. Fiona Slack-Applegate was extremely important to us and we'd like to do something spectacular in her honor."

Laughter erupted.

"Oi, if I could have your attention for a moment." Quiet ensued. "We hope you'll join us in making a large contribution to Children's Hospital in Fiona's name." Everyone sat in stunned silence. I amended the request. "Or make a generous donation to the charity of your choice—but in Fiona's name." I glanced around expectantly.

None of them hauled out their checkbooks. But every single one of them suddenly snagged their wraps and remembered they had something better to do.

"I'll tell you one thing," Addie said as the last of Mama's friends grabbed her handbag and headed out the door, "you sure know how to clear a room."

# CHAPTER TWENTY-ONE

We arrived home to find Priscilla's car parked beneath the porte cochere.

Addie's eyes darted over the grounds. "Looks like you'll have to wait to come inside."

"Didn't you get the alarm code?"

"Now how would I do that? They think my cogs are slipping. Do you actually think they're going to entrust me with the code and password?"

"You didn't even ask?"

"Of course I asked. They looked right through me."

"Did you remind them it's your home?"

"Of course I did. And then Richard said that as the man of the house, it was his job to keep the family safe; and as long as I didn't know my ass from a hole in the ground, I wasn't getting shit."

I braced my arms across my chest. "Maybe what we should do is just walk in like nothing happened and if anyone says anything, you can tell them it's part of my probation."

Addie looked at me as if I'd sprouted horns. "Have you taken leave of your senses? What's the first thing you think they're going to do?" She pulled a face and did a vigorous head bob. "Uh-huh, uh-huh." She wagged her finger in my face. "They'll call the police and have you arrested. And your probation officer—what's his name?"

"Barney Geeslin."

"Yes, that nice Mr. Geeslin will be asking what your leg monitor's doing in the Hong Kong Buffet skip."

She was right, of course.

"I'm not hiding in any wardrobes, ever again," I said, dramatic and diva-esque.

"Fine. Then stay at Broderick's until I telephone you. Then wait by the back door."

"How will I know if it's safe to come inside?"

Addie mimed a smile. "Oh, you'll know."

Broderick and I killed time eating greasy burgers and watching mindless adventures on the telly. Then I excused myself to the loo. Staying in touch with Addie worked much better now that we owned mobile phones. Made me feel much calmer. As I dried my hands, I heard Buddy Holly in the background. "Everyday" is the ring tone I assigned to let me know when Addie's on the line. Although I don't know why I wanted to give her a unique ring tone. Who else would know to call me?

For no good reason, I gave Allen his own ring tone, too— Buddy Holly's "It Doesn't Matter Anymore." Yes, it was odd to designate a ring tone for him. It wasn't as if he'd actually call. The one he used for my calls before I left this mortal coil was "Rave On." He said it reminded him of how I made him feel.

I answered my wireless. Sure enough, Addie came on the line. She instructed me to wait in the shrubs near the back door.

"How will I know when it's safe to come in?"

"You'll know." A strangely familiar response, but logical enough.

I asked what she was going to do, and ended up talking to a dead connection.

I excused myself from the carriage house and crept the hundred yards or so to the back door, to where the Hollingsworths stored their trash bins. From my place on the lawn I could see the flickering light from Broderick's telly reflected through the windowpane. A low-slung moon silvered the cobblestones. A gentle breeze whipped past my cheek, and a moment of melancholy overtook me.

I missed Allen. The void left me with an ache so strong that there are moments when I feel almost incapacitated.

If only I could talk to him again. If only I could make him see that this body is nothing more than a shell that holds my spirit. I felt the overwhelming desire to punch in his telephone number. To hear him answer and savor the tone of his voice. To hear him breathe until irritation took over, and he hung up the phone. I'd even settle for listening to his voice-mail message.

A light went on downstairs. My heart skipped.

The alarm went off.

Repetitive high-low tones blasted across the estate.

My racing pulse brought on a lightheaded rush.

I tried the knob and it opened.

Strident voices filtered in from the formal living area. Ambient blue light from mercury vapor street lamps lit the kitchen enough for me to move through it without crashing into things. I halted near the dining room, concealed by a decorative Chinese porcelain bowl that held a lush fishtail palm, and watched the drama in the formal living room play out before me.

Addie wore a long purple dress made in the style of the Victorian era, and a huge purple hat shaped like the starship *Enterprise* cocked jauntily on her head. Breasts that normally hung from her chest like flesh-tone knee-highs with a tangerine dropped into the toe of each one had been pushed up so high they now resembled biscuit dough rising above the pan.

Richard, disheveled and wide-eyed and looking deranged in his red-and-white striped pajamas, stood near the foyer. "What the hell's going on in here?"

Addie projected her voice. "I'm auditioning for *American Idol*. Cheerio."

My mouth gaped. This was her plan?

But then I realized it'd worked. I'd slipped inside and now all I needed was to creep into her bedroom without being discovered.

"Auditioning for what?" Priscilla shrilled.

*"American Idol."*

Richard's voice climbed in pitch and volume. "It's the middle of the fucking night."

Addie feigned exasperation. "It's a little after ten."

"You're not going anywhere, Mother. Get back to your room and go to bed."

Instead of coming in from her place outside on the front porch, Addie broke into song, adding dance moves to the opening bars of the "Barber of Seville" to shore up her credibility. She abruptly stopped and faked innocence. "What?"

"You set off the alarm," Richard bellowed, "that's what."

"Well if you'd give me the code, I could've deprogrammed it, and then reset it before leaving. Now which one of you buttheads is going to drive me?"

"Not me," they chorused.

The telephone rang and Priscilla caught it on the second trill. The one-sided conversation was as audible as if she'd been standing next to me. "The password?" She whispered into the mouthpiece while keeping an eye on Addie. "Rolls Royce. Yes, I'm sorry for the inconvenience. Don't call the police. No, it was a mistake. My mother—she's senile. It won't happen again. We're putting her in a home." When she hung up the phone and returned to the living room, Addie spoke with the petulance of a five-year-old.

"What's the code?"

Richard flung his hands past his chest. "What the hell? I'm

giving it to her."

"You'll do no such thing." Priscilla.

"What difference does it make? She'll forget it by tomorrow morning."

Priscilla relented. "Two-zero-one-seven. And don't write it down. I don't want the help getting it."

"I don't need to write it down. I have a photographic memory," Addie said straight-faced.

Priscilla cackled, then exchanged eye-encrypted glances with Richard.

I tried to think up a word association technique to help me remember it. Then it hit me. The four-digit code matched the Hollingsworth's street address.

Addie caught my eye through the mirror.

"You're a couple of old fuddy-duddies," she said sharply. "Dream crushers—that's all you do—ruin my idea of a fun evening. Well forget it. I'm out of the mood now." With a one-heeled pivot and an over-the-shoulder, "See you in the morning," she bustled down the hall, leaving them to figure it out.

Later, after I sneaked into her room, unnoticed, I awakened around one in the morning thinking of Allen. I picked up my new mobile phone and studied it.

I tried not to do it. I really did. But my thumb had a mind of its own. Maybe he wouldn't answer.

The phone purred.

Hearing the canned message on his machine would be enough to last me a day or two.

Allen picked up on the third ring.

I halted. Everything I'd wanted to say flash froze in my throat.

"Hello?"

I needed a defibrillator to restart my heart.

"Who's this?"

135

I started to hyperventilate.

"Who's calling?"

I tried to whisper, "Elle," but my throat closed around the name.

"Stop calling me, you hear? Or I'm filing harassment charges."

The line went dead in my hand.

# CHAPTER TWENTY-TWO

Two nights later, after the newscaster for the ten o'clock broadcast predicted another scorcher in this unending drought, it rained.

Not just any old rain. Not the kind where an angel spits and it dries as soon as it hits the cobblestones. The skies opened up and a torrential downpour took place.

It happened just before eleven. For no good reason, a huge clap of thunder rattled the windows. Suddenly, it sounded like a drive-by shooting with bullets from Uzis hitting the slate roof of Hollingsworth Manor. Then the house's alarm system engaged. As I looked around to make sure Addie wasn't to blame, I heard the toilet flush and saw the light go out. Headlight beacons came on in the driveway. To avoid the hail, Richard moved his car to the back of the property, into one of the garages beneath Broderick's living quarters.

"Do you think . . . ?" Addie ventured. "I mean, is it possible one of the ladies . . . ?"

Profanity, shouted from the drive, filtered into the house. We turned to the window overlooking the porte cochere in time to see Richard, soaked to the bone, running for the back door with his hands shielding his face. Hail the size of golf balls bounced onto the cobblestones. Tendrils of steam coiled up from the pavement as hail melted into white marbles and then disappeared. Vapors rose up from the lawn, giving the grounds a ghostly aura.

"I think at least one of Mama's friends must've come through."

"Probably Frances," said Addie.

I nodded.

We crawled back into bed and pulled the covers up under our chins. The problem with making this agreement with Peter is that we couldn't distinguish whether this unseasonably wet thunderstorm was a freakish act of nature, or provided a sign that we had four more extraordinarily good–deed doers to seek out. I fell asleep listening to Richard carping about the weather down at the far end of the hall, and holding the weather forecaster personally responsible, while threatening to sue the TV station.

In the middle of the night, a Buddy Holly ring tone roused me.

At first, I thought I'd imagined it. By the third bar of "It Doesn't Matter Anymore," I tried to incorporate it into my dream. By the time it reached the chorus, I sat bolt upright and grabbed my mobile. Allen's name appeared on the digital display.

I thumbed the talk button, put the phone to my ear, threw my legs out from beneath the covers, and headed for the loo so as not to awaken Addie.

"Allen? Is it you?" My heart drummed.

"Who is this?"

"I know you don't believe me. How could you? But it's me. It's Elle. Darling, I've missed you so."

"What do you want?" He didn't sound angry, merely resigned to the idea someone would answer, as if this was a prank phone call and he wanted it to stop. "Where are you?"

"I'm at . . ." my voice trailed.

What if he found me and only saw Sylvester Gooch? I'd be rearrested for cutting the monitor off my ankle, and reincarcerated. I'd never be able to talk four other people into doing an extraordinarily good deed in Mama's name, and this would all have been for nothing.

But it wasn't just that.

There'd turned out to be a lot riding on this, and I suddenly realized just how much.

Addie, for one thing. Those bruises all over her body. Her parchment skin didn't get that way as a result of a heavy-handed twelve-year-old. And what about the mental commitment, and the impending guardianship over Addie's person and her estate? If Priscilla and Richard could somehow be evicted from the Hollingsworth estate, then at least Addie would have the house to herself without fear of being locked away in a mental institution, or nursing home, or locked Alzheimer's unit, while Priscilla and Richard went through her money like a couple of marauding Goths.

And yet . . . I had Allen on the telephone. I was about to pour out my breaking heart when Addie walked in fisting sleep from her eyes.

"Mummy? What's wrong? What're you doing—" she sucked air "—that's Allen, isn't it? You're talking to Allen."

I gave her a strained smile. Tears trickled over my cheeks. "Hold on, darling," I said, then covered the tiny speaker and lowered the phone. "Lillibet, please. I have to—"

But my daughter strode over on creaky legs and yanked the mobile out of my hand. She pressed the disconnect button, and slid the cover back over the keypad.

"Are you crazy?" she hissed.

"Why'd you do that?" I cried. "I was getting somewhere. I was making him understand. He was coming around, and you ruined it."

"Ruined it?" she screeched. "You're the one about to bugger things up."

"Give me my phone." Instead, she hid it behind her back. I got up from my place on the edge of the tub and grabbed for it. "Give it to me."

"No." She held it aloft, swapping from one hand to the other while I implemented a few desperate swipes through the air. "Listen to me. *Listen to me.*"

I saw a new level of fright in her eyes that froze me in mid-snatch.

"Go on." I kept my voice even and metered.

"This is exactly the kind of maneuver Detective Stone would suggest. They're looking for you, Mummy. Because you didn't return to Sly's house. Because Sly's mum is worried about him. Because you cut off the electronic monitor and chucked it."

I listened. Breaths came easier. My heart stopped pounding.

"You called him before, right? And he didn't believe you when you told him who you were. I know you called from this house because Priscilla confronted me. Maybe Allen saw on his caller ID where the call came from. Maybe he told Detective Stone. They're best friends, right?"

Guilty head bob.

"And you've called him other times, too, haven't you?"

My chin dipped to my neck. She'd mastered the art of shaming me.

"And he didn't believe you then, either, did he?"

Big head shake.

"And now he calls *you*. You're the architect of this mission. You're supposed to know better. The hell, Mummy? Don't you find that odd? They're probably together right now, taping that phone call so they can sit back and analyze it using voice recognition equipment and whatnot."

I'd never once considered the possibility. But then I'd been speaking to a policeman who considered these phone calls to be pranks. Visions of Allen and Chip sitting in an interrogation room with a two-way mirror and a tape recorder set up popped into mind. Allen hadn't believed me that morning at juvenile hall, not even with Lillibet present to vouch for me. I'd been naïve to use the Hollingsworth's home telephone. The number would've shown up on the digital display of his caller ID. And if he put two and two together, the logical starting point for finding Sylvester Gooch would be through Addie Hollingsworth.

My daughter was right.

From here on out, I'd have to be careful. Needless to say, by distrusting the darkness beyond the window, I had difficulty falling asleep. Eventually, I dozed off. Startled awake, I heard a rhythmic patter against the window that sounded exactly like fingers tapping on the glass. At first, I thought it was a house cat trying to get in, but then I realized these people didn't have any pets. With trepidation, I crept to the window to investigate. Nothing could prepare me for what would happen if I pulled aside the curtain and came face-to-face with someone outside. The creepy sound turned out to be huge kamikaze locusts flinging themselves against the glass.

Welcome to Texas in August.

# CHAPTER TWENTY-THREE

The day I got Sylvester's new clothes, Addie stocked up on makeup. So when I awakened the next morning, it didn't feel strange at all to see her sitting on the vanity stool, trowelling on flesh-tone base, and whisking on powder.

"Your head looks like a sugar cookie." I hoisted myself up on one elbow and yawned into my fist. "Aren't you overdoing it a smidge?"

She pulled a face. "What can I say? I want Addie to look pretty."

How sweet.

"Yes, but those two already think Mrs. Hollingsworth's a nut. If you start changing a bunch of things about poor Adelaide, they'll only think the dementia has progressed."

"Or . . . ," Addie drawled out the word, "they'll think I'm taking an interest in myself and getting better."

But I couldn't help thinking that things such as a renewed interest in her appearance would only make Addie's daughter and son-in-law want to have her locked up faster.

"This is fab." Addie scrutinized her reflection, then fluffed on blush. "It's so smooth my skin feels luscious. You should try it."

I threw back the covers and swung my legs over the side of the bed.

"You want me to put on makeup," I said skeptically. Then again, who'd see it? Elizabeth used to love dressing in my clothes. We'd spend hours doctoring our faces with my cosmetics: Elizabeth at age five, me at age twenty-five. "I'm game."

She relinquished the vanity stool and I slid onto the cushion. It still retained the heat from her body.

While I examined the selection of skin care products, my daughter studied her reflection with cold scrutiny.

"Mummy, what would you say if it takes less than thirty days, that we get Addie a facelift?"

"Bad idea."

"How come?" She traced a finger over the wrinkles on one side of her face, then placed her hands on either side of her jaws—monkey see, monkey do—and stretched the skin back to her ears. "Addie could be a lot prettier for her age."

"What makes Addie pretty is the person inside. Besides, I've heard the recovery after a facelift hurts so bad you want to kill yourself. That would defeat the purpose, now, wouldn't it?" I snapped my fingers several times to jog my memory. "I say, didn't one of those society ladies—the famous one who wrote etiquette guides—didn't she fling herself out of the hospital window after having a facelift because the pain was so bloody bad she couldn't stand it anymore?"

My daughter scowled. "Forget it. I just thought while I'm here, I could do something nice for her."

As I picked up an eye shadow brush and shadowed my lids with the palest hint of purple, she provoked me into thinking: Why had Peter procured these exact bodies for us to occupy? Were Addie and Sly a couple of undiscovered dead people, or were they randomly plucked from their shells in order for Elizabeth and me to borrow them for awhile? Were they in here *with* us, like undiagnosed schizophrenics, lying dormant until the moment they needed to show themselves? I didn't think so, but one never knew. After all, if teaming a black lad with an old lady was Peter's idea of a joke, he could've selected these two for just about any reason.

My daughter sheared my thoughts.

"A transvestite looks better in a dress than this." Followed by, "Mummy do you think things will return to the way they were with Addie and Sly after we go back?"

"I have no idea."

"I wouldn't want her to go to a care center. To me, that'd be a fate worse than death."

"I know, darling. I wouldn't want her to go there, either."

Addie dashed out long enough for me to dress. She returned with a newspaper and enough food heaped onto a plate to satisfy the funfair fat lady.

"I told Jessie I was ravenous."

My eyes widened. "What'd she say?"

"She didn't say anything. Just pulled a face, and quadrupled the portions. Richard, on the other hand, told Priscilla I should be checked for a tapeworm."

"And what did you say?"

"Told him to mind his own beeswax," she said airily as she picked up the fork and shoveled the first of many bites into her mouth.

We sat on the bed and shared the food tray. When we finished, my daughter said, "That was so delicious I had to restrain myself from licking the plate."

"Don't. They'll think you've smuggled in a dog and come looking."

She set the empty tray outside the door, and toggled the bolt behind her. I'd already divided the newspaper into sections, and browsed the front page and the city section for stories that might require an extraordinarily good deed.

My daughter took the society pages, crawled back into bed with her feet bare and her manicured toenails pointing skyward, and perused the newspaper for fashion ideas.

"I want to buy Addie new clothes," she said wistfully. "Some of the dresses in her wardrobe look like they're fifty years old."

"Classic lines never go out of style," I reminded her.

*Cruelty to an animal . . . Family homeless after arson . . . Scout leader charged with sexual assault.* I shuddered at the headlines.

My eyes jumped to the next section and drifted over the page.

There it was: *Child needs blood donation.*

I folded the page in half, and then halved it again.

"Oi . . . listen to this. Here's a child with a blood type so rare that the blood banks are out. Doctors want him to have a transfusion because of a rare form of cancer . . ." My voice drifted off, then came back strong as I rested the article on my knee and mused aloud. "Wonder what type blood we have?"

"Red."

"Bloody hilarious," I said, but it got me thinking. As Eloise Winthrop, I had A-positive blood. My daughter had A-positive, as well. But as Addie and Sly, I hadn't a clue. "You should call your doctor and find out what your blood type is."

She got off the mattress, walked around to the side of the bed that I'd been sleeping on, and rummaged through a drawer on the night table where the phone was kept.

"What are you doing?"

"Calling my doctor like you said."

"You know who your doctor is?"

"Yes, Mum. If I hear that witch Priscilla mention Dr. Bomar one more time I'm going to beat seven shades of shit out of her with my walking stick."

I scowled. "You don't own a walking stick."

"Then I'm going to buy one. So I can beat her over the head with it. Yes, hello?" Short pause. "They put me on hold. Why do they do that? If you're calling your doctor you must be sick. So why do they . . . yes, no that's all right, just don't do it again. Now, see here. This is Adelaide Hollingsworth. I want to speak to Dr. Bomar." Short pause. "I don't care if he's with a patient. I'm not that patient. If I had any patience I wouldn't mind holding, but I don't. So I don't care if he's with a patient, my patience has run out. Do you understand? I don't know if you can help me. Do you have access to my chart? Oh, you do. Then tell me what kind of blood I have."

I waited expectantly for the results.

My daughter scowled. "Bloody hilarious. Now tell me the type. Very well, get on with it." She covered the mouthpiece with her palm. "Everyone's a comedienne." She pulled her hand away and resumed the conversation with the person at the other end of the line. "So how would I go about donating blood?" Another pause. Her eyes thinned into slits. Then she banged the receiver down on its cradle.

I arched an eyebrow.

"Stupid cow. She said, 'Get a hammer and a good-sized cup.' "

By the time my daughter quit pouting, I'd devised a plan. But to put it in motion, I'd have to call Sly's mother, Mrs. Gooch. I looked in the telephone book, and even called directory assistance, but they had no listing for anyone with that surname. Then it occurred to me that Sly's mother's name might not be Gooch. Maybe she went back to her maiden name after Sly's father went to prison. Maybe she couldn't afford a phone.

I didn't dare call Mr. Geeslin. By now, he'd be looking for me. I didn't want to call Detective Stone, either. For all I knew, they'd started a manhunt. And Allen . . .

I inwardly sighed. Just the thought of him shunning me made my heart hurt. Bottom line, I couldn't ask him either.

"Get dressed." I grabbed a washcloth, turned on the tap, and wiped the makeup off my face.

A week had passed and I hadn't returned to school. Addie

and I didn't seem to be making much headway, and if I didn't do something fast, we'd be seeing Sly's face on milk cartons.

"Where are we going?"

"To see Mrs. Gooch."

# CHAPTER TWENTY-FOUR

Priscilla had already left the house for a meeting at her ladies' club when Addie called for Broderick to bring the car around. Sneaking me past Jessie and Perry turned out to be a breeze, since Jessie was in the laundry sorting clothes while Perry thinned out the overgrowth of rosebushes at the back of the property.

We climbed into the back seat and slammed the doors. Broderick touched a button, and the door locks snapped shut. His eyes flickered to the rearview mirror.

"Where to, Madame?"

"Addie."

He punctuated the correction with a nod. "Where to, Miss Addie?"

I'd looked up the address of the cleaning company where Mrs. Gooch worked her day job, and recited it so Broderick could program it into the Mercedes's GPS. He seemed to know where it was because he did a little face scrunch.

Not a good sign.

The building was located in an industrial area, on the east side of town, in a rough neighborhood. A wealthy, elderly woman like Addie, riding in the back seat of a big fine Mercedes, turned out to be a real head turner. Every corner we turned brought more gawkers.

We pulled up to the curb in front of Blue Moon Cleaning Solutions, and Broderick hit the door lock button. Addie offered to go with me, but that didn't sound like such a good idea. For one thing, if Mrs. Gooch came after me with a broom, I'd need to run and Addie would only hold me back.

I went through the glass doors and found another glass door with a winking blue moon logo to my right.

The dark-haired lady behind the counter sat at a desk with her head bent in concentration as she typed on the keyboard. When she glanced up, clown spots of blush that rouged her cheeks surprised me. I asked for Sly's mother, she swiveled her chair toward the door. She told me Mrs. Gooch had taken off work because her son had gone missing, and police had advised her to stay home and wait by the telephone.

I wanted to cackle. Did police think someone was holding him for ransom?

I asked for her address, but the lady denied my request.

"Look," I reasoned, "I may know where to find her son."

"And you are . . . ?" She evaluated me through inquisitive green eyes that soon thinned into the expression of a skeptic. Dark brows slammed together. Then her attention darted from me, to a small office with a photograph placed prominently on the desktop, and back. I sensed the picture looked exactly like me. When she returned my gaze, she skewered me with a look.

"I'm on his basketball team." I admit it. For several seconds, the room unexpectedly went out of focus and I felt dizzy.

"I'll call her for you." She opened the drawer and pulled out a file, then leafed through it until she found the number. She flipped her pencil over, and stabbed out a number on the keypad with the eraser tip. "Myrna? Daisy. There's a kid here, wants to talk to you."

She handed the receiver across the countertop. I took it and launched into the cringeworthy part of my story.

"Mrs. Gooch? I need to talk to you but they won't give me your address. It's about Sly."

"You're Sly. Don'tchoo think I'd know my own son?" Although I tried to disabuse her of the notion, she wouldn't have it. Finally, after absorbing my words, she huffed in disgust. "Who're you?"

"I know him from school. Can I come to your house?" Said with an enthusiasm I didn't feel.

She gave me her address, and I wrote it on a scribbling pad the lady provided. I thanked Sly's mother and hung up, said good-bye to the Blue Moon girl, and trotted out the door.

Back inside the car, I handed the yellow sticky note to Broderick. He let out a deep sigh.

Addie picked up on it, too. "What's wrong?"

"I've enjoyed working for you, Miss Addie," he said. "We're going to be killed."

She swatted the air with a parchment hand. "Don't be silly. We're not going to be killed."

"Easy for you to say." But Broderick wrenched the Mercedes into gear, and headed on down the road anyway.

When we crested the railroad and turned off a rough part of Miller Street into a residential area, Addie and I were chatting each other up, oblivious to the goings-on outside.

Broderick's ominous "Uh-oh," snapped us to attention.

We looked through the windscreen and gasped. All in all, I counted three police cars.

"That rat fink." My voice pitched to incredulity. "She tattled. Turn the car around."

Broderick said, "Is that wise? It might be better if we drive on by."

I saw his point. Pulling a midblock U-turn might arouse their suspicions. Because it seemed unthinkable that an expensive German car traveling down a ratty avenue would peak their interests. They'd probably think we just dropped into the neighborhood to buy drugs. I had an inkling as to how this might play out, and didn't want to be standing in the middle of the street with a bunch of angry homeowners watching us get our arses handed to us. "What are we supposed to do? Wave at them?"

"I was thinking you could duck."

*Because in this part of town, an old woman with a chauffeur wouldn't raise an eyebrow at all. No, sir. Not. At. All.*

As Addie and I sat, gobsmacked, Broderick reversed the Mercedes. When we reached the intersection going the wrong way, he made a hard right and took off down a side street.

"Now what?" he said.

"Let's get a bite to eat, shall we?" Addie pulled a compact from her handbag, and dusted powder over her nose. "Perhaps when we're done they'll be gone."

I liked homemade cooking, but Addie wanted to eat at one of those deplorable chain restaurants. Broderick opted out of the vote, so Addie chose since she was the one paying. Note to self: The one bankrolling the jaunt gets to direct the shots. I tried to manufacture enthusiasm for what would probably be a meal of frozen food, thawed and microwaved. Ptomaine sprang to mind. The thought was gone before it settled.

Addie and Broderick ordered chicken-fried steaks, and I got a salad. Even though this boy-body craves junk food, common sense won out and I ordered from the heart-healthy side of the menu. Seated at a booth with vinyl-covered bench seats, and a knock-off Tiffany light overhanging the table, we ate in an atmosphere where particles of grease hung in the air. Addie couldn't seem to get enough junk food speeding through her digestive system. My eyes nearly popped when she asked the waiter for the dessert menu.

On our way back to Mrs. Gooch's residence, two police cars sped past with their emergency lights on. Brilliant—two that wouldn't be parked at Mrs. Gooch's.

In fact, there were no police cars at all when we pulled up directly in front of her house, a white frame cracker box with black trim and a postage stamp lawn. A rope swing hung from a large oak tree in the front yard, and children's toys in neon colors popped up like Easter eggs across the patchy lawn.

After Broderick stopped the car, I suggested he back into the driveway with the bonnet pointed at the street—a safety trick cops do that Allen had taught me.

When he looked at me funny, I said, "Hood."

"Right. We're in the 'hood."

"Just do it. In case we need to make a fast getaway."

# CHAPTER TWENTY-FIVE

After pressing the doorbell and getting no answer, I walked around to the back of the house. A huge dog, staked in the garden on a heavy metal chain, snoozed beneath the shade tree. I opened the gate and let myself inside. His eyelids snapped open like roller shades, revealing two unyielding onyx marbles. I studied his gaze as he tracked me across the grass. My heart picked up its pace. Looking into predatory, impenetrable eyes is a lot like staring down the throat of a double-barrel shotgun. The big difference is that you can reason with people. You can't reason with nature or creatures of nature. With any luck, the back door would be unlocked. And if I had to kick or shoulder my way inside, didn't I live here? A low, throaty rumble vibrated in my ears.

"Here, doggie-doggie-doggie." I extended my hand, palm up. Dogs love me. Love to lick my face. "Nice doggie. Doggie wants a bone?"

Without warning, the huge brown beast rocketed to his paws. With teeth bared and shoestring drool flying out the sides of his mouth, he charged.

"Bloody hell," I shrieked, and took off the way I'd come in. I barely made it to the gate when the slack played out of the chain, and his collar jerked him back. My heart pounded so hard I thought it would beat right through my chest. I gave up right then and there. It doesn't pay to tempt fate. I headed back around to the front when a knock on the window stopped me.

"Sylvester, you get yo' bad self in this house this minute."

Myrna Gooch's muffled demands warned me she meant business. I wished I'd been able to bring her the silk scarf Mrs. Lang gave me as a peace offering.

I cupped my hands to my mouth and yelled at the shadowy figure behind the glass. "There's something wrong with the dog. It's gone mad. We have a vicious dog."

"Nothin' wrong with the dog 'cept for you haven't been here to feed him. Now you get inside this house 'cause you owe me an explanation, and I'm gonna get it or die tryin'. Make me worry . . . um-um-um . . . I got every right to beat you senseless."

I did a heavy eye roll and ambled to the front door.

I'm not Sylvester but I'm not stupid, either. Mrs. Gooch may not realize I'm not her son but the dog sure knows.

She met me at the door with a presence as overshadowing as a gathering of thunderclouds. As I took the porch steps in twos, she unlatched the screen.

"Who that?" She jutted her chin at the Mercedes idling in the driveway. "Better not be no drug dealer on account of I'm gonna blister yo' peter if you been hangin' out with druggies."

"Mama," I said, unwilling and unable to step past the threshold, "it's just some people trying to help me."

"Help you what?" Dark eyes narrowed. She slapped the side of my head. Too late, I raised my hand to shield my face and she whapped me on the other side. "Sit yo' black ass down, boy. Don't make me go *Full Metal Jacket* on you."

I'd expected the atmosphere to be charged with hostility and suspicion, but I didn't expect to be manhandled. No way was I going inside that house and I told her so. I tried to speak like the lads from juvenile hall but I wasn't sure I could be that convincing. Funny how I'd known on instinct that Elizabeth had returned in the body of Adelaide Hollingsworth as soon as

I heard her speak. What would keep Mrs. Gooch from knowing I wasn't her son?

"Mama, I'm not comin' in long as you be hittin' me. I came to talk."

She glanced at my bare legs. "Where's yo' monitor?"

"That's not important."

Instead of arguing with me, she burst into tears and took another pop at me. It didn't hurt—well, not so much—I hardly put up much of a defense.

When my daughter was a little tyke, she walked to the convenience store with a friend. It seemed safe enough, but when they didn't return in the allotted time, we launched into an all-out manhunt. When it turned out they were out in the barn, with Elizabeth showing off her new pony, I'd been so sick with worry that I smacked her. Now, watching Sylvester's mum crumble like a fifty-year-old cookie, I wanted to cluck sympathy because I knew just how she felt.

Mrs. Gooch ran out of steam. "Don'tchoo know how scared I been? I couldn't work knowin' you was out there, maybe dead in a ditch, and now my check's gonna end up short at the end of the month."

I felt sorry for her, really I did. For no good reason, I opened my arms to comfort her and she flung herself into them, sobbing. I towered over her by a good six inches so I rested my cheek against the top of her head. She smelled of sweat and vinegar and fried chicken.

"Don't worry about money, Mama."

She pulled away enough to look up at me. "Don'tchoo see, Sly, I *am* worried. We barely makin' it now." Her voice spiraled upward in direct proportion to her downward spiraling depression.

"I'll get you the money."

Instead of being grateful, she hauled off and boxed my jaws. I tried to figure out how I never saw that coming when she ranted, "I don't want no pimp money, or drug money, and I don't want no robber money."

Comprehension dawned, and I reassured. "No, no, no, Mama, this is honest money."

"Whatchoo mean?" She looked me over like she wanted to believe whatever sad, sorry story I'd concocted, but had reserved the right to box my jaws again if she didn't believe me.

I took a deep breath. "There's this lady—"

"What lady?" Eyes thinned in suspicion.

"A fancy lady, Mama, with a big house and a big garden and house servants—"

"White lady?"

"Yeah, Mama, and she's real nice. You know what restitution is?" I remembered the term from my visit with my probation officer.

She gave me a snort of unsuitability. "I know what it means. Is yo' rich white lady gonna put you to work at her big, fancy house?"

I nodded. "Already did."

It wasn't a complete fib.

"How much she payin' you?"

"Enough, Mama. She'll give what we need to see us through the month."

"What'd you do to the dog?"

"Didn't do nothin' to the dog."

"You lie," she said, but she unhanded me long enough to wander into the kitchen.

I trailed her, halting at the sight of a little tyke in a striped shirt and overalls, sitting at the table in a booster seat, spooning cereal into his mouth.

"Say hello to your brother," she snapped.

" 'Ello little man," I said, but I was thinking, *Sly has a brother?*

Brown paper grocery sacks lined the countertop. She unpacked the frozen food first, stopping long enough between bags to store boxes in the cupboard. A single bare bulb illuminating the pantry exposed a 1960's time capsule of staples: minute rice, macaroni and cheese, flour and dried beans bagged in industrial sized cloth sacks, boxes of flavored gelatin, and jars of Miracle Whip elbowed each other for shelf space. Even the two bottles of wine—one red, one white—were low-budget, originating from places you'd never think would make wine. I found the whole thing sad until I remembered I didn't even own a bag of complimentary airline peanuts.

"Help me with the vegetables." Distress pinched her lips.

At this point, I couldn't imagine anyone in the world being so bad off that they'd need my help, not even to unload groceries. But I picked up a plastic sack of carrots and opened the cool box, having no idea where they needed to go. I must've held the door open too long because she snatched them from my hand and stored them in the crisper.

Flashes of anger sparked in her eyes. "What's wrong witchoo?"

The child stopped in midbite. When he opened his mouth, what unchewed food didn't cling to his lips dropped onto his bib. "Mama's mean 'cause the other night I wasn't hungry and so I hadn't finished my dinner, and Mama said I had to eat everything on my plate 'cause there were children starving in Africa. So I said, 'Name one,' and then she spanked me."

I barked out a laugh.

"What do you think you are—a hyena? Don't be laughin' at him. Don't be eggin' him on." Mrs. Gooch balanced an arm full of macaroni and cheese boxes in the crook of one hand so she could slap the side of my head with the other on her way to the cupboard. "You gonna be the death of me, Sly."

"I don't mean to, Mama. I'm gonna change. That's a promise.

But Mama—" I swallowed hard "—I've gotta know something. I've gotta know what kind of blood I have."

"It's red."

I barked out another laugh. I couldn't help it.

"A, B, O or AB?" I offered helpfully.

"It's AB. You got AB-positive blood."

"What kind of blood does my daddy have?"

"Whatchoo talkin' 'bout, Sly? You got no daddy."

"Everybody got a daddy."

"But yo' daddy in the pen."

"I just want to know what kind of blood he has."

"Don't know and don't care." She braced her thick arms across her bosom, and I realized that was that.

"What's his full name?"

"You know his full name—Leon Darnell Gooch. Why you axe a stupid question like that?"

"What's the name of the pen? And how do I get there if I want to go see him?"

"You ain't goin' to Wichita Falls. You got no way to get there. And he don't want to see you no how on account of he a no-account and you gonna be just like him someday. Why you want to go to Wichita Falls? You want to see where you gonna be living when you turn seventeen? That's sick. You sick, Sly."

I pumped her for more information but she wasn't forthcoming.

"I have to go now, Mama. I've got to get back to my job."

"Police be lookin' for you."

"I know, Mama. Please don't tell them I was here." I could tell from her expression she didn't like that one bit. "Please don't tell them until I finish my job and get paid."

"You a lot of trouble, boy."

I pushed the screen door open and stepped out onto the porch. "I love you, Mama."

Halfway to the car I heard the door locks snap open. I walked around the boot and opened the back passenger door.

Then Mrs. Gooch called out to me. "Where you stayin'? How do I find you?"

I cupped my hand to my ear like I couldn't hear.

She yelled, "AB."

For a few seconds, nothing registered.

"Yo' daddy got AB-negative."

# CHAPTER TWENTY-SIX

While I'd been dodging puncture wounds from the family pet, and fending off blows from a woman going mad cow on me, Addie'd been building up a head of steam in the back seat of the Mercedes.

She grabbed Broderick's headrest, hoisted herself up to ear level, and urged him to hurry. When we bounced out of the drive and onto the asphalt, she told me why.

"While you were inside, people drove by."

"It's a public street," I said. "That's how it works."

She gave a vehement headshake. "Tell him, Broderick."

"It's true. They rolled by and flashed gang signs."

"Gang signs?"

"Hand signs. And then one shaped his finger and thumb into the shape of a gun. Is somebody after you?"

"Of course not." As soon as I said it, an overwhelming sense of dread washed over me.

At the same time, Addie said, "Do you think it could be the lads from school?"

"LaVon."

"Is that the one who tripped you?"

I shook my head. "Doesn't matter. We're not coming back here. We can't endanger Mrs. Gooch." I didn't tell them about Sly's little brother.

Broderick slid me a sideways glance. "Where to now?"

"We need to go to a place called Wichita Falls."

He checked his watch. "That's a three-hour drive if you stick to the speed limit. If you want to go, we probably shouldn't leave until tomorrow."

I nodded in agreement.

Addie said, "What's in Wichita Falls?"

"Sly's—my daddy."

She shot me a wary look. "And we need to see him . . . because why?"

Over Broderick's intent regard, I leaned in and whispered, "I have an idea. A way to reach the largest number of people in the shortest amount of time."

"And they're in Wichita Falls?"

"They're in prison. And the prison where we have a contact happens to be in Wichita Falls."

"What're we going to do?"

I dug the newspaper article out of my back pocket and opened it to the story about the child with rare blood. "We're going to see Sylvester's daddy."

# CHAPTER TWENTY-SEVEN

We spent the better part of the evening in Broderick's flat above the carriage house with our long-suffering chauffeur hunkered over the computer running searches for us. He located Leon Darnell Gooch at the Allred Unit of the state's penitentiary outside of Wichita Falls, looked up directions on a map, and we plotted our upcoming day. Around seven o'clock that night, headlight beacons panned across the upstairs window. Richard and Priscilla had left for the evening; Priscilla, to her ladies' club, and Richard, to the Nineteenth Hole.

Their absence gave us enough time to enter the house, undetected, and take nice long showers before dressing for bed. While we still had the run of the place, my daughter and I sat at the kitchen table, a primitive maple drop leaf that didn't seem to fit with the rest of the glam furnishings throughout the house, devouring Richard's ice cream.

I don't sleep well in strange places, and Hollingsworth Manor gave me the heebie-jeebies. I started to imagine all sorts of bad things. Perhaps Priscilla and Richard weren't out running social errands. Maybe they were scoping out nursing homes to stick Addie into. I'd started to feel sorry for the old bird's predicament, and like Elizabeth, began to marinate in thoughts that might improve her lot with these gold-digging cutthroats after we left.

My daughter alarmed the house before we retired to her bedroom. That way, we'd hear the warning tone go off when

Priscilla and Richard returned. I'd hide in the wardrobe to ensure if they poked their noses into Addie's room, they'd see only Addie in bed, sleeping peacefully.

Reclining against the carved walnut headboard with a couple of silk bolster pillows tucked beneath my back and shoulders, I allowed my thoughts to free associate while Addie fussed with her looks in the vanity mirror.

With the newspaper article folded on my lap, I projected my voice so she could hear me through the open door. "I think we should look over Mr. Hollingsworth's Last Will and Testament."

"What for?"

"You want to help Addie, right?" She grunted approval so I explained my idea. "If we knew the terms of Mr. Hollingsworth's wishes, not to mention the law firm he used, we might be able to protect her from these piranhas. I wouldn't mind telling those two to take a running jump."

Elizabeth disappeared momentarily, and came out of the loo wearing a flowing silk dressing gown, this one in a pleasant shade of peach that brought out the undertones in her skin. She framed herself in the doorway. "Why don't we just ask Priscilla? Surely she has a copy of the will around here."

"Bad idea. The last thing we need is for Miss Priss to discover that we're plotting to keep Addie out of the nursing home. I mean—" my mind spun with bad thoughts "—what if they decide to kill her? It wouldn't take much, you know? They could send her up to the attic on a ruse, and push her down the stairs. How would anyone know it wasn't an accident? Or they could drug her food. Or overmedicate her. Really, Lillibet, I'm surprised at you. And I'm a little afraid for you, as well."

"Good point." Elizabeth turned to a mirror on her dressing table, eyed her reflection, and unpinned her bun. Silver tufts of hair floated to her shoulders, catching the light in a way that reminded me of spun glass. "Is this a good color for me? I've always liked pastels, you know?" She twisted away from the mirror to show me her new eye shadow.

I thought it a bit harsh, but she seemed pleased with herself so I flashed a smile. "Lovely. So we'll go to the courthouse this week and have the clerk pull Mr. Hollingsworth's file?"

"Brilliant."

When Miss Bossyboots and the baboon didn't come home by nine-thirty I migrated into the lounge to the liquor bar. My underpants were giving me a wedgie so I paused beside the couch to strip them off. Resting them atop the sofa, I made my way over to the wet bar and found a wine rack behind the granite countertop. I looked over the bottles until I found a white wine that looked inviting—a Montrachet 1978 from Domaine de la Rominee-Conti.

I selected two wine stems, rummaged through the drawer for a corkscrew, and toddled back to our room. "Wine?"

"Sorry we didn't think of this sooner," she said. "If Addie didn't drink before, she has good reason to now."

After uncorking the bottle and pouring, we sipped and plotted until headlights panned over the windows.

"They're home." I grabbed the wine bottle, took my glass and threaded the stem of Addie's through my fingers, took my place in the wardrobe, and waited for the alarm to trip. The warning buzzer went off about the same time I remembered I'd left my knickers in the den.

I set the bottle on the floor and cracked open the louvered doors enough to let myself out.

Addie pulled the covers up to her chin. "What are you doing?"

"Retrieving my underpants from the lounge."

"Why would you leave your underpants in the lounge?"

"They gave me a wedgie."

"And you just left them?" She sat erect, fisting the sheets in a death grip. "Have you gone mad?"

"You know, Elizabeth, this really isn't the time . . ."

"But you can't go out there. They'll see you."

I shushed her with a finger and cracked open the door a smidge. The ambient glow from the kitchen light lit the hallway enough to see the way. As I traversed the length of the corridor, I realized Priscilla and Richard had stopped to linger in the kitchen.

Deep breath.

I convinced myself they were preparing a snack, and crept into the den.

Then Richard threw a wobbly.

"She's been eating my ice cream again. She knows it's mine. I had another talk with her yesterday about it."

"Save it, Richard."

"The sooner we get that selfish old bitch out of here, the better. I swear if you don't get her under control, I'm going to . . ." He let loose with a unique tapestry of expletives.

"Lower your voice. You'll wake up the house."

A dish crashed to the floor. Panic seized my throat. Thunderous footfalls stomped through the kitchen. My first instinct was to shrink in size until I became invisible. My incredible shrinking gonads had already started the process, but the rest of me realized I'd returned to Earth without my superpowers, and now my bollocks were trying to hide behind my tonsils. With my heart beating double-time, I ducked behind a fabulous Chinese Coromandel screen with applied geishas carved out of jade.

The living room light flicked on.

Richard, still cursing, stomped over to the bar. I peered through the hinged fold that pieced two of the screen panels together. A heavy crystal decanter clinked against the counter. Richard bent over enough to open the minifridge, and dropped two ice cubes into the glass. He pulled out the glass stopper and splashed four fingers of amber liquor into the highball glass.

The strangest sensation chilled me to the bone.

For a few seconds, I was treated to a view of him scratching his privates. His attention shifted. He seemed to be looking directly through the slit in the screen.

Then he charged.

My eyes darted around in search of something that could double as a weapon, but it's impossible to beat someone into submission with a palm frond.

A lightheaded rush filled my head. I prepared to die. Again.

He came to a stop at the sofa. "What the hell?"

He'd found my underpants.

I held my breath.

Then Priscilla entered the room and turned my situation into a hell sandwich.

"Are you still ranting?" Her stance was passive aggressive; her voice laced with impatience. "Now what?"

My life seemed to pass in slow motion, like a series of film frames viewed against the light of an incandescent bulb. I sensed my eyes about to pop out from the pressure building behind them.

It was as surreal as if I were watching this catastrophe unfold through another's point of view.

Then Richard's hand darted out and everything took place in real time.

He snatched up my underpants and crushed them in his grip. He hid his fist behind his back and lifted a half-empty glass in a toast to Miss Bossyboots while I'd just experienced a new dimension of terror.

"Cheers. May the old bitch live a long life—in a nursing home, or a locked ward for dements." He belted back his drink while stuffing my underpants into his pocket.

He headed off down the hall as his wife prepared a drink of her own—Stolichnaya over ice. But instead of switching off the overhead light and joining the baboon, she settled onto the couch with her back to me, picked up a copy of *Architectural Digest* from the coffee table, and leafed through it. Leaving me standing here like a wooly mammoth in a tar pit—stuck.

"Are you coming to bed?" Richard called out somewhere behind me.

"In a minute."

As soon as the doorknob snicked shut and the sound of running water rushed through the kitchen pipes, Priscilla tossed the magazine aside and reached for the phone.

She stabbed out a number on the keypad, and listened. Then her face lit up with a smile.

She took a deep breath. "Darling, I've missed you so. When can we meet?"

# CHAPTER TWENTY-EIGHT

Eavesdropping on someone else's conversation might carry a certain allure for busybodies, but not if you're twelve years old and living vicariously through somebody else's trashy sex talk. There was barely enough room for my lanky frame wedged behind the Chinese room divider, much less me standing at attention with my musket loaded and aimed at the back of Priscilla's head.

Every lewd suggestion from this one-sided conversation sent an electric jolt to my crotch. I tried holding it down, tucking it between my legs like a tail, and breaking it in half without success. When you're twelve years old with enough testosterone churning through your body to power an engine turbine on a jet airplane, there's not a lot you can do about it if you're hiding behind an antique screen.

I prayed for relief, but in the alternative, a quick and painless death. Then Richard poked his head out again and said, "I thought you were coming to bed."

"On the way." To the mouthpiece, she whispered, "Gotta go," before hanging up the telephone.

"Who were you talking to?" he asked as she flicked off the light.

"Just calling for time and temperature."

"And?"

"According to the recorded message, it's going to be a scorcher all week."

"Yeah, well get on in here and I'll show you something hot."

The doorknob clicked behind her and I stepped out from behind the screen. I was halfway to the hall when I heard someone fiddle with the lock and the door clicked open again.

I dove for the couch, bouncing once and rolling onto the floor in front of the coffee table. I heard the padding of bare feet making their way into the kitchen when I realized Richard was setting the alarm.

Bloody alarm.

I had one minute to get to Addie's room before the motion detectors went off.

He took his sweet time getting back to the bedroom. But when the door closed again and I heard the lock turn, I pulled myself up and headed down the hall. They were already bumping tummies by the time I passed their room. I made it to Addie's sanctuary without triggering the alarm.

When I opened the door, she grabbed me by the scruff of my pink silk pajamas and jerked me inside.

"Where've you been?"

"Don't ask."

"You could've been discovered."

"Believe me," I said, "after what I just went through, discovery would've been a blessing."

She started to ask questions but I shushed her with a hand halt. "I need a drink."

We exchanged awkward looks. The headboard in the adjacent room was striking the wall.

"Like bloody rabbits," I said, and excused myself to the loo.

When I came back out, Elizabeth was propped up on marshmallowy pillows, reading a book in the incandescent glow of the light on the nightstand.

"My heart can't take much more of this," I said, alert to animal noises coming from the next room.

Moving to the wardrobe, I fished out the half-empty bottle and one wine stem. I'd no sooner taken a backward step than the doorknob twisted and the door flung open.

My daughter cried, "Priscilla," in the most strident of voices, and opened her arms for a hug. "Let me have a look at you."

I moved gingerly back into the wardrobe and eased the louvered door in place. Priscilla's such a wretched cow, and she can talk the hind leg off a donkey when she's trying to make a point. I sincerely hoped she didn't plan to stay long.

She said, "What do you mean your heart can't take much more of this?"

Peering through the slats, I saw my daughter wag the book. "It's this," she said, and held it aloft. "Just makes my heart race."

"Yes, well, we're home."

"I can see that," Addie said.

I half expected her to add that she heard them behaving like barnyard animals, and telepathically signaled her not to.

"Well, good night then."

"Good night." Addie smiled sweetly.

Thirty seconds passed. This time, I wouldn't forget to lock the door. I had a spot of time to relive the living room disaster in the dark recesses of an area I was starting to regard as my study, and I reviewed tonight's events in my head. If Richard suspected his tart of a wife of having an affair, then why didn't he confront her with the evidence?

*Unless* . . .

A creepy alternative flashed into mind.

Elizabeth hissed, "It's safe to come out, Mum."

A slant of blue light from the street lamp sliced through the break in the curtain, illuminating the room enough to navigate my way to my side of the mattress without stumbling into furniture. As I grazed my fingertips along the foot rail, I realized that I might not be the only one in this house who was still in the closet.

# CHAPTER TWENTY-NINE

On day nine, dawn broke with a clear sky and not a cloud in sight.

The doorknob rattled, jarring me fully awake. My internal alarm clock had failed.

Before I could dive to the floor and roll under the bed, the door swung open. Priscilla stood in the opening.

"Flaming Nora," I cried.

A look of utter shock covered her face. After a delayed reaction, she let out a blood-clotting scream to end all screams.

I can imagine how she saw me as she took in our appearances: me, with a mint-green mudpack smeared over my face that had dried and cracked in my sleep, black curly hair shorn close to the head and skin the shade of watery cocoa beneath my silk pajamas; and Addie, like an Old Master badly in need of restoration with her own crackled finish from the same shriveled green mask.

I drilled my fingertips into my ears to cut the noise.

Richard appeared in the doorway wielding a fireplace poker overhead. When he saw me, he let out a prolonged shriek.

Okay, now I'm certain he's gay.

Then his gaze flickered to the empty bottle of Montrachet.

He challenged us in an upwardly corkscrewing voice. "Is that my bottle of Montrachet? You drank my wine? That's a twenty-five-thousand-dollar investment from Domaine de la Rominee-Conti. Are you fucking insane?"

For a moment, it seemed he'd formulated a plan to beat me into a chocolate stain. But as he charged the room, a hand ten shades darker than mine plucked the poker from his grasp.

I hadn't yet met Perry, or his wife Jessie. But I recognized the gardener easily, standing in the doorway with his mud-crusted shovel raised like a bayonet, and a tire tool in his grip. Then Jessie rushed in dusting flour off her hands with a tea towel. She took one look at the spectacle unfolding, and—hand to mouth—let out a gasp.

Richard suddenly realized he'd been relieved of his weapon. He picked up one of Addie's shoes and brandished it. So much for this confrontation by the fashion Mafia. I expected to have to duck a stiletto being thrown at my head.

Addie tossed back the covers, slung her legs over the bedside, and reached for the silk kimono draped over the chair. She wrapped herself in it and cinched the tie at her waist.

"Silence," she screeched in her high-pitched, old-lady voice.

An eerie quiet descended over the room so quickly that the residue of their screams seemed to continue to reverberate through the air ten seconds after they had actually stopped.

Jessie spoke first. "Should I set another place at the table?"

Priscilla, fully recovered, now eyed me through slitted lids. "Isn't that the little monster who robbed you?"

Richard cowered near the wardrobe, still wielding the shoe. "I'm calling the cops. He probably has a gun." He bolted for the door.

Addie made a grab at the air nowhere near enough to stop him. "You mustn't do that."

He bounced off Perry, who stepped aside to let him pass. I jumped out of bed and dashed to the wardrobe. It took under a minute to snatch a fresh polo shirt off the hanger, and then step into a pair of clean shorts. Forget the shoes. If I had to flee, I only needed my mobile phone.

Priscilla seethed with anger. She directed her comments to Addie. "I'm pushing your appointment with Dr. Bomar forward."

"Don't do that either."

Priscilla pivoted on one heel and spun off out of sight.

Jessie eyed me with disapproval. "Just lettin' you know, Miz Addie, breakfast is ready. Will yo' boyfriend be staying?" She backed out of the doorway and padded off down the hall.

Perry, already sweaty with his threadbare plaid shirt plastered to his chest, and grime adhering to calloused hands, grinned through a mouth filled with jack-o-lantern teeth.

"What?" Addie demanded. "You have something to say?"

Perry clucked out the *he-he-he* of an old man. "I ain't one to gossip, but don'tchoo think he's a might young for you?"

Addie jammed a finger into the air. "Out."

He backed away like a shadow, and pulled the door to behind him.

My daughter turned to face me. "We have to leave."

"That goes without saying. Then what?"

"I don't know." Addie tossed me a pair of shoes. "But in a few minutes this place will be crawling with police, and you'll go back to juvenile hall; and I'll either be chased down with a butterfly net and dropped off at the asylum, or shot with tranquilizer darts and left to vegetate in the old folks' home." Addie dressed as she said this, moving at lightning speed, even for a spry old lady. "The problem is where to go and how long to stay there."

I talked fast as I tied the laces on my trainers. "I've thought this through." I had Broderick on speed dial, and told him to bring the car around. "I'll tell you the rest on the way."

I threw open the window and poked my head out. There was a bit of an unpleasant drop, and I didn't like the looks of those untrimmed hedges, but I didn't have much choice. I climbed over the sill and plummeted to the ground, and got the unique opportunity to taste a live spider when I crashed through its web. Addie started to close the window but I urged her to follow.

"I'll catch you."

Priscilla's harpy shrill carried the length of the hall. "She's barricaded herself inside, officers."

"Come on. I'll help you."

"I have brittle bones," Addie protested.

"Yes? And I'm going to jail. Who's got the better end of the deal?"

She shoved the window up as far as it would go, then slung out a leg plumped with cellulite and varicose veins. She wrenched the other leg through and sat, frozen, on the sill.

I waved her on.

She squeezed her eyes closed and flung herself out. I broke the fall. As we tumbled to the ground, a flock of birds scattered skyward from a nearby tree.

"Let's go," I rasped, helping her to her feet.

The front of Hollingsworth Manor opened onto Hillcrest Street, but the rear drive opened onto a side road. I strode purposefully down the pavement muttering curses as I walked, dragging in air with such body and heat that it felt weighty and unbreathable. As more black-and-whites squealed up to the curb in front of the house, I power walked to the Mercedes with Addie close behind, pumping myself up for the next item of business.

Tires smoking, Broderick drove us off of the estate in the Mercedes.

With a determined expression on her pale parchment face, Addie twisted in her seat enough to look out the rear windscreen. "I don't even want to think about how to handle this."

"Doesn't matter." I tied the shoelaces to my track shoes in

case black-and-whites appeared behind us and I had to bail out and run. "We have three hours to figure it out."

I realized we both still had green crackle paste on our faces but we were out of the house and that's what mattered. The only thing bothering me at the moment was that our long-suffering chauffeur seemed to be studying us like reruns of Steve Irwin in the *Crocodile Hunter.*

"Three hours?" Broderick's eyes flickered to the rearview mirror.

"Right," I said. "I was thinking this might be a good time to drive us to the Allred Unit so I can have a chat with my pop."

Then I settled back into buttery soft leather, and recounted the unsettling calamity of Richard and the underpants.

# CHAPTER THIRTY

We arrived at the Allred Unit shortly before eleven that morning. The prison holding Leon Darnell Gooch had been built with dust-colored bricks, concertina fences, and towers with guards dressed in Confederate-gray uniforms who had orders to shoot on sight anyone trying to scale the wicked coils of razor-wire strung across the tops.

Broderick wheeled the big black luxury sedan even with the entrance. A uniformed prison guard with a clipboard in hand and his bottom lip distended from a pinch of smokeless tobacco, stepped from the kiosk. Two additional guards appeared out of nowhere. They fanned out like dueling chefs with huge spatulas, and visually swept the undercarriage of the Mercedes by using long poles with mirrors connected to the ends.

Broderick announced our presence in a tone of importance. "Mrs. Adelaide Hollingsworth and Mr. Sylvester Gooch. Here to see an inmate. I am Broderick Finster."

*Finster?*

Addie and I exchanged glances.

The guard demanded to see our driver's licenses. Addie passed hers across the seat. He scraped it with his thumbnail, flipped it over and scrutinized it.

Broderick fished for his wallet, dug out his permit, and said, "We have an eleven-thirty appointment with the warden."

The man's eyes drifted over the clipboard. Midway down the page, he penned a small checkmark. "Pop the trunk."

Broderick pressed a button and the lid sprang open.

The guard bent at the waist, inclining his head enough to peer into the back seat. "Got any firearms, explosives, knives, contraband or anything else that could present a danger?"

Addie fished in her bag. "Hairspray."

The guard chuckled. "Give it here."

"Don't laugh. That hairspray can withstand a Category Four hurricane. And Tums. For indigestion."

He made a little hand motion, *gimme, gimme,* and she passed the handbag over the seat for Broderick to hand over to be searched. It seemed to appease the guard, picking at the leather, checking for false bottoms that didn't exist, and holding the analgesic up to the light.

The guard returned to the driver's window. "You wearing boots?"

A nod.

"Take them off."

Broderick opened the car door, swung out his legs and removed his boots. The guard turned them over and shook them out, then returned each one without fanfare. He moved around to my side of the car and pecked on the glass with his pen. "Step out."

Addie did a ventriloquist impression with her teeth clamped shut. "Bloody hell."

The man looked me over with a modicum of skepticism. "How old are you, son?"

I pretended to be deaf. In our haste to visit, we neglected to find out the minimum age for visitors and I didn't want to lie. At this stage of the game, telling lies would be like springing the trap door to Hell. Obviously, I had no driver's permit. I molded my hands into a few misshapen contortions that might pass for sign language, and hoped for the best.

Addie saw this and caught on. To add further credibility to

my plight, she made a few hand gestures of her own, did a couple of head bobs that further shored up the idea that we were engaging in legitimate conversation, and then said, "Can he get back into the car now?"

At best guess, they must've thought we were too pesky to deal with. At worst, they pegged us for idiots.

The guard gave Addie and Broderick a thorough going-over with a wand-shaped metal detector, and ordered them back into the Mercedes. He handed Broderick a preprinted permit and waved us on through.

"You'll have to clear a series of metal detectors inside. The watch captain will show you where to go. And here's a list of stuff not to do if you want to get invited back."

Leon Darnell Gooch padded into the family room wearing prison whites, socks and flip-flops. Chains linked his ankles together. In my opinion, he bore only the faintest resemblance to Sly. *To me.* For one thing he appeared much bulkier in his upper body. Long hours at hard labor must do that. Still, he entered the room sporting a huge grin.

"Am I glad to see you. Been a long time since I had visitors." Gooch's eyes welled.

I made introductions.

Gooch stared at the ceiling. Bits of gray in his dark hair caught the light, shining like a thousand filaments under the fluorescent glow. "Thank you, Lord Jesus." Shifty eyes settled on Addie. "Thanks for bringing my boy. Did you get heckled coming in?"

Addie shook her head.

"The screws are bad here." He thumbed at a corrections officer but looked directly at me. "So how come you showed up? Last time I saw you, you said you never wanted to see me again."

I stared, slack-jawed.

What was I supposed to do with this information? Why was Sylvester angry with his daddy? For that matter, what'd his daddy done to get here in the first place?

I decided not to answer.

"How's school?"

"I play basketball."

"You any good?"

I gave a one-shoulder shrug. "Depends who you ask."

Silence stretched between us. Leon Darnell Gooch leaned back in his chair, folded his massive arms across his chest, and stared as if he'd been asked to formulate an algorithm.

I blinked first.

"Why'd you come?"

"I need a favor."

He shook his head. "What could you possibly want from the likes of me? Got no life. No job, no self-respect. No chance of gettin' out of here." He eyed me with cold scrutiny. "Got no money." He unfolded his arms and held out his hands, palms-up. "Can't get blood out of a turnip."

But that was just it. I planned to convince him I could.

I pulled out the newspaper and unfolded it. Placed it on the table between us, and turned it around where he could read it. I pointed to the photo of a bald child with sunken eyes and a rapturous look on his face.

"I want blood," I said. "I want you to give your blood for this boy."

"Why would I do that, let somebody stick a needle in me? Boy, I'm tryin' to keep from getting the needle." He laughed without humor, apparently pleased at the reference to death row cases, and lethal injection.

"It's the right thing to do. You can help because you've got the right kind of blood. He needs AB-negative."

"You got AB. Give him yours."

I shook my head. "I got AB-positive. *You* got AB-negative. You're the only one I know who can do it."

Leon Darnell Gooch peered through crafty eyes. "I don't know him. He never did nothin' for Leon Darnell Gooch. And none of his kin did, neither. So why should I help?"

"Because of Fiona Slack-Applegate. You're doing it for her."

"Who that?"

"Somebody who meant a lot to me."

He stared uncomprehendingly. "Why I want to help her?"

"Because it would mean everything to me."

He did a quick lean-in, bracing his forearms on the government-issue table and clasping his thick hands in front of him. From my place opposite him, I locked gazes with the scariest man I'd ever met.

"Okay."

My eyes bulged. "Okay?"

He did a little head bob. "Okay."

But I wasn't sure one man's blood would be enough help. "There's more to it," I said.

"Whatchoo mean?" His eyes narrowed.

Leon Darnell Gooch had an opportunity to do something extraordinary. To change many lives for no good reason. To make up for some of the bad things he'd done, and pay back the community at the same time. All of the inmates did. I told him this and was surprised when he listened.

"I want you to start a blood drive with the other prisoners to help replenish the blood bank so that parents of children like this little boy don't have to worry about whether their child will live or die. So they don't have to be at the mercy of chance except to have a fighting chance. I want you to convince the other prisoners to give blood to the blood bank so that others will live. And I want you to do this for Fiona Slack-Applegate. In her name."

For a long time, he said nothing.

"She yo' girlfriend?"

"Doesn't matter who she is. Just do it."

"Okay." He had such a thick neck that it looked like it could support the bronze head of a life-size blackamoor, and when he bobbed his head, his shoulders moved. "And how do I go about doin' this?"

"That's your problem." I thumbed at Addie. "Mrs. Hollingsworth probably has enough influence to get the people from the blood bank to set up shop here, but you need to be the one to organize it. And time is of the essence. It has to happen in the next few days. No more than a week. Two, tops. There's a lot riding on this."

"Okay," he answered, entranced, "I'll do it. And now I'm askin' a favor of you."

"What?"

"Forgive me for what I done."

Now that was a dicey request. "What'd you do?"

"What'd I do?" He threw back his head, and roared with laughter. "Lordy," he called up to the ceiling. "This boy wants to know what'd I do?"

When he straightened his posture, his eyes were rimmed red. He might've been laughing, but this wasn't a funny *ha-ha* kind of laugh.

Leon Darnell Gooch raised his voice. "You're the reason I'm in here."

Addie clutched my wrist. Her fingers tightened around me painfully. I became aware that I'd been holding my breath.

The inmate's voice pitched to incredulity. "Myrna never told you? You're the reason I'm in here, Sly, on account of I tried to kill you when you was just a boy. You don't remember?"

"I forgive you whether you do the blood drive or not." I tapped the photo to redirect his attention. "Just help this child and don't delay."

"You're a good boy, Sly."

Tears jeweled his eyes. They teetered on the rims of his lids, moving from side to side like tiny quartz beads, then spilled over his fleshy cheeks and made two vertical tracks down his face. His shoulders unexpectedly shook.

He buried his face in his hands and wept.

I glanced over at Addie and saw her horrified expression. I did a little head jerk *Tally-ho!* and we rose from the bench and moved toward the cell door as a single unit.

We rode back to Fort Worth in virtual silence with each of us marinating in our thoughts.

If Sly's father came through for us, we'd be one step closer to redeeming the Get Out of Hell Free card. If not, we'd wasted two days working on a cocked-up plan.

I leaned back against the seat, and slumped against the door like a charred curly fry.

No wonder Sly was a mess. His own father had tried to kill him.

Lulled by the drone of tires against the asphalt, my eyes closed under a combination of sheer exhaustion and the sun's glare. Before I realized it, I'd drifted off to sleep.

# CHAPTER THIRTY-ONE

A few blocks from Hollingsworth Manor, Broderick pulled off the road. He shifted the Mercedes into park, and the sudden stop brought me fully awake. He twisted in his seat and looked over his cargo. Addie had fallen into a deep sleep. I reached over and shook her awake.

She came out of her slumber confused and blinking. "What?" She stared, wide-eyed, doing a quick look around to orient herself to time and place.

"We're almost home."

"That's the stuff."

"Any ideas on what we should do?" I asked.

Without invitation, Broderick—who'd heard the condensed version of what happened at the prison that morning—spoke up. "You don't know what happened while we were gone. If you go home, Miss Addie, they may take you away." His ball-bearing gaze shifted to me. "And if they catch you inside, they may call the police." Abruptly, he rethought the dilemma. "Or just kill you. It's hard to say what they're capable of."

Clearly, this frustrated Addie. "Tell us something we don't know."

"Well, Sly could stay with me tonight. Nobody'd be looking for him in the carriage house. But you've still got a problem, especially if they spent today making arrangements to have you . . . put away."

In the end, we decided to take in a film until the sun went

down and the sky turned dark. That way, I could slip upstairs to Broderick's flat, unnoticed.

By the time we arrived home, Priscilla's car was nowhere in sight, and neither was Richard's.

I made the decision then and there to stay with Addie no matter what.

The house was alarmed when we went inside, and I stabbed in the code with my finger to silence it. But before we could settle in—before Addie reset the alarm—I suggested we take the unguided tour upstairs.

The first room we entered had the most breathtakingly beautiful French furniture from the mid-nineteenth century that I'd ever seen. Many of the pieces were Napoleon in style but some were actual Boulle period pieces, inlaid with tortoiseshell. Modern reproductions couldn't compare with such craftsmanship. The wall sconces were obviously Doré, and the chandelier, Baccarat.

These people had way too much money—Addie's money.

This particular bedroom dwarfed the rest of the bedrooms in the house. So why wasn't this Addie's room? Perhaps because she had problems getting up and down the stairs? I moved to the wardrobe, opened the door, and switched on the light. Sure enough, clothes that could only have belonged to Addie hung on one side of the walk-in. What must've been her late husband's clothing hung on rods opposite hers.

"Would you look at this?" I pulled out the skirt of a fab green silk dress enough for my daughter to see. "And these shoes. There must be hundreds of boxes in here. And look—" I chuckled "—this must've been their bedroom and poor Buzz Hollingsworth had what? Five pairs of shoes? Amazing."

Elizabeth pushed past me. She touched the fabric of several suits. "Yummy." She stopped rummaging and stared. "Oi. What's this?" A crease formed between her brows and she stared at the shoe boxes.

I moved enough to peer over her shoulder.

"See how these stick out from the others? And yet the boxes are the same size as the ones on these other rows." She dropped to her knees and pulled at least ten shoeboxes to the middle of the floor. Sure enough, someone had hidden a metal lockbox about the size of a laptop computer. She pulled it out and blew off a thin film of dust. "What do you suppose Addie keeps in here?"

The contents rattled when she shook it.

"Bring it along." I switched off the light.

We moved silently across the Persian rug and out into the corridor.

The next bedroom had a completely matched bedroom suite from the Federal period that must've cost enough to balance the budget of a third-world country—lean lines, rich mahogany with the original finish aged to a gorgeous patina. I particularly adored the campaign chest and the butler's desk. There was even a four-poster rope bed with fringed silk throws that looked so inviting I threw myself across it. An ominous snap sent me scrambling, though, and I bounced back off and smoothed the Waterford linens enough to get rid of the evidence.

Carved cinnabar lamps and vases impressed me with their intricacies. I've always liked the color red, and these Oriental accent pieces—including the hand-knotted Hamadan rug in shades of red and blue—made the room look like it had jumped from a page out of *Architectural Digest*. I fanned the air in front of my face, taking in the scent of two hundred years' worth of museum-quality antiques.

Again, way too much money.

There was a sewing room, too—as if these people ever sat around making their own clothes. But it occurred to me that Addie probably had learned such skills as a young girl during the Depression, or she perhaps used this room as a sanctuary to retreat from her obnoxious daughter and son-in-law. It would've made a proper library if they didn't already have one downstairs.

We'd almost finished snooping when Addie dashed into the upstairs loo. Before I could continue my reconnaissance, a flash of headlights momentarily brightened the curtains.

"They're back," I shouted, and doused the lights. What I'd learned about the alarm system in the short time I'd been here was that it took a full minute to reset it. That and the fact that the motion detectors were highly sensitive.

With no chance of us making it down to her room before these insufferable people let themselves inside, I reset the alarm from the hall panel outside the bedroom and counted to myself as I ran to the loo to urge her along.

"Pull the chain, Lillibet," I shouted. "Flush, flush."

I peeked out the window, but the car had already passed beneath the porte cochere and disappeared from view.

I heard the whoosh of the toilet. My daughter turned on the tap.

I barged in, turned off the handle to the hot water tap and put my finger to my lips in a shushing motion.

Her look of irritation vanished, replaced by an understanding that we were now trapped on the upper floor.

Then her whispered protests began.

"I don't have what I need in order to be comfortably trapped up here. I warned you this was a bad idea, but no, you wanted to snoop."

"Lower your voice." The alarm's warning tone activated and quickly fell silent. I tried to be practical. "Do you have your wireless phone?"

With a pout of defensiveness, she nodded.

"Then you have everything you need."

"I'm hungry."

"You're not," I whispered, as if my saying so with enough ferocity would make it so. "Now set your phone to vibrate."

"I could really use a burger."

My head rotated in her direction like a scene pulled from *The Exorcist*. "You do realize we need to be ten percent smarter than the people we're living with."

"What's that supposed to mean?"

I stared at her, gobsmacked. "You really want to stink up the kitchen?"

We waited in the darkened room in silence, with nothing but the sounds of our breathing and the rush of cool air whooshing through the A/C vents.

A half hour went by. I poked my head out past the doorjamb and looked the length of the hallway. The indicator on the alarm's keypad glowed green, not red.

I relayed information to Addie that the security system hadn't been reset.

She mounted a strenuous argument in favor of sneaking downstairs, which I instantly discouraged. We had no idea which of these two idiots—the bipolar or the sociopath—had arrived home.

A masculine voice traveled up to our floor.

"It's Richard," I mouthed without sound. He was either talking on the telephone, or he'd brought someone home with him.

My daughter did a heavy eye roll.

It didn't take long to realize he had a male houseguest. We tried to listen in on their conversation but the voices faded in and out. Then the back door slammed shut with such abruptness I felt certain we were alone again.

We each sucked in a relieved breath, hurried to the window, and peered out through the slit where the curtains met. Richard and his mate had stripped down to their Y-fronts, and were heading to the south side of the grounds. Once the trees obscured them from view, the two of us ran to the south bedroom and headed for the window.

The featured attraction presented itself in the form of a spa tub.

I made an executive decision. "If we're going downstairs, let's do it now."

We suspected Richard had already checked Addie's room, and, finding us gone, had concluded we were still on the lam.

Once downstairs, Elizabeth changed into a dressing gown while I hid Addie's lock box in the closet.

I decided to keep my clothes on in case I had to run for my life.

I had the overwhelming desire to watch the BBC but there'd be no telly tonight. The Beeb would have to wait until we were absolutely certain the occupants of Hollingsworth Manor were in a drunken torpor or sleeping off a bender.

The back door clicked open, and snapped shut again.

Without explanation, I grabbed Elizabeth's wrist and tugged her toward the wardrobe. "In case he makes a final bed check," I said.

Sure enough, the door to Richard and Priscilla's bedroom opened and closed. My pulse thudded in my throat; my pounding heart echoed in my ears. The knob twisted and the door to Addie's room opened. The light flashed on. Elizabeth tightened her grip on my hand. Richard took his sweet time checking for signs of life in Addie's room. He moved slower than my incontinent great-uncle Basil on a shuffle to the loo. Then the light switched off, the room went pitch black, and the door closed with an authoritative smack. We should've at least been able to see shadows.

We hadn't realized we'd been holding our breaths until we simultaneously breathed sighs of relief. My eyes gradually made out shapes.

A blast of music filled the lounge. Distortion from screaming electric guitar strings gave way to ominous Druidic tones from a bass guitar. This noise pierced the walls so completely that I wanted to drive a spike through my head, but the racket gave us a chance to talk aloud without fear of discovery.

"I'm sick and tired of sneaking around," I said. "I'd feel better if we could check into a hotel. It's not like we don't have the money, yes? I mean there's plenty in Addie's current account so why don't we put an end to this madness and toddle off to a luxury suite?"

"Because we're not letting the tool and the twit take Addie's home from her," Elizabeth said with conviction, "or fleece her of her money."

In time, the dark and deafening rumble from the magnum opus ended. Silence cleared the air of any residual hang time, instantly evaporating the throbbing cadence that had built up in my head.

We didn't hear any conversational chitchat, so it seemed Richard's guest had left. While we gave Richard enough time to settle in and fall asleep, the TV came on in his bedroom and we were forced to endure the soundtrack of a porn film oozing through the walls. I poked my head out into the hall. The luminescent indicator bar on the alarm system keypad should've glowed as green as toxic waste but it didn't. The diode glowed red, cementing my suspicion that Richard wanted to be alerted if anyone entered the residence.

"Sex pervert," I muttered under my breath.

We climbed into bed.

"Want to change places?" I asked.

"Brilliant idea. From now on," Elizabeth said nastily, "I'll pee on the bathroom floor and scratch my bollocks and you can wear support hose and take Addie's blood pressure medicine."

My daughter can be quite the riot.

I took the side of the bed closest to the window for easy getaway, and checked the digital clock on the nightstand before drifting off to sleep. On some unconscious level, animal grunts and slapping noises sheared my deep slumber. In an effort to continue my Technicolor fantasies, I tried to incorporate the noise into my dream of winning the Mrs. Universe pageant while simultaneously being awarded the Nobel Peace Prize for humanitarianism. As the reigning Mrs. Universe crowned me with a tiara, and presented me with a matching scepter worth more than the Crown jewels, I unexpectedly found myself in jodhpurs and competition jacket with knee-high riding boots, astride Elizabeth's childhood pony, El Greco.

Only I'd never heard El Greco shout, "Stick it deeper—oh yeah, baby, give it to me harder. Drive me to Dallas."

That, alone, jarred me into sitting bolt upright, and fully awake.

It took a few seconds to register what was happening. Richard's sexual enthusiasm had seeped into the bedroom like a noxious gas.

The clock's digital display read two o'clock in the morning.

I looked over at my daughter lying saucer-eyed on the pillow. As the walls pounded, Elizabeth fisted sleep from her eyes.

She yawned into her palm. "Priscilla's home. Do these idiots ever stop?"

But I wasn't so sure; then comprehension dawned. The warning tone for the security system hadn't gone off.

"That's not Priscilla in there with Richard," I said.

Her eyes took on a speculative gleam. Moving closer and lowering her voice, she took my arm confidentially. "You don't think . . . ?"

"Oh but I do."

Neither of us said anything for several seconds while I developed a contingency plan.

An idea flashed into mind. This idea would either be very, very good, or so bad it was horrible. Either way, I was sick of hiding so I ran it by Elizabeth.

"One way or another, this has to stop. We'll never get a peaceful night's sleep."

"What are you talking about?"

"I'm chucking it in." I threw back the covers, slipped on my trainers and tied the shoelaces, then opened the window to make a quick getaway.

How was I to know raising a window would trigger the burglar alarm?

Ignorance is humorous.

## CHAPTER THIRTY-TWO

I'd positioned myself halfway through the window frame when Richard's scream penetrated the walls to Addie's bedroom.

He yelled, "Hide."

To our horror, Addie's door banged open and a man darted into the room stark bollocks naked. He turned around as Addie flipped on the bedside lamp.

Her mouth gaped. Forget about her keeping her eyes firmly averted—instead, they took a tour of his body.

My jaw dropped. I tried not to look but my eyes strayed on their own volition, seeing firsthand, what could only be described as one of nature's cruel creations with his perfect bone structure and lean muscular body. I'd never seen talent like that before and probably wouldn't again in this lifetime. Closing my eyes against the vision rising before me, he popped back up behind my eyelids like a reverse image of processed film.

Forget modesty. With heat in my cheeks and a smile so forced I thought my jaw would go numb, I gazed upon his naked form, feeling an enormous temperature spike as I watched his . . . shall we say . . . *confidence* wilt.

Addie's eyes telescoped back into their sockets.

The bleating security system went suddenly silent. We exchanged eyebrow-encrypted messages—*Flaming Nora*.

"False alarm," Richard called out. "The coast's clear. Back door's still locked. Probably atmospheric conditions . . ." Brimming with playfulness, he minced into Addie's room wearing a shoulder-length brown wig and full makeup, with his genitals uncovered beneath a garter belt that held up lace-top thigh-high stockings. "Now get back here and give me some more—"

He hauled up short at the sight of us gawking at the pan handle on his naked houseguest. The color drained out of his face. Raunchy talk dried up. We'd certainly foiled his plans—there'd be no more playing a solo on the pink oboe tonight.

"I can explain." He shooed the knob jockey out of the room.

Addie gave him an uninvitingly blank look. She cocked an eyebrow and stared at him with a certain degree of censure.

I resorted to code I didn't think he could crack. "Bent as a nine bob note."

Addie looked him dead in the eye. I saw in my daughter the gaze of a gunslinger, like the ones in old westerns on the eve of a duel. "We need to chat."

"It's not what you think," Richard said, his voice quivery and falling. "I wanted to try on her things. We were just playing around. It's not what you think."

Addie's eyes gleamed stubbornly.

He couldn't get any traction with her.

"It's *exactly* what we think," she said, holding up a hand before he could argue.

He gave an almost imperceptible nod. Then he dropped to his knees, clasped his hands in prayer, and spoke in the truncated speech of a sexually ambiguous cross-dresser slipping into shock.

"It was . . . just one time. Only once. Please . . . don't tell Priscilla."

Addie cocked an eyebrow. "Oh please," she declared in the face of his confession. She folded her arms across saggy breasts. Now they'd reached a standoff.

I pulled my leg back over the window sill and melted into the nearest chair in case I had to dive out again to avoid a sound thrashing. I watched with great interest as the drama played out before me.

Richard tried a new angle. "I was drunk." His shoulders wracked with sobs. "Addie, I'm begging you."

She said nothing. The fact that my daughter hadn't pulled the trigger on her temper surprised me. She'd grown fond of Addie, and a wee bit protective of her, and didn't like seeing her disrespected, especially by a lout such as Richard. He reached out to grasp her hand but caught only air as she took a backward step.

Rheumy eyes registered desperation. "I swear I'll do anything. Just please don't tell Priscilla."

Addie cupped a hand to her ear as if she'd misheard. "I'm sorry—did you say *anything*?"

The back door slammed. I went to the window and watched Richard's half-dressed guest sprint to a car. Funny, I hadn't even noticed him slip out of the room. He fired up the engine and the headlights brightened. The tag light illuminated the license plate enough for me to memorized the number. Then I reached for Addie's book and jotted the tag number down with a pencil I retrieved from her bedside table.

Evidence.

Just in case.

"Please, Addie, I'm begging you. Give me another chance. I'll never do it again, I swear."

Richard was still blubbering, bartering for Addie's silence, as I tuned in and out of the conversation. Then a serene smile settled over her face. She shrugged out of her silk kimono and tossed it at him.

"Get up, Richard. Let's go into the lounge and have a round of drinks, yes?"

He babbled something unintelligible, but rose and shrouded

himself in her dressing gown while I took a picture of him, in drag, with my cell phone camera. Call it ammunition.

We followed him into the lounge with Addie directly behind him and me bringing up the rear. Richard's hand shook so badly that he spilled more than he poured.

Addie said, "Step aside," and took over.

As he walked toward the sofa where Addie motioned him to sit, I wondered how this could possibly turn out in our favor.

For what seemed like the longest time, my daughter said nothing. Once, when Richard opened his mouth to speak, she silenced him with a glare. When he tried it again, he reminded me of a goldfish with its mouth opening and closing.

Finally, Addie put him out of his misery. "Here's how it's going to work, yes?" She jabbed a finger into the air. "One—I'm not going to a nursing home."

"No, never." He seconded the notion with a vigorous head bob, "I didn't want to send you there, it was all Priscilla's idea—"

"Rubbish."

The words he'd been so anxious to say seemed to slide back down his throat.

"Two—" up went the second finger "—this is the young man who made a mistake, yes?" She cut her eyes to me before shifting her gaze back to Richard. "I'm giving him a second chance. As you said, everybody deserves a second chance, yes?"

"Yes. Yes, a second chance," he parroted.

I stayed perfectly still, seeing where this was heading and wondering what the outcome would be.

"Three—" up went the third finger "—I have this young man doing odd jobs for me. A bit like restitution. To pay for the trouble caused by a youthful indiscretion. He has nowhere to go because of what's happened, so I invited him to stay here so I can keep an eye on him. You'd agree with me, that's the right thing to do, yes?"

Huge head bob.

Great big bobbleheaded head bob.

"In exchange for our silence—"

"Yes, yes," Richard cried, sloshing his drink as he set it down. He fell forward and wept into his hands.

Addie raised her voice so as not to be misunderstood. "In exchange for our silence, you're not going to say anything about Sylvester being here, and . . . you're not putting me in a nursing home. Or an Alzheimer's ward."

He shook his head so hard that mucous spewed from his nose, and shoestring drool flew from his mouth. "No nursing home. No locked ward."

She turned to me. "Anything else you can think of?"

I motioned her over and whispered out of Richard's earshot. "For the next thirty days, he needs to get Priscilla out of this house. Think of a way to get her out of here so we don't have to mess with her, yes?"

Addie punctuated the idea with a nod. "You're going to take your wife on holiday. A cruise." I sensed Richard about to balk. "Perhaps a second honeymoon? Just get her out of here so we can have the house to ourselves, yes?" She looked him over with judgment in her stare.

"A cruise? Whatever you say. Thirty days?"

"That's the stuff. Thirty days sounds brilliant. Might I suggest Fairbanks, Alaska? Or maybe Montreal?"

But I was thinking Mexico.

Mexico is the dregs.

They don't call it *turista* for nothing. Tourists visiting Mexico pick up all kinds of parasites and diseases because they don't have antibodies to fight off the illnesses. You don't even have to drink the water to contract "Montezuma's revenge"—but then, why would you? Don't even brush your teeth with it. If you're willing to do that, you might as well start training for your trip by drinking out of the public loo.

I went there once. Mama took me during one of my visits, and it cured me from ever wanting to go back. I'd never seen turbo-charged mosquitoes the size of hummingbirds before. And I don't even want to go into what it took to kill the freakishly large and virtually indestructible *cucarachas*—cockroaches—Mama used pointy-toed spike-heels, and doused them with mescal from the bottle she bought at the duty-free shop.

There's no sight worth seeing down in Mexico—not pyramids, not Aztec and Mayan ruins, not resorts or beaches—that could lure me back to that crime-riddled cesspool.

The only culture I absorbed came from the bacteria I picked up from using the loos, and in local eateries. Even the nicest restaurants were viral and bacterial kingdoms. Nothing turns an otherwise sane person into a mad scientist like examining every bloody morsel of food with cold scrutiny before putting it into your mouth. Assuming, of course, that the poor waiter can ferry the plate to the table without looking like he's afflicted with tics and seizures, or doing the *Jarabe Tapatío*—the "Mexican Hat Dance". All that stomping the floor and spinning around like a whirling dervish isn't just for show. They do it to drive back the mosquitoes. The solution to vacationing in Mexico, of course, is to save your money, eat out of the skip behind the worst café in town and you, too, can have the same experience without ever leaving home.

Did I mention Mexico is the dregs?

If you're a woman, this isn't the venue in which to show off your décolleté. Cover your assets and arses, hunch your shoulders and walk with a lope, a limp or a lurch. Dragging a leg as you make your way across *el parque, el mercado* or *la plaza* will serve you well. Better still; rub grime across your jaw line so it looks like you're sporting a five o'clock shadow. What do you care if they think you're a tranny? It's not like you'd want anybody in that hellhole to know your identity. Try looking scary. Or ugly and poor so you don't get pinched, groped, sexually assaulted or kidnapped. Even drooling has its place. Far better to impersonate the village idiot than the town tart where survival is concerned.

Richard should squire Priscilla off to Mexico.

I'm going to lobby for that.

# CHAPTER THIRTY-THREE

The next morning, I dragged myself out of bed on a yawn. I could've used a zap from a cattle prod to get started, I was just that exhausted. Peering past the curtain to take in the sun-dappled morning, I saw that Richard had cleared out early for work; a week's worth of tension seemed to flow out of my body.

The first I knew of others roaming the house was when Jessie turned on the cooker, and the smell of bacon filled the air. Priscilla still hadn't returned, and the newsreader on one of the local channels was forecasting another scorcher with no sign of relief for the coming week. He mentioned a cycling race in Wichita Falls—the Hotter 'n Hell Hundred, and it made me think of Mama—and the prisoner, Leon Darnell Gooch. For this to be our tenth day, we hadn't accomplished one-third of what we'd come for.

I tidied the bed and decided to have a bath. I ran hot water from the tap, adding smelly salts and gel.

After a jolly good scrub, I stretched back in the bath with my neck cradled by an inflatable vinyl pillow, and soaked in the freesia-scented bubbles. My legs were too long to fit, so my feet stretched up past the taps. Since I didn't fancy staring at Sylvester's privates any longer than necessary, I gathered foam and built a pyramid to cover my nethers and obscure the tip of the purple-headed warrior.

"Can you check the cool box?" I projected my voice in Elizabeth's direction. "I could use cucumber slices to cover my eyes."

No response. If I knew my daughter, she'd gone foraging for a full English breakfast. I doubted she'd find it here at Hollingsworth Manor, but I wouldn't mind if she returned with a plate of rashers and a couple of eggs. Famished, I ran my tongue over my lips.

Lillibet returned without the veggie. But she did have the morning paper tucked under her arm as she ferried in a food tray with pancakes, stewed apple topping with a dollop of whipped cream on top, and a side dish of bangers—sausages. I toweled off and dressed in a hurry.

I swilled down the little glass of milk and started in on the pancakes, trying to make conversation between bites. I ate with the ravenous appetite of a wolf.

"Where's Priscilla?"

She said, "Looking for her sense of humor."

"Nice one." I toasted my daughter with the juice glass. "Seriously. Is Priscilla here?"

"There's a good chance she turned into a bat and flew off."

"Stop joking."

"Priscilla's a flight attendant with Air Tabasco."

Heavy eye roll on my part. I have a passing familiarity with their work. On holiday to Mexico my near-indestructible hard shell suitcases arrived so mangled that they had to be duct-taped back together. They looked like they'd been targeted for closer inspection, and subsequently blown up by the bomb squad.

A degree of petulance crept into her voice. "Jessie says Priscilla won't be back for a day or two. This is her week to fly out."

That meant we'd have the run of the house, but only if we could press Jessie into secrecy. I decided to leave that to Elizabeth since Addie had a relationship with these people and I didn't.

I dressed in khakis and a Kelly-green polo shirt that I now

wish had been a drab shade of olive. Bad enough that I stood out like the black sheep, hiding within the flock, but to actually call attention to myself, what was I thinking? I've always fancied bright colors, but it's a good thing I chose the brown alligator Ballys and not the aubergine Ferragamos. I slid my argyle-covered feet into the shoes and cast my eyes downward to admire them.

As I gave my mirrored reflection a last once-over, I discovered a blemish. I reached for the concealer when Lillibet walked in.

"What're you doing?" she said. "You can't use that, it's makeup."

"I have a blemish."

"You're a lad. Not a transvestite."

I released my grip on the bottle. She was right. It wasn't even the proper shade.

We talked about how to spend the day, where to go, and who to contact and convince to do an extraordinarily good deed on Mama's behalf. While Lillibet returned the food tray, I had a brain wave.

A church. We should contact a church. Maybe ask someone to sponsor a potluck and charge for it. The money could be donated to the Make-a-Wish Foundation in honor of Fiona Slack-Applegate. We could challenge parishioners of other churches to do the same, but the most logical starting point would be Addie's church, if she attended. And we'd give them a week to put it all together since time was of the essence.

I was scouring the paper for additional ideas when one of the mobiles came alive.

The "It Doesn't Matter Anymore" ring tone went into the second stanza before I could force myself to react.

Allen.

I flew across the bed, bouncing once in the center before

snatching it off the nightstand. Before it cycled into voice mail, I answered.

" 'Ello?"

He breathed into the phone a few seconds. "I thought it would go to voice mail. I didn't expect an answer. I've been doing this awhile since . . ." His voice cracked. "Since . . . she left. I don't know why. I think hearing her voice makes it not feel so real."

The silence stretched between us.

My words choked me but I managed to get them out. "I never stopped loving you."

"Nor I you."

"I want to see you, darling."

"Me, too, you. It's the only way I can be sure if this is real."

He'd said exactly what I needed to hear.

My eyes burned. Tears spilled over my cheeks. "I can meet you. Say where."

He mentioned a new bistro, and was reciting the address when Addie walked in. Her expression went from serenity to one of sheer panic.

"What're you doing?"

I lifted a finger to shush her, already missing the location, and needing to rummage through the drawer for pen and paper.

"I say, darling, would you be so kind as to repeat that?"

"Mummy, you can't." When I didn't react, Elizabeth shrilled, "You can't," and grabbed the mobile, severing my umbilical cord to Allen.

Fury overtook me. I jumped to my feet shrieking. "Why did you do that? Why? You don't care how miserable I am. You're so very selfish that you can't be happy that I've finally gotten him to believe me."

I made a mad grab for the mobile, but Elizabeth clutched it in a death grip.

"He doesn't believe you, Mum. Don't you see? It's a trap."

"It's not a trap. He would never do anything to hurt me."

"You're a boy. A lad on the lam, don't you see? He's only trying to lure you where he can arrest you and lock you up. Then where will we be?"

Hateful words, strung together by vicious thoughts, tumbled out of my mouth. Even I knew that my rationale made no sense, and that my daughter was right. But it was as if I'd suddenly become possessed and my thoughts, overtaken—as if the real Elle Winthrop were suddenly governed by a stark raving mad cow.

We were both in tears when the door swung open. A roly-poly Mexican woman carrying a mop bucket and cleaning products framed the entrance to our room.

Mobile in hand, Addie whipped around. "I say, state your business."

The woman remained mute.

"Who are you? And what do you want?"

"I the maid, Missy Hollingsworth. You no remember me?" She launched into a curious mixture of broken Spanish and English, neither of which I understood in my current state. "I here to . . . *limpiar* . . . what you tell me . . . clean the *baño* . . . the bathroom."

This gave Addie a start. "Oh. Well, jolly good. Get on with it," she said, and flicked her wrist in the direction of the loo. "I say, what's your name?"

"Ana Maria Josefina Amarosa Hernandez-Vigil."

We exchanged confused glances.

"What shall I call you?" Addie said.

"Maria."

At first, we thought Maria spoke acceptable English, but it turned out the only word she commanded with any certainty was "Okay". Only she pronounced it "Ho-kay", like she was trying to clear a phlegm ball from her throat. As in: How do you get to work? "Ho-kay"; Are you an illegal alien? "Ho-kay"; Which one of those two fools hired you? "Ho-kay"; Are you gay? "Ho-kay."

"Very well." Addie smoothed the front of her frock and patted the side of her hair where I'd ruffled it, grabbing for the mobile. "Tally-ho." When Maria drew a blank, Addie said, "Just get on with it, yes?" and stepped aside to let the domestic have a go at the loo.

The presence of a third party had a calming effect on me. I considered what Lillibet said and, in my mind, knew she was right about Allen.

But in my heart . . .

"Then we'll go to the church to visit about the potluck, yes?" I said, wiping my eyes with the backs of my hands. "Call Broderick for the car and we'll be on our way, yes?" She nodded, and I closed with, "And do give me back my mobile in case we get separated."

She reluctantly returned it. I stuck it in my pocket while she called for the car. As we waited by the front door with me hiding, once again, behind the Chinese Coromandel screen, she served as a lookout for Jessie as we went over our plans.

# CHAPTER THIRTY-FOUR

We struck out at the church Addie belonged to, so we went to ten others. None of them wanted to support our brilliant idea, either. But after grousing to Broderick, I had another brain wave.

Substance Abuse Counseling.

He'd let it slip that he was a member—I suppose because this was one of his meeting days and he needed Addie's permission to go while on the clock.

"I think it's a brilliant idea. We can just explain to them what we need and make it a challenge with the other substance abuse groups."

Broderick wasn't so enamored of the idea. "The thing about SAC is that it's anonymous. Members are comfortable going there because they don't have to tell anyone that's where they are. And what you say in meetings is confidential so you don't have to worry about others blabbing your problems. I was a boozer since I was thirteen. I've been a recovering alcoholic for two years, three months, fifteen days and—" he checked his watch "—four hours and fifty-three . . . no, fifty-four minutes. And I don't have to tell that to anyone I don't want to."

"Mazel tov." This, from Addie.

I stared. She can be so funny.

"I think you should go to Broderick's meeting with him. Advance this idea and see how it goes over." To Broderick, I said, "You'll help, won't you?"

He nodded. But I sensed that he thought we'd lost our minds.

When we arrived at the designated meeting place, I volunteered to wait in the car. "We don't want to scare them," I said good-naturedly, but I was really hoping for the chance to telephone Allen again and set up a rendezvous.

None the wiser, Addie and Broderick left me in the parked car, under a shade tree, with the windows down. Seeing the last glimpse of Addie, her dress swishing through the door, with Broderick on her heels, I rang Allen up.

Heart pounding, I listened to his recorded message as the mobile cycled to answerphone. I thumbed the mobile off and tried again after five minutes. When he answered, "Carswell," on the third ring, it put me off a smidge. Sounded like business, and I thought he would've had my number programmed in with Buddy Holly's "Rave On" ring tone like he did before, well, before my untimely departure.

"It's me." Long pause while I assembled my thoughts. "I'm not catching you at a bad time, am I?"

"I'm at work, but if you'll hang on a sec I can move where it's more private."

A visual of him putting a bit of distance between him and his colleagues flashed into mind.

"Are you in the office?"

"No. In the parking lot next to my car."

Long pause. I couldn't understand why I was handling this so clumsily. Why beat around the bush?

"Look, darling, I want to see you. That is, if you want to see me." On the one hand, I wanted him to move on. Unconditional love—blah, blah, blah—and all that. It's pure crap, you know? On the other hand, jealousy moved me to want him to grieve for me.

"Of course I do," he said through a pained breath that choked me up as soon as he spoke. "When?"

I looked at the door Addie and Broderick had disappeared through, and knew they'd be gone a good half hour. More, if the pitch for the potluck turned out to be successful. Scouring the area with my gaze, I spotted a popular coffee bar. "What about Java Joe's on Camp Bowie?"

"Be there in ten." As an afterthought, he said, "How will I know you?"

I suppressed a giggle. "Don't worry, darling, I'll find you."

A local jewelry store had a huge clock designed into a lamp-post outside their door, and I checked the time from the back seat of Addie's car. As I counted down, a police car passed. Less than a minute later, another rolled by. A dreadful thought occurred to me, and I wished I'd memorized the unit number printed on the back of the first black-and-white. Perhaps it'd been the same patrol car circling the block, I told myself re-assuringly.

But maybe it hadn't.

I found these black-and-whites intimidating. They reminded me of tarantulas ready to swoop down and sink their fangs into you. The Fort Worth police department was undergoing an automobile transition, replacing the older solid white vehicles with black-and-whites. Both cars still bore the rust-colored cow head decal on the doors and they both had WHERE THE WEST BEGINS and DEDICATED TO PROTECT in block letters on the sides of the patrol units. But to me, the white ones conveyed images of Officer Helpful saying, "Howdy, ma'am, is everything all right?" while the black-and-whites conjured up Gestapo visions.

An unmarked car passed by and I spotted it immediately. The driver pulled into the bank car park next to Java Joe's. A plainclothes detective jumped out and trotted into the bank. A moment later, he returned with a slip of paper, and I watched him count his money on the way back to his car.

The thing about dating a policeman is that you learn all kinds of useful information. Like where the best restaurants are. Or how to locate the speed traps before the motor jocks clock you on radar. Where to expect traffic cameras, and how to spot them. And how to recognize an unmarked patrol car with its tiny antenna and recessed emergency lights behind the grill below the bonnet.

Now that I'd agreed to meet Allen, second thoughts consumed me.

Had he betrayed me?

I shook off my doubts when the car pulled away from the bank, left down a side street, and disappeared from sight.

It took less than a minute to cross against the light and saunter through the parking lot. Allen's unmarked patrol car pulled up directly in front of Java Joe's. I loitered near a string of postal boxes where I could watch without being seen as he backed into a parking space.

Allen's quite punctual. He doesn't like it when people are late. He's always where he's supposed to be with plenty of time to spare, so I dared not be later than a minute.

Seduced by the location, I still remained cautious, waiting through another light change, surveying cars, and trying to identify ones that might have police in them. My gaze flickered to the front window, a huge glass pane with the name of the coffee bar stenciled on it, and a "cuppa Joe" painted below. Allen selected a table facing the door the way he always did— they do that in case of a robbery. Same way he backed into the space in front of Java Joe's. For easy getaway, yes?

I trotted to the corner of the bank, walked along the pavement beneath the awning, and stopped in front of the coffee bar. As I opened the door, a tiny bell jingled overhead.

Allen, wearing a ball cap with the Fort Worth Police emblem stitched on the front, apparently didn't see me because of the bill pulled low over his forehead. He seemed preoccupied with his half-empty coffee cup, and didn't bother glancing up. I did a quick look about.

Teenagers occupied a bistro table positioned against the wall opposite the room. A newspaper obscured the face of a lone man sitting at the back of the café, and an elderly couple paying at the cash register had yet to select their seats.

The tiny bell above the door jingled. Expecting the worst, I jerked my head, wincing as the door creaked behind me. But it was only the postal carrier bringing in the post stacked atop two parcels.

Allen glanced up from his cup. My knees turned to jam.

" 'Ello, love," I mouthed and waited for him to motion me over.

He pushed back from the table and stood. As I moved toward him, he said, "Can I get you anything?"

"I'd like a scone, please, and a spot of tea if they have it."

"I'll see what I can do." Blue eyes coolly narrowed. A look that fell somewhere between shock and anger brought a flush to his cheeks. He dragged a chair across the rough-hewn plank floor and motioned me into it.

When he returned with a biscuit and hot tea, I sat opposite and waited for him to speak. He looked me over without judgment in his face. Still, I moved uneasily under his intent regard.

"You took an awful chance." He picked up his cup and held it aloft. "Cheers."

"I had to come." I lifted my teacup and clinked it against the mug. "I want to explain. I know it sounds unbelievable but if you'll spare me a moment I can make you understand—"

"Of course," he said but his face said *No way.*

I wanted to tell him how I was able to come back, but my throat closed around the words.

In an instant, the air pressure had changed. At that precise moment, the reflection of a black-and-white flashed in the mirror behind the bar like a subliminal message sneaked in between film frames to make you want to buy popcorn at the movies. Only this one told me to run.

Allen took off his ball cap and placed it on the table.

That dried up the conversation.

A frisson of genuine fear overtook me.

For no good reason other than instinct, my attention shifted to an advancing blur out of the corner of my eye. Action moved in slow motion—everything except me, that is—then accelerated in real time.

I'd been deceived.

The couple I'd mistaken for teenagers jumped from the table and rushed us. The female yelled, "Don't move."

Those two words turned into the actual sound of my heart collapsing in on itself, and turning into a heart raisin.

My gaze flickered to the rear exit. I wanted to bolt in that direction but the lone customer lowered the newspaper, revealing the face of Detective Chip Stone. His shirt was ringed with sweat so I wondered where he'd dump my body.

Allen mimed a smile.

"Donkey!" I ejected from my seat, turning over the chair as he made a mad grab and swiped the air in front of me.

Detective Stone charged my way, closing off the rear exit. I yanked the front door at the same instant the door on the black-and-white opened up and a patrolman jumped out.

Amazing how fast my Thoroughbred legs could travel with my head in the wind and hot air brushing my cheeks. Should've worn my trainers, I thought, but it turns out leather-soled shoes work just fine when you're trying to avoid kiddy prison. The odor of jail and the smell of freedom is very distinct. And when compared, I preferred inhaling air noxious with the smell of dead gas from a nearby petrol station and the exhaust of moving traffic to and from juvenile hall.

I wasn't conscious of having circled the strip center but when I reached the rear of the bank, the back door to Java Joe's lay behind me.

The groan of a freight train carried in the distance.

A loud bang of metal against mortar filled the air. Without a backward glance, I heard the fire door to Java Joe's fly open and hit the brick wall. Stone, in all his bluster, had flung himself out the opening and into the chase behind me. Beet-faced and swearing, he called Sylvester's name. I could almost feel his foul breath blistering the back of my neck.

The sound of grating metal from the black-and-white hitting a dip in the road carried on the breeze like a demon's shriek. The squeal of accelerating tires, followed by a grinding roar, helped me flee in earnest.

The gate to a nearby apartment complex yawned open. I dashed through it with three angry men and a fleet-footed woman gaining on me. The patrol car screamed to a stop. I ran past the swimming pool and the launderette, past the office, and through an alcove between apartments. Turning left at the skips, I inhaled a lungful of putrid air from rotting garbage.

And past the Dumpsters, the red bricks of Camp Bowie Boulevard beckoned me onward.

So far, I've had a few concepts hammered home: One, Priscilla's a psycho; two, the Fort Worth police will trick you, and; three, betrayal by your lover hurts.


After the SAC meeting ran its course, Broderick introduced Addie Hollingsworth.

Elizabeth said, "I know this will sound unusual, but I need a very big favor. I wondered if the group would assist me with a potluck dinner at the pavilion at Trinity Park this coming Sunday?" She paused to let the murmurs die down, watching the members with interest as they turned to the person sitting on either side for their reaction.

"You see," she went on undaunted and wagging a signup sheet, "what I'm asking is for each of you to bring a dish, and to bring five friends and have each of them bring a dish. We're going to open it up to the public for a donation as long as the food lasts. The money we take in will go to the Make-A-Wish Foundation to be donated in the name of Fiona Slack-Applegate—"

A female in the group let out a shriek.

Everyone turned in a collective movement and stared.

A woman who looked to be in her early sixties rocketed from her seat. Elizabeth watched as her face drained of all color before flushing beet red. The angry shade of crimson contrasted sharply with her purple silk sundress and outright clashed with her champagne-colored hair.

"Over my dead body," she shouted, holding up a deadly finger with a Beverly Hills manicure. "My name is Sugie, and I had the horrible experience of knowing Fiona Slack-Applegate. She's as evil as the day is long, and I can assure you she's the sole reason I have to attend these meetings as a condition of my probation."

Deathly silence snared everyone in its grip.

"Fiona Slack-Applegate stole my husband from me."

Elizabeth's stomach went hollow. This was Sugie Rowenstein, the woman her grandmother's friend, Bitsy, had spoken of at the country club.

It didn't seem possible for Sugie's voice to get any louder or shriller, but it did.

"When I walked in on them in our marital bed, I went crazy. I got my gun to kill her, but she grabbed my poor, gullible Sheldon and used him as a shield. If you read the papers, you know how it ended. If you didn't, let's just say Fiona went on to destroy other people's lives, I was tried for murder, sentenced to ten years on probation, and court-ordered to AA meetings as a condition of my freedom. Thank God the jury bought the crime-of-passion defense."

Elizabeth's stomach clenched. She stood, gobsmacked, as the wide eyes of AA members thinned into slitty-eyed stares.

Sugie's voice came close to piercing eardrums.

"So I don't know how you have the audacity to attend this meeting, encouraging members to memorialize this fiendish lunatic—" she turned on the group "—but if anyone dares to participate in this little scheme, I'll consider it a traitorous act and deal with each of you accordingly . . ."

Everyone sat, stricken. The threat hung overhead like a guillotine.

". . . even if it means getting my probation revoked."

# CHAPTER THIRTY-FIVE

The "Everyday" ring tone chimed from my pocket. Addie and Broderick must've returned to the Mercedes to find me gone. I crossed against traffic with tires squealing all about and my leather-soled shoes pounding the brick road. Motorists showed me rude hand gestures, but I'd hit my stride. Alligator loafers hydroplaned on my own dripping sweat.

I dug for the phone and thumbed the on button.

"Lillibet, tell Broderick to drive around back of the building."

"Where are you?"

"No time to explain." Me, again, breathless.

"Bloody hell. You called Allen, didn't you? Have you gone soft in the head?"

"Please, Lil, I'm in a bit of a sticky wicket, yes? So if he can wheel the car around and open my window . . ." I shut my mobile down and hoped for the best.

I rounded the final corner. Allen and his motley lot were gaining on me, especially the girl, but the black-and-white got caught at the traffic signal. With the whoop of the siren, I suspected he'd gone through the light and would be pulling a midblock U-turn any second.

The Mercedes rolled past, slowing enough for me to dive through the window opening. Which answers the question, *Is she really dumb enough to jump into a moving vehicle?* The answer is yes. I fell across Addie, completely exhausted, and pulled my feet inside. Broderick hit the electric window button and the tinted glass hummed shut.

"Hurry. I have police behind me," I bleated from the floorboard like a tethered sheep.

Broderick made a sweeping U-turn and gunned the big V-8 engine. My neck immediately snapped back as he tried out his backup career as a Formula One racecar driver. The Mercedes roared out onto the motorway just as Addie warned of the black-and-white rounding the corner.

Broderick's knuckles whitened against the steering wheel. I sunk farther into the floorboards as Addie opened her handbag and nonchalantly began powdering her nose.

From my place on the carpet, I looked up expectantly. Addie's sign-up sheet remained unsigned.

"What happened?"

Like a television newsreader, Broderick gave me a blow-by-blow account as the traffic in front of us ground to a halt.

"We're stuck in line, waiting for the traffic light to turn green. Do not get up, Mr. Sly. The cops have gathered in the parking lot behind the building. They look flustered—wait, make that pissed. Two men, a woman and a pissed off patrolman who just pulled his gun and checked it for bullets," he said, throwing his voice from the side of his mouth like a ventriloquist.

This is the moment the needle on my day moved from simply horrible to completely sucking on the suck-o-meter.

"Thankfully, the light just turned green and the cars are inching forward. Stay down. We're almost through. They think we're part of the snafu. Apparently nobody saw our car drive off the lot."

My stomach twisted as the big Mercedes slumped forward and bumped onto the bricks. As we rolled to safety, I couldn't help but wonder why Allen had betrayed me.

I touched Addie's leg. "I know you're upset, but I've had a terrible morning. A real *National Lampoon*-level disaster."

"You've had a terrible morning," she yelled so loud that I drew back. "*You've* had a terrible morning? I feel like I've just had a heart attack, dipped in a stroke with a side order of cardiac arrest. While you were out fleeing the police, Broderick and I were nearly shot by a crazy woman."

"Is that why you didn't get any signatures?"

Her eyes bulged. The spit of fury spewed from her words. "Signatures? You're worried about a sign-up sheet for a potluck? We were lucky to leave without having our scalps grooved down the middle."

She recounted the tale, with Broderick periodically insinuating himself into the conversation when she neglected to mention interesting tidbits. By the time she finished, I considered it a draw as to which of our adversaries had taken the bigger piss on us.

I directed my next question to Broderick. "I say, old chap, shall I get up?"

"The coast is clear."

I hoisted myself up onto an elbow, wrenched myself from the floorboard, and grappled with the seat.

"Where to, now, Miss Addie?" Broderick asked as I unfolded my legs to get the circulation back and eased into my seat.

"Courthouse."

I stared in disbelief. "Pardon me, but is your head soft?"

Addie glared. "Spoken by someone who's only one dumbass away from getting on the six o'clock news."

"I can't believe I just ran from the cops and now you want to pay a visit to the courthouse."

She blinked.

"So we can run from more cops? Are you daft?"

"Oi. I didn't tell you to get yourself into a bleeding Barney Rubble—you did it to yourself. If you don't want to go inside, I'll get the documents myself."

"That you'll do, missy. I'm not moving anywhere but at gunpoint."

"That can be arranged," Addie said. She pulled herself up by the headrest until she was even with Broderick's ear. "I say, Broderick, do we own a gun?"

"I wouldn't know."

"Can we get one?" She flopped back in the seat, disappointed, and made eye contact with him through the rearview mirror.

"There's a three-day waiting period."

"You don't say?"

"It's so they can figure out whether you're crazy, or a felon wanted for crimes."

"Do you suppose Richard has a gun?"

Broderick said, "I sincerely hope not."

I wanted to know why we needed a gun, but Addie silenced me with a glare. As I pondered possibilities, Broderick pulled up in front of the courthouse and engaged the flashers on the Mercedes.

With a "Be right back," Addie alighted from the vehicle and walked spryly into the building.

She returned within fifteen minutes, long enough for us to be warned to move along by a traffic enforcement officer checking parking meters. Since the courthouse covered the entire block, Broderick and I orbited the building like Mars's moons, Phobos and Deimos. Believe me, the irony of that particular brain wave isn't lost on me: Phobos means "fear" and Deimos means "panic."

Broderick was the first to glimpse Addie. He rolled up to the curb, shifted into park, and jumped out over the watchful eye of the meter reader long enough to open her door and close her safely inside. We drove off without a hitch.

It occurred to me that I was hungry again, and I talked Addie into having Broderick stop for lunch. Since I knew she was still holding a grudge, I let her pick the place. It delighted me when she chose a pub that specialized in fish and chips. In the dimly lit room, as we waited for food, Addie pulled a copy of Walden Hollingsworth's will out of her handbag and read it to us. The document turned out to be a fifty-page megillah.

"I'm screwed," she said when she finished. "Unless . . ." I followed her eyes to the clock on the wall. "We should pay a visit to the solicitor's office."

When we returned to the car, Broderick climbed behind the wheel and started the engine. His eyes flickered to the rearview mirror. "Where to now, Addie?"

"The law office of Thompson and Winters." She found the address on the court documents and read it aloud.

We didn't have an appointment, so it took a bit of a wait to see Mr. Winters. His receptionist informed us he'd be in court until three. Since we didn't have anything better to do, we released Broderick for a few hours and waited in the foyer with Addie leafing through a fashion magazine and me taking stock of the room.

The law office waiting area had a calming effect with its curious mixture of Danish modern furnishings intermingled with rattan pieces. I'd assumed Buzz Hollingsworth's attorney would have an office decorated much like the room of mounted game heads back at Hollingsworth Manor, but this place couldn't have been more different. Colorful Puerto Rican art hung on walls that had been whitewashed in a chalky shade of pale lime green—a pleasant backdrop in which to showcase festively-painted accent pieces of wooden animal folk art. White plantation shutters, sized to cover the windows, had the slats shifted open to reveal a bright golden sun slanting past leafy banana trees growing outside near the windows.

When I sat on an upholstered sofa, dust shimmered up from the cushion. It danced in the sunlight a few moments before settling onto the yellow blooms of a potted plant.

Around three-thirty that afternoon, Buford Winters walked in loaded down with court files. He deposited them on the receptionist's desk, shrugged out of his navy blue blazer and hooked it over a peg on the hall tree, then met us in the foyer with an outstretched hand.

"Why, Mrs. Hollingsworth, this is a treat. But I thought you were Mr. Thompson's client."

"I was. Now I want you." She finished shaking hands and then introduced me.

"Is there a problem?"

"Not if you don't make it one. I want my will rewritten. I want to provide for Sylvester and his mother."

"I don't understand. When Walden—Mr. Hollingsworth came here with you some years ago, you executed what's known as Mom-and-Pop wills with your daughter as beneficiary. Isn't your daughter still alive?"

"Let's just say she's become *persona non grata* and leave it at that," Addie said.

His brow furrowed. "Mrs. Hollingsworth, are you feeling well?"

"Why? Don't I look all right?" She tried to keep her voice light and convincing.

"I mean . . ." His voice trailed.

Addie and I exchanged eyebrow-encrypted messages. We shared a simultaneous thought—that Winters had just questioned Addie's mental health.

An hour and a half with the lawyer convinced him Addie was in fine form, but the rest took time. As he explained it, videotaping the proceedings would be a major safeguard—just in case Priscilla tried to contest the will by calling Addie's sanity into question. By doing it his way, the tape could be shown to the judge or a jury. Hopefully, they would see that Addie was perfectly normal, knew what she was doing, and had good reason to do what she did when the changes were made.

We left Mr. Winter's office on an emotional high.

Then "It Doesn't Matter Anymore" sounded from my mobile. I glanced over at Addie, and her whole body seemed to sigh.

She flip-flopped her hand toward the Mercedes pulling up at the curb. "Don't answer it."

When I thumbed the talk button, she walked away as if by mutual agreement.

This time, I said nothing. After a minute of listening to each other breathing, the mobile disconnected on Allen's end, and I caught up to the car, disappointed, but not really surprised.

# CHAPTER THIRTY-SIX

Four days later, after awakening to the brilliance of a tangerine sunrise, I turned on the telly and volumed the sound down low on my way to the loo. The newsreader was giving the drive-time weather report. As I ran warm water in the basin and washed my face, snippets of phrases drifted in and out of my morning routine. Words like "scorcher" and "drought" and "triple-digit temperatures" not only filled me with an overwhelming sense of discouragement, I found it downright depressing.

My mobile went off, sending a lance of apprehension through me. Addie was on a reconnaissance mission to score a lumberjack's breakfast from Jessie while simultaneously getting the scoop on Priscilla. But when "It Doesn't Matter Anymore" trilled out, I found myself running to the bed to silence it. As soon as I picked up my phone, the force field of Allen's psyche invaded my brain, and I felt the pull of him urging me to answer.

I thumbed the on button but withheld the greeting.

"Elle? Is that you?"

He practically slapped me with every word he spoke.

Tears blistered behind my eyeballs. I had two weeks and one day left to complete the journey, and, so far, I'd had almost nothing but disappointment. For two days. I'd played a mean game of hide-and-seek with the lunatics of this house, I'd been roughed up by thugs from my school, chased by the cops, and just generally been made miserable yearning to rekindle a love that I couldn't have. At least Elizabeth had the right attitude.

Not once had she mentioned the young man she'd made friends with while on holiday here, and as far as I knew she'd made no calls to get reacquainted with him.

"I'm sorry, Elle," Allen said. "Please give me another chance. Please?"

*From the spoils of conflict rise the flames of desire.*

*Who wrote that? Dante?*

I wanted to believe him; truly I did. But I couldn't work through the betrayal. The last thing I needed was for my daughter to return and shame me yet again for being such a stupid, lovesick cow.

I disconnected the call with a push of the thumb and a hearty, "Sod off."

As I toweled my face dry and reached for my toothbrush, a frightening explosion of immense proportions rocked the house. For a moment, I thought the gas cooker blew up. Then I heard a horrible drumming. When I ran to the window and peered past the slit in the curtain, I saw what appeared to be thousands of baseballs dropping from the clouds onto the cobblestones. Nearby, sirens blared so loud that I barely heard Jessie scream-ing for Perry to shelter their old car beneath the porte cochere.

Then the skies opened up and a waterfall poured out.

The newsreader was still speaking about a hot, muggy day when Addie hurried in, white as a sheet.

I said, "What's that wailing noise? It sounds like an air raid."

"Severe-weather sirens." She rattled the newspaper at me. The headline showed the body count for American troops serv-ing in the Middle East.

"Not there," she panted. *"There."* She finger pointed.

I opened the page. The piano key grin of Leon Darnell Gooch stared back at me from a photograph. He was holding a picture of the little boy with the rare disease.

Addie squealed, "Read it."

The story must've hit the AP wire and got passed on nation-wide.

*Ailing blood banks get transfusions.*

I blinked at the headline, gobsmacked.

"Aloud," Addie prompted.

" 'Convicted felon, Leon Darnell Gooch, sparked a statewide blood drive to replenish ailing blood banks' . . ." My mouth gaped. "So the lad gets the blood?"

Addie nodded. "And other tykes, too. Read on."

My eyes drifted over the article but the words strung together made no sense. I saw my mother mentioned by name—Fiona Slack-Applegate—and refolded the paper.

"Just tell me the rest." I slumped against the edge of the bed.

"Sly's father gave blood, but he didn't end it there. He organized a blood drive to replenish the banks with the help of the rest of the inmates. They all donated blood—except for the ones with diseases and such—and it turned out to be such a rollicking good time, making them feel good about what they were doing, that it turned into a competition. Before long, the rest of the state prisons joined in."

"Why would he do that?" I whispered uncomprehendingly. "*How* could he do that?"

"Probably has Mafia connections within the prison, yes?" she offered sweetly. "I hear they're big on gangs."

I didn't bother to figure this out. As best I could tell, we had two successes to our credit, Mama's friends coming through for her, and Leon Darnell Gooch coming through for me . . . and only fifteen days to accomplish three more.

I finished dressing while floating on a cloud and marveling at the enormity of it all. Then Priscilla drove into the driveway and ruined everyone's moods.

As soon as she pranced in through the back door, I had just enough time to grab my mobile before escaping through the window into the driving rain.

*So much for Richard getting this cow out of our hair.*

And where was Richard anyway? We hadn't seen him in five days.

# Chapter Thirty-Seven

With my back to the exterior bricks, I listened as Priscilla gave Addie's door a brusque tap, then opened the knob and waltzed in.

"I'm home." And then, "Since when do you watch the BBC?"

"I do a great deal of things you people don't know about."

I peeked through the window in time to see Priscilla cross the room and shut off the telly. She took the chair next to Addie's nightstand, and eyed her mother with disapproval. "Jessie says you've been eating like a hog."

"Jessie should mind her Ps and Qs."

"I think you've put on weight."

"Really?" Elizabeth said innocently, "Well I think you may've lost thirteen stones."

"What?"

"Pounds. A hundred eighty pounds of gristle." When Priscilla didn't react, Elizabeth filled in the blank. "Richard—he's gone."

"Are you . . . being British again?"

With rain dripping down my face, I caught Elizabeth's eye. Accusing my daughter of being British was like blaming a longhorn for having long horns.

She said, "Let's get on with it. I'm a fat, lazy bastard. So what? Toddle off, now, won't you?"

"We have an appointment with Dr. Bomar in a half hour."

Elizabeth set her jaw.

My mouth gaped. This was about the conservatorship so

Priscilla could stick Addie in the nursing home and steal her house. Part of me wanted Addie to run screaming into the storm. But that wouldn't help the old woman once we left. Perhaps the best thing Elizabeth could do for the old bird might be to go see this Dr. Bomar and set the record straight.

As Elizabeth hazarded a glance, I caught myself head-bobbing.

*Keep the appointment,* I telepathically encouraged her.

When it came to filling out forms chronicling Addie's medical history, Elizabeth demurred. Better to let Priscilla fill out the form on her behalf than to bugger up something as simple as her date or place of birth. After Priscilla finished updating the questionnaire, she passed it across the chair for Addie's signature. In the blank space next to Reason For Visit, Priscilla had written "mental health evaluation."

The right side of Elizabeth's brain wanted to send a signal to her fist to knock Priscilla into the next room. The left side wanted to send the same signal, but only after acing the physical and mental portions of the exam.

Elizabeth felt an easy confidence about the appointment. She knew something the thick cow sitting next to her didn't know— that, in her own right, she possessed the closest thing to a photographic memory as one could get without becoming a national weapon. When she scanned the paper for errors, she committed Addie's facts to memory. The way Elizabeth had it figured, the only way Priscilla and Richard had any kind of chance at all to get Addie into a nursing home would be through black ops.

Dr. Bomar didn't look at all as she'd expected. When he met them at the door and called her into the inner office, his age and demeanor surprised her. For one thing, he was half her age and boyish looking. For another, they were about the same height. And the wire-rim glasses that were a bit too large for the shape of his oval face made his warm brown eyes look larger.

"Do come back and let's get your weight, Mrs. Hollingsworth." He urged her onto the scale and immediately moved the big weights to the right. It was as if the small, fine adjustments were irrelevant. Ball park seemed good enough, as he tapped the weights until the balance settled midrange. Then he measured her height. "You're up seven pounds. What's going on with that?"

Elizabeth said, "Don't worry about me—worry about Priscilla. Her thighs are starting to look like bridge supports."

"Actually, I'm pleased you've put on weight."

"Hot weather makes me hungry. And I'm preparing many of the foods that I like. And I've taught Jessie, our cook, to make the things I don't have time to cook."

"That's good. So you're using the stove?"

"How else would I make a meal? Don't worry; I won't burn down the house. Did Priscilla tell you that?"

He opened the door to one of the patient rooms. With a swashbuckling gesture, he waved her inside. She took a seat in the patient chair and waited for instructions.

After wrapping her arm with a blood pressure cuff, Dr. Bomar seated the ear tips of the stethoscope into his ears and placed the circular chest piece over her pulse at the crook of her arm. Soon, he began asking innocuous questions.

Did she know the date, what day of the week it was, and who held the office of president? Elizabeth suspected these questions were designed to see whether she was properly oriented to place and time.

She decided to make a preemptive strike and did a quick lean-in. "I know why I'm here. Priscilla wants to put me under a conservatorship."

"Guardianship," he said.

"Whatever. Here's the thing. I don't need that. I can manage my finances all by myself. And if I can't, I have the good sense to hire an accountant. I remember to take my blood pressure pills, which, by the way, how's my blood pressure?"

"Amazing, actually."

"Well, isn't that nice? I don't need the pills but if you say I have to take them, I will. My memory's good and my attitude's even better. Don't sign those papers."

Dr. Bomar sandwiched her hand between his. "Mrs. Hollingsworth, we're only concerned about your welfare. Nobody wants you wandering off or getting hurt."

"Rubbish." Elizabeth pulled away. She reached for the germicide dispenser, pumped the bottle twice and rubbed her hands together with a vengeance. When she saw him looking at her funny, she said, "Multi-resistant staph. Who needs it?"

He agreed.

"Look, Dr. Bomar, if you think I'm bonkers, why don't you ask Richard? He can probably be fairly objective. If he thought I was nuts, he'd tell you, wouldn't he?"

After excusing Addie to the waiting room, Dr. Bomar motioned Priscilla inside. With her backside moving with an exaggerated sway, she went in with a smile. Five minutes later, Addie's daughter came out, white as a sheet, with a scowl on her face.

"What's wrong?" Elizabeth asked.

But she knew.

The doctor wasn't going to sign the guardianship papers.

Not today, anyway.

Now if she could only do something to enhance Addie's chances of avoiding the nursing home in the future . . .

# CHAPTER THIRTY-EIGHT

Later that afternoon, while Elizabeth and I sat at a café snacking on potato crisps and sipping fizzy drinks, she asked what I knew about the six degrees of separation.

"The small world phenomenon?"

"Yes," she said emphatically. Then she explained it in detail. "So we use that theory to get to enough people so that maybe out of the hundreds of thousands of contacts, one will do an extraordinarily good deed in Grandmummy's name and it'll count toward redeeming the Get Out of Hell Free card."

I nodded mechanically. "At this rate, the only way we'll reach enough people is to shanghai a TV station and take the newsreaders hostage. With our luck, we'll be shot dead before we ever reach the studio."

Elizabeth's eyes grew large, and the slack went out of the tissue paper skin that surrounded them. "That's it."

This triggered an eye roll on my part. "What? We're taking over a TV station?"

"No. The Internet." She went on to explain. "If we could commandeer a computer, we could write an email and forward it to everyone on the contact list asking them to pass it on to everyone in their contact list, and on and on and on."

In other words, a mass email pleading for a good deed for Fiona Slack-Applegate.

"No good," I said. "All the emails that start out like chain letters end up threatening people with bad luck or disaster."

"Or they promise good luck."

"Right. Annoy your friends and see how many acquaintances you can alienate. Is that the idea? Besides, I always delete those things. Why wouldn't everyone else?"

"It only takes one. Imagine if we inspired one person—like Leon Darnell Gooch. You saw what effect that's had, yes?" Elizabeth said.

The thing about my daughter is that she can be almost irritatingly optimistic, and I find this mystifying. You say lemons; she says lemonade. You say mad cow; she says new boots. You say feast; I say salmonella.

"I don't know . . ." my voice trailed. "Fifteen days?"

"Remember how that famous tennis player's pics traveled the Internet with lightning speed?"

"I suppose you'd want one of us to post a naked picture, wouldn't you? I think it should be you."

I considered our plight. With Leon Darnell Gooch, we had a bit of leverage. He was only doing a good thing in order to rehabilitate himself with his son for trying to kill him when he was little. But with strangers who had no vested interest in us—or Mama, for that matter? I didn't see how it could work.

That afternoon, we hijacked the computer in Richard's study. At first, I thought I'd have to log on using Allen's password and send the mass mail out as if it had originated with him. But Elizabeth opened the desk drawer to search for a pen and there it was on an index card—the passwords to Richard's email account, the bank accounts, and to a couple of online catalogues, as well. I experienced the overwhelming desire to order new shoes, but the voice of reason overtook me: by the time any packages arrived, we'd be gone.

With my face bathed in the pale blue glow of the computer monitor, I sent a heart-wrenching email request to everyone in

Richard's address book, and typed in his name at the end of my plea.

The whole operation took less than a half hour.

While pensively gnawing my bottom lip, I surveyed my good work. Then a new idea sprang to mind. The angel on my right shoulder tried to talk me out of it. The devil on my left shoulder goaded me to follow through.

Elizabeth interrupted my internal struggle with a suspicious, "What?"

"Allen has a huge email base. He's in the police officer's association and he networks with other law enforcement agencies in and around the state."

Expecting opposition, I was pleasantly surprised to find her on board with the idea.

Lapis-blue eyes took on a strange sparkle; laugh lines bracketed her thin lips. "Go for it. And check Priscilla's, too. She's bound to have a few friends . . . although I can't imagine anybody being so bad off they'd sit around listening to *her* complaints."

When we finished sending our email to practically every cop in the world except for INTERPOL, we started in on the socialites.

Then another brain wave struck.

My daughter's and my email accounts were renewed annually. Since the email couldn't exactly come from us, we each set up a dummy account using our middle names, and began the blanket email by saying that we'd discovered a final request from Elle Winthrop and her daughter Elizabeth and wanted to share it.

Email requests went out to all of the people in our address books—including members of the Southwestern Cattle Raisers Association, who we hoped would be particularly moved because of our untimely deaths in their city.

When we finished, we logged out of Richard's computer, and opened another bottle of wine from his collection.

"This is positively brilliant, Mum. If either of these louts runs across the emails, they'll think the other one did it. Neither would ever suspect poor Addie, who's so feeble and addle-brained that she practically needs to be institutionalized." Elizabeth cackled wildly at the irony. *"Who's the nut case now?"*

Then my daughter fell silent. Pensive and on the verge of brooding, she came up with an idea of her own.

"Remember those black billboards with white letters that started popping up a while back that were supposed to be messages from God?"

I remembered Allen explaining one that read: *Invite me to your school.–God.*

Apparently no one knew who'd originated the idea, only that someone had taken their nondenominational campaign to an advertising agency, and that's how the phenomenon got started.

My favorite was: *You think it's hot here?—God.*

And that made me inwardly wince thinking about Mama. We had to get her back. We simply had to. Because if we didn't, we'd never be able to make up for all the years she didn't have time for Elizabeth and me.

I went to the kitchen for a glass of ice water. When I returned, I made an announcement. "We need an ad agency."

"What else?" Elizabeth pulled a pad out of her handbag and scribbled.

"Where should we place them?"

"Where they'll do the most good."

Sometimes my daughter annoys me with her mind reading.

"I know that." I screwed up my face and it made her laugh. "Give me a location."

For a moment, she stared into the distance, chewing the inside of her mouth the way she did when she was a little tyke and had a problem to figure out. Then she said, "At the airport."

"Positively brilliant."

"Tally-ho."

We met with an advertising agency about the billboards later that afternoon. I'd found a photograph of Mama on the Internet, but it wasn't that flattering so we mutually agreed not to use it. In truth, Mama wore the expression of a rightfully accused serial killer, unmasked, complete with a look of outrage on her face. It had been snapped around the time of the Rowenstein shooting. By the time we finished at the ad agency, Addie had purchased two billboards in Fort Worth, four in Dallas and four near the DFW Airport arteries. For extra cash, they agreed to have our billboards printed and posted within five days.

It's a good thing one of us came back rich, or we wouldn't have been able to pull off that little coup.

Maybe Peter knew what he was doing after all.

# CHAPTER THIRTY-NINE

Five days later, after we'd forgotten about the billboards and were off spinning our wheels in a new sand trap, I dug through Addie's closet looking for clean clothes and came across the lock box we'd taken from the master bedroom upstairs.

I pulled it from its hiding place and carried it to the bed with reverence. It did, after all, belong to Addie.

We stared at it a few seconds, studying the lock to get an idea how to defeat it.

"I think we'll have to force it open," I said.

Elizabeth scrunched her brow. "Addie obviously wanted to keep what's in it a secret or she wouldn't have hidden it behind all those shoe boxes upstairs. I'm afraid she'll be upset when she finds out someone broke into it."

In the end, we had no choice. We were running out of time, and there might be something inside that could help us in our endeavor. While Jessie carted out the trash, Elizabeth sneaked into the kitchen and brought back a dull-bladed knife. When the knife didn't work, she returned with a meat cleaver.

"So much for Addie not discovering the burglary," I said.

The box came open after two well-placed whacks. At first glance, we noticed a piece of woman's clothing. As I lifted it out, I heard the crackle of paper, and carefully unfolded the fabric to find a journal, a stack of newspaper clippings intermingled with purchase receipts, an envelope large enough to hold documents or photographs, and an accounting ledger.

Elizabeth echoed my thoughts when I suggested we keep the contents in order.

After removing the journal, I lifted out the rest of the contents and placed them, upside down, in the middle of the bed. The journal belonged to Priscilla, and was one of those books that apparently played the sound of a woman screaming bloody murder when opened. This, of course, alerted anyone in the house to what I'd done.

We exchanged awkward looks. Then Elizabeth threw the deadbolt to the bedroom door, and jiggled the knob to make sure it locked.

I pulled the first newspaper article off the top of the stack.

Holding it close where my daughter could follow along, I read the headline: *Socialite arrested in husband's murder.*

From this clipping, we learned how Sugie Rowenstein had come home to find her husband, Sheldon, in bed with Mama. According to the story, Mrs. Rowenstein pulled a small-caliber firearm from her Judith Leiber handbag and fired at Sheldon Rowenstein's lover—identified as Fiona Slack-Applegate—at the same time my mother used the victim to shield herself from the gunplay.

Elizabeth paled noticeably. "Sugie Rowenstein didn't exaggerate at the AA meeting."

"You all right?" I asked before turning the next article upright.

She nodded. "I don't understand. Why would Addie save an article about Sugie Rowenstein? Do you think they knew each other?"

"Pass."

"Because Mrs. Rowenstein sure didn't act like she knew Addie when we were at the SAC meeting."

I turned over the next article.

*Oil baron, Hollingsworth, found dead in Fort Worth luxury hotel.*

"Oh dear," I said, and we began to read.

Walden Hollingsworth had checked into a fancy hotel with a woman not his wife. The maid found him dead the next morning, and the woman, gone.

Elizabeth fell into a somber mood. "How embarrassing for Addie. To have her husband running around on her—and then it becomes public knowledge when he dies."

"Don't take it personally."

She looked up with huge blue doe eyes. "How can I not, Mum? I know her. In a weird way, it's almost like we're friends. I like her." She cleared her throat. "I love her."

"I know." But I didn't know. Not really. I turned over the next article and we read it together.

*Police blame poisoning in death of oil baron.*

Elizabeth said, "Who'd poison Addie's husband?" She gasped. "What do you bet it was the woman he was with?"

"Pass."

"He wouldn't commit suicide. I know it in here." She fisted her chest near her heart. "He had Addie. He loved her."

Big headshake. "He didn't love her that much if he was running around on her."

Elizabeth lifted the next story. It unfolded the length of two long columns.

*Medical Examiner rules homicide in Hollingsworth death.*

The toxicology results in Walden's death pointed to arsenic poisoning.

We reserved comment.

The next item of business turned out to be a contract for a storage unit. It had been signed, and paid up for a year.

"What's the significance of this?" I leaned in enough to show my daughter.

She shrugged.

"And this?"

We examined a hardware store receipt where someone had

purchased . . .

*Two bags of lye?*

*Rat poison?*

My stomach went queasy. For a moment, the room blurred. This was a lot like asking for a miracle to turn a jug of water into wine, and getting an old paint can filled with bodily wastes instead.

Forcing myself to continue, I picked up the next article. This one was so long it continued with a jump site onto another page, and had been taped together with transparent tape.

*Socialite missing. Police believe foul play involved.*

"Oh no." I sent a trembly smile to my daughter. Blood pounded in my ears.

This story began with Mama's witness status in the Rowenstein murder, but ended in veiled speculation that she was the woman last seen at the hotel with Walden Hollingsworth the night he died. The author of the piece suggested that without their star witness, prosecutors would have trouble convicting Sugie Rowenstein of the murder of her husband.

It took a few minutes to digest the news. On the strained hope that I'd misunderstood the information, I gave it another read. Witnesses told police that Walden Hollingsworth offered Mama a ride home from the debutante ball. He dropped Addie off at Hollingsworth Manor because she wasn't feeling well, and Priscilla reported him missing the following afternoon after he didn't return home that night. He'd been having trouble with a couple of roughnecks who worked for him, and Priscilla suspected foul play.

I massaged the headache that had formed behind my eyes. "I think I'm going to be sick."

Walden and Mama, snogging in a hotel room. Imagine that. My gaze shifted to Elizabeth, to the tears rimming her eyes.

"Why would Grandmummy do such a thing?"

"Pass." But what I wanted to say was that I'd seen a pattern here.

We covered the next few articles, moving sluggishly, as if we'd fallen into a hypnotic trance.

*Hollingsworth daughter and son-in-law to appear before grand jury.*

We looked over an invoice from a private investigator specializing in marital issues. A cancelled check written by Addie to cover the PI's services had been stapled to the bill.

I did a double take.

What I saw chilled me to the bone.

The time-and-expenses invoice wasn't billed for investigating Walden's affair with Mama. It covered billable hours for spying on Richard. I opened the envelope paper-clipped to the accounting and emptied the eight-by-ten, black-and-whites onto the bed. What I saw made me want to run to the loo.

*Richard with Mama outside a nightclub.*

*Richard with Mama going into a hotel.*

*Richard with Mama kissing in the elevator.*

*Richard with his hand cupping Mama's . . .*

"Don't look at these." I snapped.

But Elizabeth set her jaw. "In for a penny, in for a pound."

What we were doing had a voyeuristic bent to it; I wasn't at all certain I wanted to know any more details about my tramp of a mother. Numbed by the facts, I read on.

*Victim or murderess? Slack-Applegate investigation still ongoing. Police stymied.*

Followed by: *Wealthy doyenne falls into mysterious coma as police continue investigation.*

I handed that one to Elizabeth. After a minute she said, "I think someone poisoned Addie." She crushed the article to her breasts and stared at some distant point beyond the window.

The next one read: *Toxicology results point to arsenic poisoning*

*for Hollingsworth widow. Widow taken off ventilator. "Progress poor"*
*doctors say.*

The next newspaper clipping bore the headline, *Wealthy*
*widow off life support. Doctors call full recovery a miracle.*

I handed the second one to Elizabeth. "Somebody poisoned
Addie. Here's the one where she gets better."

We read our respective articles in silence, mentioning only
the salacious parts, or the parts that continued to puzzle us.
When we were done, we traded.

Then I had reason to get excited. "Listen to this." I read
from the next article.

*Widow unable to testify in grand jury investigation. 'Lacks*
*capacity' says prosecutor.*

"Priscilla cooked this story up, I'm sure of it," I said, feeling
a shudder ripple up my back. "Don't you get it? Now her
mother can't be dragged into this mess."

But Elizabeth didn't see things with quite the same clarity.
She picked up the clothing from where I'd placed it, shook it
out and examined it with the vengeance of a forensics specialist,
starting with the label on the garment. After several minutes,
she rendered an opinion.

"Or, Priscilla was behind this. She discovers her father's having an affair with Fiona and kills him." She picked up the maid's
uniform and apron, pressed it to her nose and sniffed it. "It
smells like Priscilla's perfume."

The act of calling her grandmother "Fiona" was not lost on
me. I sensed Elizabeth distancing herself from the woman whose
tentacles had infiltrated this wealthy community, and then
destroyed the lives of so many people. *The woman we were trying*
*to rescue from Hell.* I couldn't help but feel that Peter's decision
to send us back as Addie and Sylvester was no accident.

As gently as possible, I tried to shape my concerns into just
the right words as I offered an alternate theory and delivered it

in a trailing voice. "The uniform could've fit Addie."

But my daughter wasn't having it. She clutched the dress to her breasts and squinted fiercely. "Addie didn't do it," she said with conviction.

This journey Peter had sent us on was breaking my heart. "Darling . . ."

"No, Mum." She fixed me with a wounded expression. "With enough time, I can prove it."

"We're almost out of time."

Now I wanted to unravel the mystery more than ever.

I scanned the next three articles and then handed them, one by one, to Elizabeth.

*Investigation ongoing in case of missing socialite. Police fear victim dead.*

*Rowenstein offered plea agreement in husband's death.*

*No jail time in Rowenstein plea deal.*

By the time we got around to reading Priscilla's diary, I was hungry and asked Elizabeth to check out the cool box to see if Richard still had a carton of ice cream. Once she left the room, I wrapped the incriminating journal along with the rest of the evidence back up in the maid's uniform, and stuffed it into an unused, shirt-sized cardboard priority mailbox that I found in a drawer in Richard's office. After scribbling a short note, I put it to the attention of "The Detective In Charge of the Walden Hollingsworth and Fiona Slack-Applegate Cases" and addressed it to the Fort Worth Police Department homicide unit. And in the bottom corner, I added: "Requested Evidence."

Then I stuck enough stamps on it from Richard's drawer to get it where it needed to go, and shoved it under the bed until such time as the mailman dropped off the post the following morning.

# CHAPTER FORTY

We were still reeling from the shock of our discovery when the local newscast came on at six o'clock.

After breaking news and continuing stories, the slim, red-haired newsreader stared at the teleprompter through luminous green eyes that begged to be trusted.

"And finally—this just in: Who is Fiona Slack-Applegate, and why do we need to do an unselfish deed on her behalf? Billboards are cropping up all over the metroplex—" a picture of the billboard popped up on the chroma key wall behind her "—like the campaign for God several years ago. The advertising agency refused to comment on the sponsor, an anonymous client, but said their switchboards have been jammed ever since the first one appeared two days ago. The person viewing the billboard is asked to do an extraordinarily good deed on behalf of Fiona Slack-Applegate, but who is she? If anyone knows, we ask that you give us a call . . ."

Elizabeth and I exchanged guarded looks.

We watched in rapt silence until the story ended, then switched to another channel. No matter which station we turned to, a variation on the same theme appeared on competing broadcasts.

Two days later, while watching Daxi Ree Cisco on CNN, the buxom blonde broadcaster with the big Texas hair and aquamarine eyes stared into the camera, looking efficient and trustworthy as she addressed viewers.

"And now, there's an unusual phenomenon sweeping the nation. Who is Fiona Slack-Applegate and why are people being asked to do good deeds in her memory? It started in a Texas prison when Leon Darnell Gooch, an inmate with the most rare blood type, AB-negative, donated blood to a child with a rare form of myeloma. This began a ripple effect the likes of which hasn't been seen since the largest and most progressive grassroots network of breast cancer survivors."

The program cut from Daxi Ree Cisco, to a film clip of a prison interview with Leon Darnell Gooch.

Gooch, huge and intimidating and practically bursting the seams of his prison whites, braced his forearms across his massive chest. He stretched back in an uncomfortable government-issue chair in gunmetal gray, and flexed the toes on his calloused feet against his plastic slides.

"My son, Sylvester Gooch, told me 'bout this woman, Fiona Slack-Applegate. He axed me to give my blood to a sick baby on account of I got rare blood and this baby—he need it—and wasn't nobody else helpin' on account of the blood banks didn't have no blood to match. Only I was a match and my son, Sly, he say do it for Fiona."

The prisoner broke into a grin that made him look like he'd swallowed a harpsichord keyboard.

The interviewer asked about the difficulty enlisting the help of other inmates to start such a massive blood drive.

Gooch sat bolt upright. His feet slapped to the floor. He sat erect, a giant of a man, looking like a rugby hooker in the scrum's front row. Fleshy cheeks automatically hardened. Eyes glowered beneath the light of the camcorder beacon. I half expected him to turn green, snap the links on his handcuffs and belly chain, and rip the bars off the window behind him.

"Wasn't no difficulty. They wanted to donate. On account of they could either go peaceful or I'd make a shiv, stick 'em in the ribs, and hold a cup under 'em and get it like that. Mostly everybody wanted to give of his own free will." He rested his hand over his heart. "On account of, like my boy Sly say, it the right thing to do. Some of 'em didn't."

The grin spread over his face again as he relaxed into a huge, toothy land shark.

"What happened to the ones who didn't give blood?"

He swatted the air. "They in the infirmary . . . gettin' transfused."

"Seems like that would defeat the purpose."

Leon Darnell Gooch gave a slow headshake. "Not really. There's always a certain amount of waste you have to factor into the problem."

"How were you able to inspire the inmates in other prisons across the state to join in what has now become the most massive blood drive in the state's history?"

"Put out the word."

"Beg your pardon?"

"Connections."

"Connections?" she parroted. "Like . . . friends?"

"Gangs."

Elizabeth slapped her knee. "Told you," she squealed. "Didn't I tell you?"

I felt the lightheaded rush of someone wanting to conquer their fear of heights by going on the kiddy scream machine, only to find that the roller coaster's metal safety bar failed to engage.

For a moment, I went in and out of the interview again.

Then Gooch said, "Then Texas inmates challenged prisoners in Louisiana, Oklahoma and New Mexico to do the same thing. Then they challenged inmates in other states, who challenged prisoners in other states and now we got a lot of people givin' blood. On account of it's the right thing to do. And they ain't goin' nowhere. So they's easy to catch if they don't want to co-operate."

My stomach clenched.

Then I heard Fiona's name mentioned again as Gooch put out a new plea for others to join the nationwide blood drive.

Then the reporter turned to the camera. "So who is Fiona Slack-Applegate? Sylvester Gooch, you started this move-ment—if you're listening, please call in."

A number flashed on the TV screen. I sat, numb and unblink-ing, on the edge of the settee.

The video clip of Leon Darnell Gooch cut away to Daxi Ree Cisco. "We have our correspondent from Fort Worth, Texas. Alana Timms, weigh in on this. You're the one who interviewed Leon Darnell Gooch, am I right?"

"Yes, Daxi."

An image of a lovely redhead popped up on the screen with the hostess. The reporter didn't seem much older than Eliza-beth. She looked so trusting, standing before the camera in a green shirt that made her eyes practically jump off the screen. As she pushed the ear fob deeper into her ear, chills swarmed over me.

"We're asking Sylvester Gooch to contact us, Daxi, but we're told this young man is wanted by police. Perhaps more people would do a human kindness for no good reason if . . ."

I was in and out of the broadcast, considering the ramifica-tions of showing myself, when Elizabeth called out from across the room.

She had the telephone cradled against her shoulder to muffle our conversation. "They want to interview you." Excitement flushed her cheeks. "How soon can we get down to the sta-tion?"

"What? You called them? Has your head gone soft? I'm on probation. There's probably a warrant for my arrest by now. We have two days left and you want to spend part of it sitting in a TV studio . . ."

"Oh, they don't need us at the station. She's coming here."

Anger blurred my vision. The last thing I needed was to have my location traced to the Hollingsworth's house.

"Hang up. *Hang up.*"

Don't think for a moment I wouldn't have liked to lie about on the couch the rest of the morning while pretending to enjoy life as a sweaty fat bastard. And I would've, too, had it not been for a TV truck rolling up to the curb, disgorging a camera crew. They scurried about like ants, setting up their equipment in front of Hollingsworth Manor.

Before I could escape out the back, Jessie let them in through the front door. Instead of being able to make a dignified getaway, they swooped through the house with camcorders rolling and caught me with one leg inside and the other lopped over the sill, halfway out Addie's bedroom window.

# CHAPTER FORTY-ONE

Six days had passed since the first billboards were erected.

Reality hit as I pulled my leg back inside the window and tried to convince myself that this type of exposure could be the break Elizabeth and I needed to get Mama out of Hell. And if we couldn't redeem the Get Out of Hell Free card, then we could at least do something to make things better in the lives of the two people we'd become a part of.

On that note, the last thing Sylvester needed was to be videoed running from the TV crew. So I pulled Addie aside and asked her to be the spokeswoman.

"I have a really bad feeling about today," I said. She looked like she needed convincing so I said, "Call it instinct. Call it insanity. We need to wrap things up here. And before we do, I think you need to have a conversation with Priscilla and tell her about the will. If you want to protect Addie, she'll be less likely to contest it if you level with her now."

She said nothing but I could tell she was mulling it over. For now, that was all I could hope for.

"As for the TV people, I don't want to be interviewed here. Tell them we'll meet them in Dallas. It'll give us a chance to hone our images, and make a better first impression." By "us" I meant "me."

Elizabeth gamely informed the media: We'd come to the TV station that afternoon so they could shoot the interview in the studio, edit the video, and replay the footage on the evening and late night broadcasts.

This actually worked out better. Because of the timing, my shots would become breaking news that would interrupt daytime viewing. Then I'd get another bite at the apple during the news broadcasts.

The news crew was packing up the last of their gear when Priscilla drove up in her Jaguar. When she came inside through the back door muttering curses under her breath, Jessie had the good sense to find something else to do.

Addie was already waiting in the kitchen when the soon-to-be-disenfranchised heiress dragged in the last of her flight bags.

"I want to talk to you, Priscilla."

"Not now, Mother, this was a turnaround flight and I'm tired."

"You can sleep later."

Priscilla gave her a heavy eye roll and proceeded through the formal dining room and down the hall toward her bedroom. Addie followed close behind. Anger pinched her lips.

Priscilla was already inside her quarters, unpacking, when Addie got her attention.

"I've changed my will. I'm telling you as a courtesy."

I was hovering just outside the door where Priscilla couldn't see me, but I wanted to be available in case something went terribly wrong.

Instead of getting angry, Priscilla cackled. "You can't change it. You're non compos mentis."

Calm as a Hindu cow, Addie said, "You'd better hope not, because if I'm declared incapacitated, you won't be able to call me as a witness in your murder trial."

Dead silence filled the air, as lethal as if a noxious gas had been released, and the canary took a nosedive off its perch.

"You're insane." Priscilla.

Addie continued. "I understand why you'd want to kill Fiona.

What I don't understand is why you'd harm your father."

"I don't know what you're talking about. You're forgetting I was on a flight and missed the debutante ball that night."

"I know about the rat poison." Addie carefully modulated her tone to conceal her anger. "I found the receipt."

"What receipt?"

From my place by the door frame, I couldn't tell if Priscilla spoke in the emotionless voice of a sociopath, or with the stricken tone of an innocent person.

"I loved your father. Did you ever stop to think maybe he really did *just* give her a lift? That maybe walking her to her room was an innocent gesture on his part?"

"Stupid old woman—Richard saw them together. They were in bed. In the throes of a wild sexual encounter."

"How do you know? Were you there?"

"Richard told me."

"I don't understand. How could he know that?"

"He watched them go into the hotel. They were playing grab-ass in the elevator."

My stomach clenched. Unless Priscilla had lost a lot of weight, that dress was closer to Addie's size than Priscilla's. But it wasn't Priscilla dressed up in Richard's clothes that Addie and I saw the night his company came over. It was Richard who came into our room wearing a wig, garter belt and stockings.

Pulled from eavesdropping by instinct, triggered by the breaths of an interloper, or the sweep of air from a quietly opened door, I shifted my attention to the end of the hall.

*Richard.*

Or rather the shadow cast by Richard, brandishing a huge gun and lowering the barrel.

My heart went dead in my chest.

With all my strength, I shoved Addie into Priscilla's room, following her in as the first gunshot rang out.

Footfalls thundered down the hall. Priscilla stood near the bed, gaping and speechless.

My stomach went hollow. I toggled the deadbolt, then jumped to my feet in a frantic attempt to herd Addie to the window. We'd been living with a sociopath and a killer—perhaps even two killers—certainly a small but decidedly creepy couple who meant to do us great bodily harm.

Priscilla stood, inert, as if she'd been blindsided.

Then the alarm went off—not the warning tone, but the panic alarm. Richard kicked the door as I threw open a window. I pushed Addie through the opening, following her out as the second kick splintered the door. Her tissue-paper skin had turned a ghastly shade of white, and I wondered as I lay on top of her whether I'd killed her when I landed.

A distant trill rang in my ear—the alarm company calling to see if police were needed.

I heard Priscilla scream as I pulled Addie to her feet, and my spine realigned itself. From the halting way she moved I could tell she was having trouble catching her breath. I tightened my grip on her arms painfully, pulling her along as we plodded through the flower bed. We reached the corner of the house when the second gunshot blasted the bricks, sending chips of mortar glancing off my skin. I wasn't conscious of having pulled Addie across the lawn to the next estate but when I reached the neighbor's front door, the melee we'd just escaped lay behind us.

As I watched in horror, expecting Richard to come after us, he suddenly pitched, headfirst, through the open window.

A scream died in my throat.

He didn't leap to his feet, as I'd feared, the way the villain in every horror movie routinely springs back to life. Perhaps the fall knocked the wind out of him? I took a second look. Richard wasn't going anywhere.

And when I shifted my gaze, Perry stood, framed in the window, holding an upraised shovel in his hand like a bayonet.

# CHAPTER FORTY-TWO

Under the blue sweep of a cloudless sky, while Jessie and Perry dealt with the police, Broderick drove Addie and me to the TV studio in Dallas. As we dressed in the back seat of the car with the clothes we managed to snag before officers arrived, he pulled down the sun visor and darted glances at us through the rearview mirror.

By the time we arrived, I'd wrangled into my new designer suit, dress shirt, and tie. I also brought along a second tie in case they wanted me to have a different look. And I wore the alligator loafers, of course.

Broderick elected to wait with the car while the interview took place. On the walk into the building, Addie and I agreed not to mention what had just happened at Hollingsworth Manor. With any luck, the newsreaders wouldn't know about Richard being locked up in jail or possibly dead. I really didn't want to know myself. For now, it was enough that the evidence in the deaths of Mama and Mr. Hollingsworth had gone out in this morning's mail, and was on its way to the appropriate detective.

From here on, let God and the government sort it out.

As the makeup artist dusted what looked like powdered chocolate over my face to cut the sheen caused by the heat of the studio lamps, Sylvester Gooch resembled a young gentleman instead of an ordinary little street thug.

Addie was a vision of understated elegance in one of her new frocks—a cashmere prayer coat with its shawl collar and open front, patch pockets and side slits, over a matching sleeveless knit dress in a muted shade of light brown called winterhaze. I warned her it'd be too hot to wear on a blistering, muggy day like today, but she claimed she'd been chilled by the morning's events so I didn't obsess over it.

That's the thing about old people. They get cold easily. Poor circulation and all, I suppose.

I'd never been inside a TV studio before, so I glanced around with mild curiosity. There was a mock parlor built near the area where the newsreaders delivered their reports, and we were asked to sit on a small settee while the reporter took her place in a tufted leather wingback. Someone had placed a white bakery box full of petite palmiers on the coffee table, and the sight of fresh goodies made my mouth water.

I assumed the reporter, a lovely redhead who introduced herself as Alana Timms, was clairvoyant—either that or she saw me eyeing the cookies—because she asked if I'd like one, and then sent one of the crew to bring me a beverage.

"Gin and tonic," I said without thinking and reached for a pastry.

When she didn't react, I shifted my gaze from the box. The expression on her face telegraphed my gaffe. "Just a little joke. I'd like a fizzy drink." She blinked. "A Big Red if you have it. If not, sparkling water will be fine."

Addie asked for a margarita but the reporter laughed it off as if she'd made a joke. We were brought two bottles of Perrier, and while Addie cupped hers in her hand, I unscrewed the top of mine and drank the first of many swallows.

"I'm going to ask you about Fiona Slack-Applegate," said Alana Timms. "Then I'm going to ask you about yourself."

I shot Addie an *Uh-oh* look.

"We'll have about three minutes to do the live interview—"

I tuned out the rest of her statement. If I could drag out the part about Mama, that would eat up most of our time.

A musical trailer sounded, and I stiffened against the seat back. Addie looped an arm around my shoulders in a grandmotherly fashion as the producer stood by and gave Miss Timms the countdown.

The interview went swimmingly. As the producer gave us a spinning finger gesture, *Wrap it up,* I appealed to viewers to become inventive and do an extraordinarily good deed on behalf of Fiona Slack-Applegate.

Then we got the finger-to-throat slitting gesture and we were off the air.

Alana Timms said, "That was wonderful." She touched my knee and locked me in her green gaze. "If you could give us a little more time, we want to continue the interview with a Q-and-A."

I blinked.

"This is for our Thursday show. Don't you watch us? Well— never mind—we do a features program for the six o'clock news on Thursdays and this would be wonderful."

I was thinking, *What could it hurt?* and reminded myself that I'd brought along the red silk tie that would give me a completely different look. In my vast experience as a late forty-something woman, *What could it hurt?* usually acts as the predecessor to *No good deed goes unpunished,* which probably should've gone on my headstone instead of *"Here lies Elle, who lived her life well, helped those less fortunate, to avoid an afterlife in Hell."*

What can I say? My father had a sense of humor. He chose a more fitting epitaph for Lillibet. It simply said: *The good die young.*

I shook off my sudden melancholy.

We were already here and the red silk tie really did make me look hot for a twelve-year-old from the poor side of town.

Addie said, "What do you think, Sly? Maybe a bit longer? For Fiona?"

"Sure."

The TV people gave us time to grab a quick bite, so Broderick drove us to a nearby eatery. Before heading back to the TV studio, we put away chicken-fried steak and key lime pie like a pack of ravenous jackals.

Back at the TV station, we were halfway through the interview when Alana Timms asked how Addie and I met.

"We met at a convenience store."

She scoured her notes. "It says here that you robbed Mrs. Hollingsworth."

I had a sick feeling and didn't like to think where this was all headed.

Then Addie jumped in and rescued the interview.

"Rubbish. That's the thing when you're trying to do something good for someone. Take me, for instance, the police got it all wrong about Sylvester. He's a jolly good lad—"

Alana Timms stiffened.

Addie realized she'd regressed to the British accent, and quickly backtracked. "—an absolutely fabulous young man and a fine basketball player, as well. He has a good work ethic and helps me with chores. We've been having a lovely time starting this grassroots campaign to encourage people to be good Samaritans—"

Instead of the lightning bolt I expected to strike us both dead, my attention strayed to the reporter. She focused on something past my shoulder, and her expression hardened. A couple of Dallas police officers filled the studio doorway. And behind them, Mr. Geeslin, my probation officer.

*And Allen.*

*With Detective Stone.*

255

I let out a shriek, ripped off my mike, and hopped over Addie like a reincarnated puma.

I spotted the fire exit and dashed out the back with the alarm ringing in my ears.

As if I didn't have enough trouble, "It Doesn't Matter Anymore" started ringing in my pants pocket.

*Sod off,* I thought and picked up the pace.

I shed the coat. It's hard enough running in hundred-degree weather without being overheated by extra clothing. Then I ripped off the shirt. The last thing I wanted to ditch was the fabulous designer tie, but I didn't want them to have anything to grab onto if they got close enough to catch me, either. I fled through the streets of downtown Dallas, dodging this way and that, until I unexpectedly stumbled upon a re-creation of a cattle drive in the form of bronze sculptures—longhorns on a cattle drive, driven by three horse-riding cowboys.

I kept running. When I glanced over my shoulder, flashes of color from Allen's red plaid shirt, popped up in my peripheral vision. My lungs burned. How could a middle-aged man keep up with me? I have the majestic legs of an Olympian, coupled with gazelle-like speed, yet every time I looked over my shoulder I saw that fat Hall of Fame bastard, Stone, gaining ground, and Allen, ten steps ahead of him.

I reached a produce market crawling with people. I ducked beneath the tent, pulled out a handful of coins from my pocket, and deliberately dropped them onto the floor.

This gave me a reason to bend down to pick them up without looking cagey.

The table I'd chosen to do this next to had a cloth thrown over it, with wooden boxes of avocados, Japanese eggplants, artichokes, and bundles of asparagus stacked on top. I crawled beneath the table pretending to search for change, and saw police fanning out nearby.

A vendor of Asian descent said, "You buy?" He held an avocado up to the light. "Nice?"

"Yes, I'll buy. A moment, please."

He must've guessed what was going on because he began sacking avocados for me.

As I sucked in several calming breaths, I watched the police cross back opposite from my hiding place. Then I came out from under the table.

"Jolly good." I shoved a five-dollar note into the man's hand, snatched the bag, and fled deeper into the market.

My mobile sounded again—the "Everyday" ring tone. It comforted me knowing Addie was searching for me.

I stopped by a watermelon stand, put down my little sack of fruit, and shoved my hand into my pocket. I thumbed the button on my mobile, catching it before it cycled into voice mail.

" 'Ello, Lillibet, you must come find me." I jammed a finger in my other ear to cut the noise. "I'm lost in a produce market near baskets of watermelons. The police are everywhere. Have Broderick drive the car around, and stay close to the curb. I'll come out when I see you."

I realized I'd been doing all the talking. Now, I awaited the response.

"Oi. Did you hear me? I'm in the market."

For a wistful moment, I thought my mobile had dropped the call. That would've been preferable to the alternative.

"Lillibet? Are you there?" I pulled the mobile away from my ear enough to stare at the digital display. Sure enough, it still showed an active connection. "Darling, can you talk?"

Too late, the hair rose on the back of my neck.

I had the skin-crawling feeling of being watched.

A snapping noise came from behind me and to the right. If asked to identify the sound, I would've said *The clang of a jail cell slamming shut behind me.*

I turned. Allen studied me from several feet away.

He held Addie's phone aloft.

His mouth tipped at the corners.

Something moved at the limits of my vision. As I looked around to make my getaway, Detective Stone stepped into the other end of our row, effectively closing off my escape.

# CHAPTER FORTY-THREE

For no good reason, the skies stormed over and the wind picked up. Huge drops pelted the overhead awning like a thousand drummers beating off-cadence. In the distance, the blacktop steamed.

I vaulted over the watermelon table in a single bound. Allen followed suit and the table collapsed under the extra weight. Melons dropped to the floor with a sickening splat. Detective Stone's curses faded as I put real estate between us.

I didn't dare look back and plodded ahead blindly. I'd only visited Dallas once since coming to the states; even then, a tour guide had shown us around. Now, landscape features that had seemed so prominent when I'd first been shown the city, looked like Everywhere Else, USA.

I didn't slow until my lungs gave out. Bent over at the waist and heaving, I sucked air.

Water soaked my trousers and my undershirt had become plastered to my back. My Ballys were covered with gelatinous muck and I felt like I'd been rucked in a rugby match.

Allen caught me in a flying tackle.

The impact knocked the air from my lungs. I hit the ground, hard, and he pinned me. Python arms, tight against my ribs, kept me from taking a breath. My lungs burned from oxygen deprivation. Gasping for air, I rolled onto my back and came face-to-face with the man I loved and had once hoped to marry.

For a moment we just stared at each other making silent assessments; me, wondering how to get away; him, wondering how to hang on.

"Sod it—I give up."

Rivulets of rain streamed off his hair and doused my face. We were close enough to get squidgy with each other. The part of me that my right brain controlled wanted to kiss him; the part of me that my left brain controlled wanted to knee him in the 'nads and sprint to safety.

He breathed heavily, the way he used to do after we'd finished an evening of carnal gymnastics.

"Get off me," I said, seriously winded from this sad, sorry chase.

"You won't run?"

"Don't know if I can. My knee's cocked up."

"Where'd you learn to talk like that?"

"In bloody naffing England, lovie."

"What'd you do, you little burglar? Break into her house? Window peep? Stalk her? What the fuck did you do to her?"

Breaths became shallow. I had to get him off of me. "You're crushing my ribs."

"I'll crush your head if you don't tell me." He drew back his fist.

I thought he was going to hit me, and closed my eyes so I wouldn't see it coming. In anticipation of a sound thrashing, I burst into tears.

"Allen, stop," I cried. "You don't understand. I tried to explain but you wouldn't listen."

Unassailably indifferent, he came up off my ribs. I drew in a sweet, cleansing breath. The sky had turned nearly black, and rain was running up my nose like a turkey in a thunderstorm.

Stone, with his finger pointed skyward, called out in the distance. "Tornado."

A blast from the Mercedes' horn filled the air.

I hoisted myself up on one elbow. Allen climbed off me, and pulled his handcuffs from the back waistband of his blue jeans. He jerked me to my feet, spun me around, wrenched my arm up and ratcheted one cuff on. But before he could get the other secured, I talked fast.

"I saw you the night I died. I looked down upon you. Stone was patting your shoulder telling you not to cry. You said . . ."

He stood with his mouth gaping.

"You said, 'I'm not going to stop loving her just because she's gone.' "

His grip on the handcuff went slack.

"And he patted your shoulder while the others watched you cry like a baby."

He let go. The other handcuff ring clattered against the small of my back.

Stone closed in. I wrenched my arm from his grasp and made a mad dash for the Mercedes.

I reached the sedan to the sound of electric locks unsnapping. The back door popped open and I dove inside.

Then I heard it—Allen's plaintive cry through the waterfall of rain—as I shut him out of my life.

"Elle. Elle, come back. I believe you."

I jammed my fingers into my ears, closing my eyes while Broderick sped us away.

# CHAPTER FORTY-FOUR

We were already on the motorway, headed toward Fort Worth in the blinding storm, when Addie demanded to know what had happened. Blustery gusts drove sheets of water into the windscreen, making it necessary for Broderick to slow the Mercedes to a crawl. Smears of red flashed from the brake lights of cars in front of us. When we could no longer see out the windows, Broderick halted the car on the shoulder and we sat, frightened, in the driving rain.

I grabbed Addie's wrist and tightened my hand around it. "I want to go back."

"We're not going back. Broderick, drive on."

"He knows it's me. I told him something only the two of us could know." At this point, having Stone back at the market, waiting to arrest me, didn't even factor into the equation.

"No." She ignored the rest of my plea and spoke only to our chauffeur. "Get off of this bloody road before a truck runs us down."

"But Addie, there's a guardrail."

"Drive around it."

"We'll get stuck in the mud."

"Not if you drive fast enough."

"I've never seen anything like this." He addressed the steering wheel.

Clearly, the weather unnerved him. Half of the sky had turned as green as an emerald. The other half, as black as onyx. We were headed for disaster and Broderick knew it.

I flopped back into the leather seat wanting to cry, while simultaneously wondering how our chauffeur could see past the driving rain as it sluiced down the windscreen. "We're almost out of time. We can't return to Hollingsworth Manor. The police will be waiting for me. We should go to Mrs. Gooch's. Perhaps she'll let us stay the night."

Addie nodded. "I mean it about getting off this motorway, Broderick," she said with authority. "We're down to the wire, and I want to take Sly home to his mother's."

Broderick set his jaw. His eyes flickered to the rearview mirror, where they lingered a few seconds before cutting away.

"As you wish, Madame."

"Addie."

"Yes, Madame."

Addie went quiet and sunk into her own thoughts. Broderick had resorted to formality, the way he'd done when we first met him. I suspected he no longer intended to indulge us, and fleetingly wondered if Priscilla had gotten to him.

He broke the long silence by turning on the radio, tuning it to the weather channel so we could monitor our bleak travel situation.

The announcer warned listeners to run for cover.

"I think we should park the car and take shelter inside a building," Broderick said. "Maybe a hotel for the duration. Do you have enough money on you, Madame?"

"Just drive." This, from Addie.

"But, Madame, we're in a storm the likes of which I've never seen. It's not safe . . ." He went suddenly quiet and inclined his head toward the radio.

Addie alerted like a dog on point.

The announcer spoke of a team of scientists who were headed for the metroplex, prepared to study the bizarre phenomenon that made the skies open up for no good reason.

Addie said, "Pull over."

Broderick crept along at a slug's pace.

I hoisted myself bolt upright and stared out the window. I saw what Addie saw. A hotel vacancy sign flickered in the distance.

"Pull over."

"There's no exit, Madame."

"Then make one."

"But, Madame . . ."

"Have a whack at it."

Broderick sucked air. His eyes darted to the mirror, and cut back to the windscreen. Whipping the car off the road, hard right, we plummeted over the embankment. Screams died in my throat as we skidded across grass and mud, fishtailing to the service road below.

"That's the stuff." Addie clapped him on the shoulder. "Simply brilliant. Now pull under the portico."

When he slid to a stop, he shut off the engine, and got out of the sedan. He opened Addie's door. But before she climbed out, she turned and gave me a pointed look. "Stay right where you are," she said, in her ventriloquist voice.

As the chauffeur stood beside the door, waiting to escort her inside the hotel, she demanded the car keys. "I need to get something out of the boot."

He stared uncomprehendingly. "Boot?"

"What you Americans call the trunk."

He did one of those sour lemon face scrunches. I suppose it didn't really matter if he decided she'd gone mad. We had so little time left. But I worried how such slips might affect the real Addie Hollingsworth once we were gone. I concluded that we'd done everything we could, and that the old lady would have to bounce back on her own.

He moved toward the trunk, but she dodged him as well as any of the lads on the basketball team.

"I'll get it," she said emphatically. "You go inside and let them know you'll be needing a room." She fished in her handbag and pulled out a fistful of bills. "Take this. If it's more, come see me."

His brow flinched. His forehead furrowed as if he were trying to make sense of her instructions.

As an afterthought, she added, "See if they have a vending machine and buy a sack of potato crisps for Sly." To me, she said, "You'd like that, wouldn't you?"

I couldn't have eaten if I'd wanted to; my stomach was still tumbling. But I nodded to go along with her, and it seemed to appease Broderick, as well.

Addie tracked him with her gaze as he sprinted into the building. When the last bit of trouser fabric disappeared behind the door, she slammed the boot shut and jumped behind the wheel. Before I could react, we were off.

The last thing I saw through the rear windscreen was Broderick flinging himself out the door wearing a look of utter shock on his face.

# CHAPTER FORTY-FIVE

Because of the downpour, what would've normally been a forty-five minute drive to Sylvester's house from central Dallas turned out to be almost double. Water had risen over the roads, making it impossible to see the divider lines. Some roads looked too deep and treacherous to cross. When we arrived at Sylvester's house, Mrs. Gooch was standing inside the open doorway, peering out through the screen. Seeing her there made me thankful to have a safe place to go.

When she realized I'd returned, she came out onto the porch wrapped in a lightweight sweater and stood, gobsmacked, as Addie shut off the Mercedes. We ran toward the house with me holding Addie's arm to keep her from slipping. Once we climbed the steps and stood beneath the leaky awning, Sylvester's mother hugged me with the strength of a circus bear.

Then she commenced to give me a bloody good smacking about the head and face, all the while screaming, "Why you make my life so hard? Why you do this to aggravate me? Why you make me worry?"

"That's enough," Addie said sternly She squared her shoulders, and with her head held high and her jaw defiant, used a no-nonsense tone that caused Mrs. Gooch to retreat into the house.

I reluctantly followed.

Addie said, "I'm sorry for the trouble. I have Sylvester's wages, and we thought we'd drop them off." She fished in her handbag, produced a wad of cash, and handed it over to Mrs. Gooch without counting it. "And I have a proposition for you."

Mrs. Gooch's eyes thinned into slits.

"Hear her out, Mama," I said.

"I want you to come work for me."

"I have a job."

"I know. But I'm old and I need help. And I don't care if you work me in when you're not doing your other job."

"Jobs. I have three of them." Sly's mother's jaw tensed.

"Maybe I can make it so you only have to work two jobs. If you like working for me, you can quit them all. I'm only asking you to try it."

"How much it pays?" Mrs. Gooch's head did a strange sort of chicken movement, pushing forward and drawing back as she spoke. "On account of I don't work for peanuts. I'm a good cleaner, and I don't make a mess, and I don't ruin people's stuff, and all I ask is a decent wage, and maybe a sandwich on my break. I don't fool around when I work. I clean, and I clean good."

She delivered this information with the momentum of a windup toy.

Addie let her wind down. "How much do you make now?"

"Minimum wage."

We exchanged baffled looks. Addie said, "How much is that?"

"Not near enough."

"How much would you want to come work for me?"

We could almost see the gears turning inside Myrna Gooch's head as she ciphered the amount she'd need in order to make it worth putting up with us.

She said, "Two hundred dollars per weekend. I'll work ten hours a day."

Addie said, "I'll pay four hundred."

The counteroffer had a jarring effect. "Say what?"

"Four hundred . . ." And to clarify, ". . . per weekend."

Sylvester's mother stood near a threadbare sofa, and she slumped onto the nearest seat cushion with the energy of a ragdoll. "You want me to work for you for four hundred dollars per weekend," she said in the flat monotone of a madwoman. *"You want me to work for you for four hundred dollars per weekend?"* Her voice crescendoed to a feverish pitch. She jumped from her seat and began to dance around the living room, repeating the words with different inflections in her tone. *"You* want *me* to work for *you* for *four hundred dollars per weekend."*

Addie nodded.

She let out a joyous scream and shouted at the ceiling, "Thank you, Lord Jesus." Then she resumed her dance, chanting the words like a mantra. She pulled me by the arm and placed my hands firmly against her waist, then turned her back to me and pulled me along behind her. Addie joined in the conga line as Mrs. Gooch led us through the rest of the house, a ramshackle dump in need of a good fixing up.

We ended up in the kitchen, seated around a chipped Formica table.

"May I offer you something to drink? Grape punch? My other boy, he love grape punch. Only he don't get to drink it in the living room on account of it stains."

Addie said, "Nothing for me, thank you."

I said, "No, thank you."

Mrs. Gooch did a double take. "Did you just thank me?"

I cast my eyes downward. Once I left, I hoped Sly would have a greater appreciation for his mother.

"We need a place to stay, Mama. Miz Addie can't go home tonight on account of . . . well, she can't go home. The police are looking for me, and they think she helped me get away. If we go back to her house, we'll get arrested."

Mrs. Gooch slapped me on the side of the head. I drew back,

and raised my hands to shield my face. She said, "Whatchoo think? Some white lady can come here overnight and be safe?" She pointed in the direction of the driveway. "With a car like that? Boy, you know yo'self, first thing in the morning that car will be up on blocks with everything stripped off but the frame."

"Can't we hide it?"

She broke into raucous laughter. And she probably would've still been laughing if gunshots hadn't rung out.

Glass shattered. Bullets peppered the side of the house. We dove to the floor with our hands over our heads. I threw myself on top of Addie and hugged her close.

Then all went quiet.

Outside, neighbors shrieked. Their screams carried a bit of hang time as I tried to assimilate what happened.

Then a loud banging rocked the screen door.

"I don't know what you done wrong, Sly, but I been afraid this would happen." Mrs. Gooch worked her way up on all fours, then to her knees, then steadied herself against the sink as she pulled herself fully upright.

As she headed for the front door to intercept the neighbors who were trundling up the steps, I gave Addie a weary headshake.

"We have to get out of here. I don't want to die this way."

# CHAPTER FORTY-SIX

While the neighbors piled onto the Gooches' porch like rugby players in a scrum, Addie and I went out the back door. I'd no sooner opened the gate than the family dog came up out of a dead sleep and rushed the fence while simultaneously chomping at my rump roast. He ripped my trousers from the seat to the knee but I didn't care. We'd gotten safely beyond the gate, and that's what mattered.

Addie and I hurried to the Mercedes with purpose in our steps. Police sirens wailed in the distance. I sensed they were speeding in our direction.

As soon as Addie started the car, the neighbors turned toward us in a collective shift. The blaring radio muted Mrs. Gooch's words, but I knew in my gut she was calling us back.

Addie bounced out of the drive like she was auditioning for a guest spot on one of those British daredevil programs. The big car slumped heavily down the street in water so deep it made a groaning noise as the tires pushed the rainwater aside. We hadn't passed more than a handful of roads when she said, "Uh-oh."

"What's wrong?" I was still looking through the rear windscreen, expecting a car full of thugs to pop into view. We hadn't passed any police cars, but I'd lowered my window halfway down to enable me to hear the sirens.

"We're almost out of petrol."

"What?" I twisted in my seat to look at her. She stared straight ahead unwilling to make eye contact. *"What?"*

She shook her head. "We'll have to stop."

"Can't we get out of Sylvester's neighborhood first?" From my place in the passenger seat, I couldn't see the car clock, but I estimated that it couldn't have been later than six. Still, the lampposts were all lit up with a hazy mist around them, and the sky was as dark as if it were midnight. I couldn't think of any worse place to be than where we were at that exact second.

"We're on fumes. I don't think there's enough petrol to go very far before we're afoot."

I swallowed hard. The rain was still pouring down with a vengeance. Water rushed over the road so fast and furious that it formed a swift current. Addie slowed for a traffic signal that no longer functioned, trying to go the distance before the car choked and died, while I prayed we wouldn't be swept away in the flood.

"First petrol station you see, pull in."

She nodded bravely. I could almost smell the fear.

Shop lights flickered on the horizon. "Bet there's one up ahead," I said, not knowing, but wanting to offer comfort. Elizabeth has such a gentle soul. When things go wrong, she occasionally panics. But posing as Addie Hollingsworth had given her a new sense of fierceness.

She broke the silence stretching between us. "I want to do something for Sugie Rowenstein before we go. I want you to write this down on a piece of paper, and I'll sign it."

I looked around for something to write on but saw nothing. She eyed her handbag and I rummaged through it. I came up with a check slip from the bank, turned it over and gave her the go-ahead.

"I, Addie Hollingsworth, do hereby promise Sugie Rowenstein . . ." She paused to let me catch up. ". . . the sum of one hundred thousand dollars . . ."

With the tip of the pen poised above the paper, I stopped and looked at her.

She nodded for me to continue.

". . . on behalf of Fiona Slack-Applegate, to make partial amends for the pain and suffering caused by stealing her husband and using him as a shield."

I snorted, but wrote the words as she spoke. We didn't have time to argue about the lack of eloquence. Elizabeth had known the right thing to do and had tidied up nicely.

"You're a brick, darling." I made a line for her signature and penned the date at the top. Then I reached across the seat and tucked it under the sun shield.

"Do another one. This time, make it for the police."

I dug for more paper. "Ready."

"My name is Adelaide Hollingsworth, and my daughter, Priscilla, and her husband Richard have been trying to kill me."

She spoke slowly, prompting me on as I finished each phrase.

"Richard was administering poison until I caught him pouring powder into the vitamin shakes he brought me. If I should be unable to speak out, please perform whatever tests you need to prove this. Start with arsenic." She nodded. "Leave a blank for my name."

I did as instructed, and drew a line for myself as a witness to her signature.

She spoke without making eye contact. Both hands whitened against the steering wheel. The force of the current washed us into the next lane. "Do you think this is how we'll go, Mummy? That we'll be swept off the road and drown?"

"Pass." My pulse throbbed.

"Do you think drowning is painless?"

"We're going to buy petrol, and pull into the nearest hotel." I tried to infuse confidence into my voice "Then we'll order room service and wait out this horrible storm while watching bad programming on the telly. That's what I think." My heart drummed in my chest.

We drove the last of the street in anticipation. I wondered whether we'd end up on the side of the road . . . or if we'd make it in time.

My mobile suddenly chimed out a melody.

"It Doesn't Matter Anymore".

"Mummy, please don't do it."

My daughter looked over at me through Addie's blue eyes, and I swear for a moment I could see my child's soul at the core of the old woman.

"I won't say anything." I fumbled in my trouser pocket. "I'll just listen."

Tears bubbled up, teetering along the rims of her lids like tiny opal beads. "But you won't. You'll talk to him. And you'll tell him where we are. And he'll come for us again, just like before."

I thumbed on the talk button and pressed the mobile to my ear.

"Elle, is that you?"

I looked beseechingly at my daughter. Tears rimmed her eyes red. When making the choice between my daughter's well-being, and my desire to have what might be my final conversation with my one true love, I chose my daughter.

I quietly pressed the end button and dropped Allen's call.

We moved along at a crawl. Water rose above the street and over the curb as it crashed into the gutters, making whitewater so high you could raft in it. For the first time all day I felt a sense of serenity. Even if we had to walk the rest of the way, we'd driven close enough to take shelter and return with enough fuel to start the Mercedes again. We'd all but resigned ourselves to running out of fuel when an illuminated sign from a petrol station glowed pale in the distance.

As we rolled heavily up to the pumps, we breathed a collective sigh of relief.

"Give me the money." I held out my hand.

"First, we sign the papers." She scrawled her name on both pages, and I penned mine as a witness to what might turn out to be a deathbed alert.

Addie dug into her handbag and handed over a fistful of cash. I didn't even bother to count it. I jumped out of the car and ran for the door.

I called to her over my shoulder. "Want a fizzy?"

"And a Zinger."

We hadn't eaten since lunch and I was anxious to stuff myself with restaurant food, but Elizabeth had grown fond of the coconut-raspberry cakes and I decided to pick out several.

As I stood at the work surface counting out the money for petrol and snacks, a look of utter panic washed over the store clerk's face. For a second, I thought a robber had followed me into the shop. What sounded like the cry of a mewling kitten reached my ears. Then I looked out the window and saw what riveted her attention.

A black fellow jumped from a nearby car. He fisted Addie's hair savagely.

She screamed bloody murder but held onto her handbag.

He fisted her face, bloodying her nose. I watched her fall as he grabbed the purse strap and gave it a yank.

I never anticipated the murderous fury inside myself that focused me in the form of an adrenaline rush. I dropped the money and bolted through the door, calling her name and threatening bodily harm.

Then everything moved in slow motion.

Addie's head hit the pump at an unnatural angle. Her eyes went wide, staring at me as she collapsed to the pavement limp as a rag doll.

The driver jumped out.

*LaVon.*

I knew instantly who'd shot up Sly's house. I didn't recognize my voice or understand the words being fired from my hair trigger tongue. I only knew I had to get those thugs away from my daughter.

LaVon pointed at me.

An orange burst of fire shot out of his finger.

For a second, I thought I'd slammed, face first, into an invisible wall. Momentum forced me backward, into a fall and onto the ground, rendering me powerless as I watched my feet fly up and crash down again.

A shriek shrilled in my ear.

Then the Buddy Holly ring tone played. Calmed by the melody, I closed my eyes.

As rain pelted my face, a peaceful darkness shrouded me against the harsh fluorescents buzzing overhead.

# Chapter Forty-Seven

Blaring police radios roused me into consciousness.

*My side hurts.*

*Lying flat on the pavement makes it hard to breathe.*

I pulled in a breath of gauzy air so thick and muggy and heavy with the scent of death that each intake left an unpleasant taste in my mouth. Screams filled the air. With hesitation, I cracked my eyes open, not really wanting to see whatever I might see. Memory deserted me, but I forced myself to remember.

*I'm at a convenience store . . . yes, that's it. I went inside to pay for gas.*

*I don't recall driving here. Wait. That wasn't me. It was Addie. Addie Hollingsworth. Addie took the fancy Mercedes and drove us.*

*Wait. Where's Addie?*

*Somebody please help me. I think I'm dying.*

*It's all coming back now.*

I paid for the gas as a black man jumped out of a big car and grabbed Addie's handbag. The strap broke but she wouldn't let go. He punched her in the face with a closed fist.

She reeled backward, dazed, as I ran to help, but the man didn't seem to fear me.

*"Get away from her."*

He struck her again. Thick drops of blood stained the sidewalk like spilled paint. She fell to the ground and hit the concrete island next to the petrol pump. Blood formed a dark pool beside her. The side of her head appeared to be caved in, just a yawning crimson fissure. As rainwater thinned the pooling blood, ribbons of pink washed across the pavement.

*And the driver—wait—I know him.*

*It's LaVon.*

*The one who thought I chatted up his girlfriend. I don't even remember her name.*

*Stella. That's it. Stella.*

LaVon jumped out of the car. He pointed at me. A blast of orange fire left his finger. Then came a crack so loud and forceful that it rang in my ears and knocked my feet out from under me.

*It's so cold. Does anybody know I'm here?*

*And where's Addie? I can't see her anymore. Did she get away?*

Tires screamed against the asphalt. Car doors opened and closed. Beacons of red, white and blue ricocheted off the store windows.

*I'm dying and there's nothing I can do.*

A shadowy specter moved toward me. I blinked, and the hulking form of a man came into focus.

*A policeman.*

"I warned you, Sylvester, if you continued these crime sprees, you'd either end up dead or in jail."

A female voice I didn't recognize came to my defense.

"He didn't hurt that old lady—he tried to save her. And a dude shot him. I wrote down the license plate. Here."

A black velvet sky sparkled with a million mirrors, reflecting the desires of dreamers.

*My dreams are dying.*

"Stay with me, Sly," the cop said, and patted me on the head for reassurance.

"I'm not Sly. I'm Eloise—Elle for short."

*I accept that we were in a wreck.*

*It runs through my mind in slow motion.*

*Someone should tend to Elizabeth.*

I sharpened my gaze, but a wave of dizziness overcame me. Excruciating pain made me wince. When I touched my ribs, even the slightest pressure blinded me. My hand came away sticky.

*I must've hit the steering wheel.*

*Yes, I hit the steering wheel and the car flipped.*

Blood spurted from my mouth as I tried to speak.

"Don't move," said the cop. "Help's on the way." He put his hand under my head. Even though his face blurred, I recognized the voice. Chip Stone. Allen's friend.

"Help Elizabeth" I said. I wanted to tell him what happened, but as soon as the words formed in my throat, they dissolved.

A commotion broke out.

An unfamiliar voice shouted, "Stay back, Carswell, you'll contaminate the crime scene."

"Let him in," Stone bellowed.

"Hold my hand?" I clutched at his sleeve and missed. "I don't want to die alone."

"You're not alone. And no, I won't hold your hand. I brought along somebody else who'll do that for me. You remember Allen, don't you?"

"Allen's here?" I tried to smile.

I blinked several times, and Allen came into focus. He grabbed my hand and squeezed, pressing it to his cheek and holding it tightly in place.

"Cold. So very cold."

He let go of my hand, whipped off his jacket and wrapped it around me.

"Freezing."

He threw more cover over me and bundled me tight. "I'll buy you a new one," he said to Chip Stone. Then he sat next to me, lifted my shoulders slightly off the pavement and cradled me in his arms.

"Where's Elizabeth?"

"She's . . . I think the ambulance already took her."

"Good."

*She'll make it. She's young and has a lot of life left to live.*

Snippets of memory returned. I said, "I should never have disrupted your life."

Allen's protests sounded tinny and distant.

"It's just—I love you." Pain knifed through me. The more I tried to talk, the weaker I felt. "Have to go now. Have to say . . . good-bye."

I wasn't conscious of having left my body, but when I took in the entire picture, a crime scene lay below me. Floating above them, I hovered in the misty gray haze somewhere between life and death.

*I don't see myself anywhere.*

*Allen's cradling a young black lad, sobbing into his neck, but it's my name that he's calling.*

"I love you, too, Elle. Please come back."

*Déjà vu.*

*I've done this before.*

As I looked down upon the chaos, paramedics shook out a Mylar blanket and covered the body of an elderly woman. Where'd she come from?

"What's happening, Mummy?"

Startled at her voice, I realized Elizabeth had joined me, asking a question I couldn't answer. Still, I did my best. "I think we're having the same dream."

Below us, Chip Stone faded into a smoky blue shadow, but his voice remained clear. "The TV cameras are here. Put the boy down, Allen. Last thing you need's a photo of you hugging him." And then more urgent, "Do what I said, damn it. You don't want them to get the idea you're a sick motherfucker."

The boy went limp. Allen eased him back onto the ground. The image of Allen grew hazy, but I heard him as clearly and distinctly as if he had whispered into my ear.

"It's her, Chip. It was Elle. And now she's gone again."

The sky opened up. A deafening clap of thunder rolled over us. Cannonball hail crashed against the pavement like the bombs over England in WWII that my mum and dad used to speak of. This turned out to be a mightier rainstorm than any I'd ever witnessed.

Engulfed by a light so white and brilliant that I could no longer distinguish the fading forms below, I gave in to a weightless ascension. Gravity could no longer hold us in place. I took Elizabeth by the hand and held on tight.

Then the storm cleared, leaving only a refreshing residue of mist bathing my face as the scene on the ground vaporized and my daughter and I floated away.

# Epilogue

"Take your time," Thomas said as he walked us to the front door of our magnificent Tudor mansion. "He'll call for you when his golf game is over."

"But how will we know when to be ready?" I asked.

Thomas sighed. "You'll know."

We went inside to the comforts of home. Our pets bounded over to greet us. I checked their bowls and saw that they were full.

"Do you think . . . ?" I tentatively began.

Elizabeth gave me the one-shoulder shrug.

The dog brought my slippers and dropped them at my feet. But when I put them on, they turned into Jimmy Choos in a rich shade of purple that matched the beautiful dress that had suddenly sculpted itself to my body.

In the blink of an eye we found ourselves standing in St. Peter's office. Without making eye contact, Peter held up a finger for quiet. He settled his golf shoes into a stance, reseated his grip on the putter, and tapped the ball into a glass turned on its side.

"Congratulations," he said as it jumped the rim and clattered against the bottom of the glass. "Do you wish to redeem your card at this time?"

Mystified, I scrutinized his expression to see if he was mocking me.

"You mean—"

He nodded. "Be absolutely certain." His brow furrowed. "Some things cannot be undone."

I gasped in disbelief. Inwardly reeling from the knowledge that we'd accomplished what we'd set out to do, I said, "When do we get to see her?"

"Well, that's the thing—" he leaned against the putter "—first, I need the card. Then you get your mother."

I opened my handbag and fished it out. The mere act of touching it sent heat radiating from my palm up to my shoulder. I'm not a hundred percent certain, but I think that Get Out of Hell Free card had a pulse. I held it out for him, eager to avoid scorched fingertips.

Instead, he gave us a brittle smile. "Just so you know, she'll be on probation."

*News to me.*

Elizabeth and I exchanged awkward looks. We gave him a couple of shoulder shrugs, *Whatever you say.* Since we were already halfway to eternity, how difficult could probation be?

*Easy peasy.*

He took the card. "You sure?"

We nodded in sync.

"When do we get to see Mama?" I asked again.

A seismic thunderclap came out of nowhere, rattling my senses and vibrating my toes. Elizabeth grabbed my arm and held on tight. The air around us turned violet. It undulated in waves like heat snakes on hot asphalt. I glanced down in time to see the pale downy hairs stand straight up on Elizabeth's arms.

A force field of electromagnetic energy charged our shared space. Charcoal haze dissipated to a smoky shade of gray, bringing with it an odor that smelled of sulfur, copper, excrement and decay.

And then, with electricity crackling all around us, she materialized, standing before us with eyes glowing like embers, wearing iridescent red chiffon that glimmered like flames, with a long cigarette holder sticking out of scarlet-gloved fingers.

My jaw went slack.

I shook my head in disbelief.

Elizabeth's mouth opened and closed like that of a washed-up trout.

Words popped out before I realized I'd been thinking them. "I don't know how to tell you this, but there's been a terrible mistake."

# ABOUT THE AUTHOR

**Laurie Moore** was born and reared in the Great State of Texas where she developed a flair for foreign languages. She's traveled to forty-nine U.S. states, most of the Canadian provinces, Mexico and Spain.

This sixth-generation Texan majored in Spanish at the University of Texas at Austin where she received her Bachelor of Arts degree in Spanish, English, Elementary and Secondary Education. She entered a career in law enforcement in 1979. After six years on police patrol and a year of criminal investigation she made sergeant and worked as a district attorney investigator for several DAs in the central Texas area over the next seven years.

In 1992, she moved to Fort Worth and received her Juris Doctor from Texas Wesleyan University School of Law in 1995. She is currently in private practice in "Cowtown" where she lives with her husband and a rude Welsh corgi. After more than 33 years as a licensed, commissioned peace officer, she recently retired from law enforcement but continues to practice law in the Cultural District of Fort Worth.

Laurie is the author of *Constable's Run, Constable's Apprehension, Constable's Wedding, The Lady Godiva Murder, The Wild Orchid Society, Jury Rigged, Woman Strangled—News at Ten, Couple Gunned Down—News at Ten, Deb on Arrival—Live at Five, Wanted Deb or Alive,* and *Deb on Air—Live at Five.* She also wrote a young adult novel, *Simmering Secrets of Weeping Mary—A*

*Deuteronomy Devilrow Mystery,* using the pseudonym Merry Hassell Frels. Writing is her passion. Contact Laurie through her Web site at www.LaurieMooreMysteries.com.